Life On The Edge
For Mumbai's Middle-Income Family!

Sandesh Singh

Ukiyoto Publishing

All global publishing rights are held by

Ukiyoto Publishing

Published in 2021

Content Copyright © **Sandesh Singh**

ISBN 9789355979896

All rights reserved.
No part of this publication may be reproduced, transmitted, or stored in a retrieval system, in any form by any means, electronic, mechanical, photocopying, recording or otherwise, without the prior permission of the publisher.

The moral rights of the author have been asserted.

This is a work of fiction. Names, characters, businesses, places, events, locales, and incidents are either the products of the author's imagination or used in a fictitious manner. Any resemblance to actual persons, living or dead, or actual events is purely coincidental.

This book is sold subject to the condition that it shall not by way of trade or otherwise, be lent, resold, hired out or otherwise circulated, without the publisher's prior consent, in any form of binding or cover other than that in which it is published.

www.ukiyoto.com

Dedication

To all Mumbaikars,
Salute your human spirit to keep the city running, at all the times!

To my Parents,
Ma & Papa, I could never exist without you.
Your blessings, and unconditional love has shaped me.
Smile on your faces, is more important to me than anything else.

To my siblings,
For happily sharing, and constant caring.
Growing up with you, was the best thing to happen;
for all those beautiful memories to cherish for life.

To my wife Suman, and Kids Ankanaa, Aashani and Abhiram
Without you and your support, this would not have been possible.
You are the reason; my life has not gotten closer to edge ever.
You make my life beautiful each day. Lots of love.

Author's Note

Mumbai, earlier referred as Bombay, is not just another city. It fulfils boundless aspirations, it feeds crores of families, it engulfs so many human stories within its fold. The vibrancy of the city, ever accommodative and liberalistic attire, never-die and can-do spirit, and its ever-lasting magnetism has always fascinated me. One book can never cover what the city is about, I just touch one facet on the surface in this book.

This book is a tribute to our middle-class society. They are the ones, who drive the aspirations, unfazed by the edges of life, who try their bit to go above and beyond, baselining the new 'normal'. They are the ones, who define, nurture, and uplift the values of social ecosystem. My deeper gratitude to all those unrecognized and unsung heroes of our middle-class society.

Most importantly, I extend my deepest respect to all the mothers, sisters and daughters, without whom this world would not have been kinder, a better place to live as it is now. This book brings few orthodox aspects of our society at certain time; with no intent to encourage patriarchy or stereotyping. Women are 'the' important part of our society, and they must be regarded well.

This is my first book, and more to come. Requesting your love and blessings on the journey.

Thank you

I must thank all those people in the backend who have helped me develop the overall craft.

Hari, Anasua, Apoorva, my sincere thanks to you. Without your help, this book would not have been complete.

I would like to thank the Ukiyoto Publishing, for giving their prestigious platform to a new author. My gratitude to the entire Ukiyoto team for their thorough professional approach in bringing this book to market.

Thanks to my wife for staying by my side, being the constant support during these eight years long journey of bringing this book to reality (indeed it took so long). Most importantly, she has designed the cover page of the book – beautiful piece of imagination.

Thanks to all my friends, colleagues, and well-wishers, for always encouraging, and supporting me.

CONTENTS

1. **GIRL AGAIN!** — 1
   - 1a. Baby Born — 1
   - 1b. Double Whammy — 6
   - 1c. Baby Arrives At Home — 12
   - 1d. Mrunali Goes To School — 16

2. **GIRLS GROWING UP** — 18
   - 2a. Girls Growing Up — 18
   - 2b. Need Of The TV — 22
   - 2c. First TV, And Then Refrigerator — 28
   - 2d. Mrunali's College And First Job — 35
   - 2e. One Diwali And Shruti's Trouble — 43

3. **POLITICS AND SHREE PARTY** — 48
   - 3a. Ganesh Introduction To Shree Party — 48
   - 3b. Shinde Bhao — 53
   - 3c. Ganesh And Politics — 58
   - 3d. Disenchant With The Party — 69

4. **RIOTS, FAMILY, AND SOCIETY** — 77
   - 4a. Structure Demolished — 77
   - 4b. It Hit Chawls — 83
   - 4c. Yakub Being Questioned — 91
   - 4d. Yakub's Family Under Threat — 98

5. **VIVEK, THE FIRST LOVE** — 105
   - 5a: Mrunali Found Someone — 105
   - 5b. Parents Do Not Always Agree — 113
   - 5c. The Other Side — 119
   - 5d. Calmness, Takes Aggression! — 124
   - 5e. Unthinkable Happened — 127

6. **SHRUTI AND HER STRUGGLES** — 134
   - 6a. Shruti Discovering Herself — 134
   - 6b. Deepak, Another Fling — 140
   - 6c. Developed An Interest — 144
   - 6d. Shruti Shames Family — 148

7. **MRUNALI's MARRIAGE** — 155
   - 7a. Mrunali To Agree — 155
   - 7b. Rejection Again — 162
   - 7c. Sakhar Puda — 168
   - 7d. Quest For Maruti 800 — 173

8. MEANWHILE SHRUTI AND JAYA	179
8a. Shruti Meets Mangesh	179
8b. Not To Be, Or To Be	187
8c. Shruti Too	196
8d. Meanwhile Jaya	205
9. NATURE, DISASTER, AND INJURY	211
9a. Heavy Rains Causes Havoc	211
9b. Divorce, A Social Stigma	219
9c. Train Blasts, Hit The City Hard!	225
10. CHANDEKAR BUILDERS	230
10a. Builder's Entry	230
10b. Jaiswal's Murder	237
10c. Ganesh To Not Pursue	244
11. LIFE HAS TO END, ONCE!	251
11a. Life Is Uncertain	251
11b. Back To Native Home	256
11c. The End, For Another Beginning!	267
ABOUT THE AUTHOR	274

1. Girl Again!

1a. Baby Born

Life paints a rosy picture for a second, when there is none. And such moments do come often just to keep eyes open, mind intact and pulses bright. People say, it is hope. But, to have hope, there must be some motion.

When life stays like a pond and does not move; ignored from the world; being hidden at a place, where there is no sight of any disturbing activity to give it a momentum; that it desires; to talk, to express, to demonstrate its beauty. Alas, it is not meant to be part of the world!

That's what happened in Tamhankar family. Till today, there was hope, that things will change. It will be a D-day, a day of celebrations, and joy, and fun. Years gone, months gone, Days gone, and today, hours gone, and minutes gone. The lady nurse came out and said 'Congratulations, you have a baby girl.'

One could easily notice the change of expressions on Ganesh Tamhankar's face. Eyes, which had hope until now, are now filled with hopelessness. Here is the third girl in the family!

He had his second daughter Shruti in his hand. He composed himself from the shock, looked at Shruti, saw the excitement, happiness in her eyes. He looked at his newly born daughter, and clinched his fist, and dropped it in fraction of seconds. That is it, that is how he could display his helplessness.

'Thank you,' he could mumble to nurse with absolutely no expression on his face.

Lady nurse did not take much time to understand the pain, that this man was going through. She had earlier seen such 'lost' moments, moments filled with disappointments and teary eyed. This was better than those, where relatives have jumped on her bringing such 'bad' news; with disbelief that this could happen to them. She immediately went inside and locked the door.

Eyes were silent, focused on that encircled zeroes, an imaginary figure. Ganesh was here, but not very much here. He was delighted, when his first baby was born. He was one of those open-minded folks, who were willing to welcome a baby girl or a baby boy in the family. Yes, he and Ramya, his wife both were ready for any outcome with their first. They were just happy that the baby is going to fill in the vacuum that was there in their lives for such a long time.

It was a long wait, more than twelve years after their marriage. They did everything possible to get a child, someone who would take their family ahead. They met doctors, sadhus, ojhas and all those who claimed to produce results. They reached out to everyone, who offered even a slightest of hope. But nothing positive happened. They were getting hopeless with every such meet being failed, with no results. They had the pressure from family members and relatives. The society is not easy to live when a married couple does not have their own child. And when the interval since marriage is long; the society views them with a bad karma; uses that as an argument to taunt. Desperation was at its best. They kept trying and trying in the capacity they could. Their hopes shattered at many moments. There were times, they felt devastated. So, when they got to know that Ramya is pregnant; it was the happiest moment of their lives. Life has taken several twists since then.

Ganesh realised that he was holding Shruti tight. She was getting uncomfortable, trying to come out of his arms. He released the pressure, went in front of Lord Ganesha's idol. A symbol of 'hope', 'wealth', and 'beginning'. He has never forgotten HIM, in times of worry, in times of difficult situations, in times of happy moments. HE was the cause in Ganesh's eyes. Again, he was at HIS mercy! Will HE show the path to him today? HE was smiling with Ladoos in his one hand, and weapons in the other.

'Oh Lord, why did you do this to me? Why? I prayed and prayed. I visited Siddhivinayak temple multiple times. Not for this. I have two daughters. Didn't have a problem. But wished to complete my family with a son.' Ganesh cried in front of Lord Ganesha.

'Why didn't you? Have I done anything less in worshipping you? Please…please tell me.' Ganesh was crying, with drops of tear dropping on either side. But Lord Ganesha was still smiling.

He wiped his face. He quickly glanced in both directions. Nobody was watching him. Then, he went to meet his wife.

***

Ramya was lying on the hospital bed. She was amid many other women busy with their new-borns, and family members. Her moist eyes were constantly eyeing for somebody. Someone of her own. She is still trying to sort out the emotional complexities she has just gone through. Yes, she knows that the third addition to their family is a 'Girl'. Again.

She was distressed recounting each day of past nine months. She and Ganesh together have gone through thinking, and planning around this new baby. They have been positive this time, very hopeful. Again, they did everything possible they could to get a son in their family. Ramya knew that it is not easy to live through the whole life with just daughters; sons are needed to grow the family, continue the generation. A son can give them the shelter and support during old age. She was vocal about it. She has been praying to have a son in their family from the beginning. However, it was Ganesh, who always encouraged, and wanted to have a daughter in the family. She confronted complicated emotions each time she delivered a baby girl. Then she recuperated with a hope, 'The next time!'

An undefined, unsaid pain she suddenly experienced, 'There is now no next time.' She shivered.

Ganesh is in front of her. She saw Shruti first.

Shruti smiled, hugged her. 'Mama, I have one more sister. She is beautiful.'

Shruti was delighted. Her little tongue jumped up and down while expressing the triumph, she just witnessed. She was a small girl, about to complete four in few months. She is not the age to weigh right versus wrong; good versus bad. She was yet to be taught the implicit rules of the society. She could afford sheer innocence.

Shruti is beautiful. Her eyes are like her mother, dark, intense, and big. There was always much to read from them, than what she spoke. She is jubilant, excited; not worried about what her parents are going through. She probably is yet to understand the words of silence; unspoken words always hurt the more. It was that moment, Ramya had a brief smile. It again turned soar. She turned her face the other side.

Ganesh puts Shruti down, and asks her 'Go out Shruti, and play.'

He pulled a creaky stool nearby and positioned himself next to Ramya. She is facing the opposite side. None of them are comfortable to initiate, knowing the feelings of their companion. Both knew vividly what the other one is going through in mind, and heart.

Ganesh looked at his wife. She looked dry. She was calm, but exhausted – physically and emotionally. He understands, it has been a long journey for her, enduring everything while being pregnant. And, after a long nine months of wait, and labour; if the expectations are not met; it can have severe effect on mind and soul.

He noticed, that Ramya is thinking, thinking too much about it. He wanted to bag her attention and wanted her to be positive about all of this.

Just a while ago, he had an emotional break-down, but this time he should be strong. Ramya is going through the same pain, that he is. It is difficult for both, so one needs to be strong, and support the other. It should be his responsibility to take care of her.

'So, what should we name her?' Ganesh took the initiative. Ramya, this time turned to face him. Their eyes met and blinked. They were expressing support to one another. They have done it the best, standing for each other, and be a force for the other when it was needed the most.

'Where is our baby?' Ramya finally asked after a short spell of silence.

Ganesh now realised that the baby was not next to his wife. Why? He did not know.

In case of their two children earlier, he found their new-born lying next to Ramya covered up with cloths. He remembered; the babies cried every twenty-thirty minutes when they were born. It was said that they get hungry and feeding the smaller doses of milk pacified them quickly.

But today; the new-born baby is not with them as yet. Ganesh thought for a moment and said 'Doctors may be doing medical check-ups. She should be back in some time.'

Hours gone, however, they still had not heard from anybody on where their new-born daughter is. Ramya got nervous, 'She is still not here?'

'Let me go and find out. You stay relaxed.' Ganesh jumped from the stool.

1b. Double Whammy

Mrunali is a five-year-old, a grown-up girl for her age. She is quite mature and understands the world in a sane way. She knows that her parents are in the hospital to get the delivery of their third sibling.

She has been waiting for this day for a long time now. She came to know about this news from her neighbour Mhatre aunty, around four months ago. She vividly remembered, Mhatre aunty telling her, 'Muni, you will have a baby soon. Do you know?'

Mrunali had thought over it for a moment. Then she just smiled. She did not respond to it. She was surprised but didn't want Mhatre aunty to know that she was not aware about it. She was confused, why would her mother hide it from her.

Immediately she went to her mother, and asked 'Aai, is it true that we will soon have a baby in our family?'

Her mother had plainly asked, 'Who told you?'

Finally, when her mother said 'Yes, soon you will have a baby to play.' Mrunali had positively responded 'I want bhau. I and Shruti will play with our brother…It will be fun.'

She could not very well understand what her mother wanted to say at that time. However, she was less bothered about it. Since then, Mrunali had fondly discussed over this topic with her sister Shruti several times. They planned various games that they will play with their brother, and with the other kids in the neighbourhood. Mrunali wanted to name his brother as Jitendra. She had once seen a movie, where she enjoyed watching the actor named Jitendra dancing, and singing. She liked those flashy cloths and funny dance moves.

A knock on the door brought her to present. She was watchful. When her mother experienced the pain early in the morning, her parents left her in the house instructing to lock the door from inside, and not to open the door unless she knows the person. She quietly came closer to the door and heard someone shouting her name. 'Aha, that is Mhatre aunty.' Mrunali opened the door. Mhatre aunty came inside the house; she had brought Shira and tea with her.

She placed the Shira in front of Mrunali, and asked her 'Mruni Betaa, how are you? You excited?'

Mrunali nodded her head.

'Don't worry, everything will be good. Your parents should return by the evening or possibly tomorrow. Eat this and have tea.' Mhatre aunty comforted her.

Mhatre aunty has always liked Mrunali. She always felt close to Mrunali and had always shown motherly affection towards her.

Mhatres and Tamhankars have been neighbours since their chawl society came into conception; precisely seven years ago. They were the first ones to buy the house in this society. Since then, they have taken care of each other. Mhatre family includes Mr and Mrs Mhatre, and they have a son and a daughter. As they said, they are a complete family. Mr Mhatre works in a bank, and earned enough to live a little better lifestyle, that the others in the middle-income society would be envy of.

Mhatres and Tamhankars became closer when Mrs Mhatre had fallen ill due to Malaria. Mr Mhatre was out, to a different town to attend his bank related training. Mrs Mhatre was running high temperature, she felt helpless. Ganesh and Ramya came to know about her worsening condition. They got her immediately admitted to a hospital, paid all the bills, and took good care of her. When Mrs Mhatre got discharged from the hospital, Ramya continued to care for her and ensured that Mrs Mhatre gets well soon. When Mr Mhatre returned from the training and came to know about all the help Ganesh and Ramya provided; he and his wife felt indebted to Tamhankars. And since then, they have bonded well like a close-knit family.

Mhatres and Tamhankars had a reason to get close. But in general, this is the beauty of middle-class society; the neighbours and close by develop such an intimacy, which is not defined, bound, or limited by blood relationships. They are available during their happy occasions and go to any extent to help during difficult times. The celebrations are truly unbiased, less fake, more from the heart, being together.

***

Ganesh had to come to find whereabouts of his new-born. He asked a nurse, 'Me, Ganesh Tamhankar. My new-born baby is still not there.'

'Wait there.' Nurse was rude, 'let me get back.' She came back after a while, 'doctor is examining her.' She stumbled, 'It may take some more time before they discharge her.'

He patiently waited outside the doctor's room to see his daughter.

After a while, he peeked inside. Doctor was pointing to a baby, 'This is a special case. This new-born girl, she is affected with a disease. Only one in thousands, or tens of thousands new-born cases across the globe.'

Ganesh was not sure, if the doctor was talking about his baby. He looked around; this was the only baby in the room. He continued listening to the conversation.

'These are rarely seen in West India, specifically in Bombay.' Other practitioners were eagerly listening to the doctor. They looked junior, Ganesh thought.

'This new-born did not have the left eye formed. It looked like a plain surface in place of left eye.' Many of the practitioners had not seen such a case earlier.

'This was not picked up on any of earlier scans performed. So, this came as a shock.'

'It is entirely possible that this might not have been clearly visible during the scans, or completely ignored. This is a case of Anophthalmia, where one part of eye is not developed. Generally, in such cases, there is a possibility of more birth defects. But we just finished the tests, and investigations. Fortunately, the baby is otherwise fine.' Other nurses and practitioners were nodding their head.

Ganesh was clueless. He was not very sure, what the doctor was saying. But he understood that there is some problem to his baby girl. He went inside, 'Is this my baby?'

'What is your name?' doctor hesitated.

'Tamhankar. Ganesh Tamhankar.'

Doctor verified a few things, 'Yes, she is yours.'

'What were you saying just now?' Ganesh shouted.

Doctor handing the baby to him, said 'Look here, her one eye is not developed.' Ganesh got the rude shock of his life. He could not believe what he was seeing. It looked weird, extra mass in place of eye. He turned his eyes away from his new-born. Life has never been easy on him, but it was hard for him to handle the turn of events today.

'Why, why is it?' He cursed the hospital, and the doctor.

'Why didn't you do your job perfectly? I visited Dr Pagare regularly. We got as many scans as he ordered and treatments that he said. So, why this has to happen?'

Doctor calmly said, 'It can happen to anyone.'

'What does that mean?' Ganesh retorted back. 'Why to me?' 'You all don't care for the poor. Would you do this to a rich person?'

He has never been so much out of control, but he was unable to help himself.

Doctor put his arm around Ganesh, 'see, we understand your situation. But it can happen to anyone. Even to riches. This is God given.'

Ganesh sobbed, but shivering with anger and helplessness. Doctor took the kid for some final check-ups; and asked him to wait outside.

Ganesh's whole world has come crashing down. This was the least expected to happen to them on this devil day. Flurry of tears poured floating through his eyes. He just could not control it. It could not have been more tragic than this.

He tried remembering if he has done anything bad in his life which has come back haunting him. God must be punishing him for his sins, and now gifted him the suffering, for life.

'How would I see my daughter without one eye, how will she grow? Who will marry her?' Ganesh was deep in his thoughts with numerous questions, with answers to none of them. He was heralded with the thoughts and questions that society will ask him. They will talk about the punishment from God, bad karma, devil's act, and what not. How will he face those eyes and loose talks, what will he explain to his relatives? His eyes dried out, but the pain in those eyes not yet.

'Oh, I forgot. Ramya must be waiting.' Ganesh came out of his grief, remembering his wife.

He anxiously muttered to himself, 'What should I tell her, how would she react?'

Finally, he was given his child. Doctors mentioned to him that it is important to take lot of care of this baby, and frequent checks would be required so that her other eye remains safe; and no other new things pop up. He tried to hear the doctors and make sense of medical terminologies around her daughter's case. He could not grasp any more than that it is a rare case, and generally such kids are given special powers by God to happily live their lives.

He is worried. He was not this tense when he was told by doctors several years ago that it is rare for them to become parents. However, today is different. He is faced with a dilemma. He knew he must face his wife and tell her the truth. He has to be cruel and put the facts as is.

***

Ramya was ecstatic to see the face of her new-born. It brought a smile on her face. She could not comprehend the dim face of her husband. Probably he is still running into those emotions of having a baby girl, hence she discounted. 'Aha, she is so beautiful. Fairer than both sisters.'

She thought. The baby did not resemble any of them, however she looked like herself a bit.

Then, Ganesh slowly leaned towards her, and adjusted the cloths on the baby a bit. Ramya noticed but was not sure of what she is seeing. She was stunned, she could not utter a word. She looked at her husband. He patted on her hand with the glumness on his face still on. She is staring at her new-born, with drops of tear falling from her face. This is the most-tragic day of their lives.

Ramya fetched her daughter near her chest, kissing her and loving her. She has made up her mind that this daughter will need the utmost attention, and care from her and Ganesh. She has held her new-born very tightly on her left. She looked at her hubby, put her hand on his hand. Their eyes met one more time. That sense of sympathy is what they needed for each other, to survive this cruel day.

Two human-beings, being married, have taken vows to take care of each other, stand for each other, and be there for the other during the most difficult times. They become the support system for each other, medicine to heal and cure, punching bag to defuse anger, a shoulder to cry upon. It is a special bond, like how mind and soul is in one's body. In being together, in being oneness, many a times they don't realize the presence of the other. This is what makes it easy for them to live, live together and longer. Ramya and Ganesh are living that life, without knowing that they are synonymous to successful relationships. One has said, your bonding strengthens during difficult times; and Ramya and Ganesh have lived many such moments being together.

1c. Baby Arrives At Home

Finally, Ramya and her newly born daughter is discharged from the hospital. After several discussions with doctors and taking opinions from various experts, they had come to acceptance that there is no hope to revive their daughter's eye. They had by now consoled themselves. They were now ready to face the world.

They reached their home. It was a 100 by 120 square feet home in a chawl, called 'Jagardev Compound'. People living there, would not like it being equated to slums. All the chawls in this neighbourhood maintain utmost cleanliness, and hygiene, albeit the smaller space they were living in. Every individual room was internally decorated and given a good look and feel inside the house. Although it could not match the decorum of tall buildings, these folks enjoyed where they stayed, and wanted to care for it.

In their house, there was a mattress kept in the living room, and a radio occupied the place next to it. Just adjacent was a kitchen with an attached open bathroom. Tamhankar was always pleased, that he decided to buy this house particularly in this neighbourhood; where people tend to be neat and clean, respectful to each other, and most importantly for his neighbour, Mhatre family.

As soon as they were about to enter the house, Mrunali came running, 'Aai…Aai…' She called her mother.

'Show me the face of baby,' 'give her to me.'

Ramya consoled her, and said 'she is soft, delicate.' 'Not now.'

Mrs Mhatre gave a symbolic gesture to stay put, and not to come inside the house as yet. She has to perform 'Grih Pravesh' rituals. She came out with a pot filled with water. She spelled some prayers, and performed aarati of Ramya and new-born, and then let them in.

Finally, Mrs Mhatre took the child in her arms to play with her, 'my sweetie.' She quickly unwrapped the blankets over her. It could not be hidden anymore. She saw the missing eye. She looked at Ramya, and found her eyes staring at her, waiting to meet. Ramya could not control herself. She cried and wept her heart out. She was inconsolable. Mrs Mhatre hugged her tightly adjusting the new-born in the other arm.

Mrs Mhatre was the biggest support to Ramya currently. She was consoling Ramya to have courage and faith in God. 'Everything that HE does is for good, and for specific purpose, Ramya.'

Mrs Mhatre continued with a pause, 'You and Ganesh are good human beings. God will have special plans for you both, I'm sure. Keep faith. This girl will be more blessed and will do wonders for you.'

***

Ramya kept thinking about what Mrs Mhatre said to her. She consoled herself out of the situation. She asked Ganesh, 'why did God do this to us?' Ganesh did not immediately answer.

'I'm really not sure, what is upsetting to me more, that our baby is a girl. Or she does not have an eye.' Ramya just let it out.

Ganesh looked at Ramya with affection, took her hand in his hand, folded it. She closed her eyes, put her head on his shoulder.

He said, 'She is our daughter. She is a sister to Mrunali and Shruti. We'll love her the same way.'

Ramya wiped her tears, 'You know, what Mhatre Tai said? That, God may have some purpose behind this. Our baby would be very blessed.'

Ganesh was calm 'Yeah, for sure. Everything happens for a reason.'

They kept consoling each other, until late in the night. The next morning, they woke up; and they had a name for their newly born baby 'Jaya', a goddess name. Jaya, someone who will achieve triumph against all odds.

***

Next day, neighbours started romping Tamhankar's house. This is a normal in middle class communities, for neighbours to just arrive; no intimation needed, no prior permission asked. They don't care, rather not worry about the time of the day; or what the host would feel; obviously lacking the sophistication of upper-class society. It is not guided by any other intentions, just out of their duty to make a visit; convey their thoughts, give their warmth, shower the love, and share the pain.

Neighbours came, they took the new-born Jaya in their hands, glared at her, made faces, expressed their emotions, shared opinions; and left. Ramya sat silently, listening to each one of them. It was a moment of grief not only for her, but the people in chawls as well.

Some of them were caring for Jaya and Ramya. They brought in goodies to eat, clothes for new-born, creams, and oils to use for post-pregnancy. They gave the words of support and strength. They praised how beautiful Jaya is, and good that Ramya & Ganesh came up with such a good name for the girl. They also said that the three girls will be nice with each other and be great siblings.

Some talked about Karma from the present birth, or from the past births; and how, what you do yesterday, impacts your present. It becomes part of your destiny. You cannot avoid it. You have to accept it graciously and do your best to live it.

Some even said, it may be a curse for the wrongdoing of forefathers, and ancestors. Hence it is said, one should be truthful, and good in its own conduct, else it affects your children. Your generations to come will bear the impact.

Some even attributed it to an evil act. Ramya may need to perform pooja, rituals to take care of it; so that no more wrongs happen to her family.

Someone claimed, this is a liberated society; and still accepts women who produce only girls, and that too three. Otherwise earlier, they used to not take it kindly to such women and do worst things to them in the name of honour.

Ramya, not for a moment felt, these discussions were intrusive, meant to hurt her, or meant to offend her. She knew, it was out of their love and caring towards her. Though she looked grim and tired, she had graciously welcomed each neighbour who visited her.

At the end of the day, Ramya was not sure if these visits and said words from the neighbours have calmed her down, or further aggravated her. But one thing was sure, it has further solidified her inner strength. More she talked, more she justified, the more she became attached to her new-born, indeed to all her three daughters.

***

Ganesh had come early from his job. Just because he has a new-born in the family, he cannot keep away from the job. Each day, he has to make his livelihood to survive. Ramya has composed herself and brought tea for him.

She sat next to Ganesh and asked, 'How was the day?'

'No, not bad. I was just thinking about you and Jaya.' He placed his hands on the top of Jaya, stroking her small hairs.

'What were you thinking?' Ramya was curious.

'It was very usual. You would be thinking the same. How was your day?'

Then, Ramya narrated the entire day to Ganesh about how the neighbours visited, and what they said.

She talked about how Jaya has been a nice girl throughout the day; and did not trouble her at all. Whenever she was hungry, she cried; but otherwise, either she was sleeping or playing cheerful. Also, about how Shruti and Mrunali were playing with Jaya, they were so happy to touch Jaya's cute little fingers.

'It was so pleasing to see both excited and cheerful with Jaya. Jaya was responding to them as well. I think, these three will bond well.' Ramya said. Ganesh nodded.

1d. Mrunali Goes To School

Life moves on. Tamhankar family has moved ahead. There were times when they thought of trying for the next child; however, they consoled each other. They decided to be happy with what God has given them, their three daughters; and provide them the best that they can.

Things were never meant to be easy for Ganesh and Ramya. With the big family, they felt the pain of their lives more often. When one does not have enough to feed their kids and cannot afford to fulfil their small wishes, the heart cries. There is a rush of blood from top to toe looking for that clue, looking for that small hint, an idea to go, and find that small pinch of luck or anything; that can translate that very moment into a joy. Alas it hardly happens in reality!

Innocent, that very sparkle in the eyes of those kids. It is hope. Ganesh always gets hopeless seeing those eyes. He often goes through this emotional turmoil. Sensing the desire to get up, and do that right or wrong, which is there in his might to achieve that thing. Howsoever small or big it is, to give that momentary happiness to his kids. However, that is the irony. It never happens. That inability to do anything, feeling of being handicapped, helplessness, powerless. That creature he was!

There is always a reason, on why the nature has grafted itself the way, it has. Poverty will never end, there will always be people in that bracket, probably with the baselines changed, definitions altered.

Girls were growing up. Ramya and Ganesh were in a dilemma whether to put Mrunali into a school or not.

'Kids at her age are going to school,' Ramya said to Ganesh.

'Girls don't go to school.' He was quick to respond.

'But I would want my kids to go to school. Mrunali should go to school sooner.'

'The world is progressing. If they don't study, what will be their future?'

'Ramya, no girl goes to school. I go pass that school in the morning, and I see only boys. They do all funky things there.'

'I don't know all this. If boys go to school, then our daughters must go too.'

'Can we afford the cost of schools? What will we achieve?' Ganesh innocently put it across. 'You know it, we are surviving somehow. Anything more will be a strain on our finances.' The pain of not able to give the basic things to his children, not able to fulfil his wife's only wish ached him deep within.

Mrunali's eyes would brighten up on seeing the kids in the locality going to school, holding heavy backpacks. Ramya would have tears. It took lot of courage on her part, to ignore the sparkles in those little eyes of her elder one.

Mrs Mhatre persisted with Tamhankar family, 'Bhau, people say this 'Mulgi Shikli, Pragati Jhali' for a reason. Mrunali is such a bright kid, she must go to school.'

'I am also going to put my girl to school next year. She will accompany Mrunali. Ganesh, Mrunali is like our own daughter. We will not think wrong for her.' Mr Mhatre added a personal touch.

'Also, it will not be difficult financially.' Mr Mhatre explained his rationale, 'The public schools offered free education until seventh standard. So, the cost is not much.'

'When it becomes costly, you can stop. Let us strive to have our daughters educated as much as we can afford.'

Ganesh nodded to this.

Tamhankars decided to pursue the education of their daughters. And Mrunali starts going to school.

2. Girls Growing Up

2a. Girls Growing Up

Time is truly the only thing in the world, which keeps flowing, flying and moves on. It never stops. It is the only thing, which never does any discrimination. Be it a happy moment, or a moment of grief. Be it for rich, or for poor, cuts across religions and castes. It changes. And it changes gracefully, with universal acceptance; no complaints from any one or any quarter.

In its multi-folds, it hides multiple stories; unknown to many, untold to many. It does so with immense pride with no intentions and reservations howsoever from anyone.

Lot of time has passed. Tamhankar girls are growing up fast. Ganesh and Ramya are proud of their daughters. Each of them is unique, gifted with talents, and ready to face the world.

Mrunali was growing more mature amongst the lot. She takes pride in whatever she does. She going to school, paved the way for her siblings. She will realize this at some age; she is the reason for the education of her sisters. She wants to study as much as possible and go until 15th standard. That is how she and the others in the neighbourhood referred higher education. After junior college (12th), three years of degree is referred as 15th standard.

There is a slight arrogance that has crept in Mrunali. There was a reason. The other girls in the society were not given as much as she was. Ganesh always loved her and gave his best to educate her; and fulfilled all her wishes. She further distinguished herself from the rest with her focus on education. She took lot of pride in the fact that she is the one amongst few girls in the society who is doing well in the studies.

Middle girl Shruti is growing more beautiful. She has an attractive face with a beautiful smile. She looked gorgeous with her fair skin, big black eyes, sharp nose, and thinner lips. To many in the community, she was prettier than many of the female actors around at that time. However not to forget, she was born in a lower medium class family. She knew, she is beautiful; she loved every bit of herself. However, thought of getting into acting or modelling never crept into her head, not even in dreams.

She is very frank and approachable to people. Her friend circle was getting bigger in schools, and in the neighbourhood. Boys wanted to be in the vicinity of her, around her. She enjoyed the attention and adulation, but her parents always wanted her to be careful of her acquaintance.

Little one, Jaya is silent, naughty, being pampered by two elder sisters. Though she was small, but she has already understood the limitations of being born as handicapped. Having to live without an eye, she has been managing to cope with it. She has learned the art of emotional balance; she kept to herself, all that she was going through internally, completely to her inner conscience.

Ramya would always think that Jaya is the most mature amongst the siblings. She would always want to be with her parents supporting them, being with them in all small or big things.

Ramya and Ganesh were grateful that their three daughters would always be together, supporting one another all the time. They would care for each other. Such bonhomie is not often found in siblings. But may be because they were girls, they bonded so well.

***

Mrunali played the perfect big sister to Shruti and Jaya. All three enjoyed playing in bigger groups. Mrunali and Shruti would drive the play for the group. Mrunali used to command, and kids in the community would listen to her directions.

'Run' and kids ran. Rajesh threw the ball at Shruti.

This was the game of 'Khorcha'. The popular game amongst kids, they can enjoy in groups. Mrunali had laid the rules well for all the kids to follow.

'Mangesh, hit Dhawal.' Mrunali shouted, she and Jaya were in the same group. While Shruti was in the other team.

But Mangesh hit the ball again to Shruti. Tarun shouted, 'Hit Shruti.' Shruti was running all around, getting hit; trying to save herself.

'Hey, why only to her?' Mrunali shouted, realizing that this is not with an intention of winning, but getting the attention from Shruti.

'What is going on? You two,' she pointed at Mangesh and Tarun.

'You want to play or go and sit at home.' 'I'm here. You cannot misbehave with my sister.'

Tarun retaliated, 'We are on the same side, Mrunali. This is not about your sister.'

'Can't I see? Don't try to fool me. Wait, let me speak to your mother.' Mrunali abandoned the game.

Tarun ran after her, 'Please not…let it be.'

But Mrunali had made up her mind; she ran to Tarun's house; and complained to his mother. His mother gave him two tight slaps, and a message 'Learn to behave with girls.' Then she turned to Mrunali, 'Beta Mruni. I trust you. Please forgive him. Let me know if he does any mistakes again.' Mrunali happily returned home with Shruti and Jaya.

***

It was a republic day celebration in the chawl community.

People in chawls would celebrate this day with great rigor, do prayers for the well-being and arrange events to enjoy as a group.

Mrunali was everywhere, she took the lead in grooming the flowers, decorating all the walls across, and prepared for all the events of the day.

'We are here because of such freedom fighters; they gave their lives for us so that we enjoy this freedom. This freedom is hard earned, so respect it, love it, and enjoy it. Jai Hind. Jai Bharat.' Mrunali ended her speech on how India achieved freedom. She exhibited a greater understanding of history, a command over the language and exhilarating confidence in front of several people.

Her mother, Ramya was proud of seeing her daughter on the stage with such a command. She saw the spark in the eyes of Mrunali. She saw people's admiration for her. Her eyes got moist, it was as if all the admiration and adulation is for her. It was as if she was living her life on the stage.

Later, it was a dance event, where Shruti and Jaya together performed a dance on the stage. Everyone enjoyed the performance. That was the Tamhankar family all over the community event.

2b. Need For The TV

Television brought the biggest change in the lives of the individuals, families, and societies. Not everyone could afford a TV those days. It was an esteemed possession. This was still days of black and white TVs. A few in the community would afford a TV, and the others would romp into their homes. You can get into arguments with anyone, but not with those having a TV in their homes.

The days, when doordarshan channel (only channel those days) would put the mega shows such as Friday movies, mythological programs on Sundays; all the people in the neighbourhood would romp into the homes with TV. It used to be a big gathering. If someone missed to make it in time to watch an episode of a serial, then he would get a thorough update from the other members of the family. The narrator would recount the second-by-second description of events as if it is unfolding in front of the eyes; including the commercials that came in between the episode. A little pause from the narrator would antagonize the listener; in the eagerness to hear the whole episode in quickness. Elders who have read and heard about mythological scriptures; would watch such serials with lot of enthusiasm. They would critic the portions of episode with truth vs false; right vs wrong. Hearing the anecdote from the elders would add an interesting flavour to the story.

The best days were watching the game of cricket, it was undoubtedly the unifying force in the society. People from all castes and creeds, all ages used to get together, and watch it for the India team. The individual houses having the TV would get filled from left to right, one side to the other side, on the windows and outside the doors. There was commentary on the TV, and then outside, everyone was expert, they had opinion, they had views, they had strategies. Passions would flow, emotions would run high. There would be favourites, but GOD of Cricket, Sachin was universally accepted.

Slowly in few years, the black and white TVs were replaced with colour TVs. However only a few could afford it. Another challenge was going beyond the doordarshan channel. Not everybody could afford cable network. Those who could, were categorized into upper middle class and above. This was super-luxury.

***

One day, Ganesh came home looking extremely happy, this was after a long-long time. Ramya was pleased to see this pleasant change in her husband. He looked more like his older self. He was constantly worried about the well-being of kids, and how to grow them. She would find him fetching Jaya in his arms, staring at her with sympathetic eyes, un-nerving her many a times.

She could not get him to share his concern with her but wordlessly shared her husband's pain. However, she never wanted her daughters to get any negative thoughts.

She set about making him tea while he took time to shrug off his shirt. Though not one of the most handsome, Ganesh has had a good physique. The kind of body one develops after years of toil. Ramya loved her husband and how gentle he was despite working with work-travel roughened men.

Ramya who was playing with Jaya, supposed that something must have happened today and there must be a reason the creases on her husband's face had reduced. She called out to Mrunali who was studying in the makeshift study created out of a loft close to the ceiling. One of the modifications everybody in Mumbai did to their kholis to eke out every inch of available space.

Mrunali came down the iron stairs and picked up the baby as her mother got busy making tea for her father. She smiled at Ganesh without saying anything and he smiled back at his eldest child. She was growing into a fine woman. She would soon be of marriageable age, he realised with a pang in his heart.

Shruti was playing outside. So Mrunali took her youngest sibling and sat down on the veranda from where she had a view both inside and outside.

He liked Ramya's ginger tea made extra strong with oodles of milk every evening and that was the time the couple got to spend time together seeking solace in each other. Ramya served him tea in the small steel glass, inside a slightly larger steel bowl which served as a saucer. He loved to pour the tea into the bowl and take small sips, blowing into it as he savoured the flavour and its taste. Few of the luxuries he craved on coming back from work.

She handed him two khari biscuits which again was the usual accompaniment along with his evening tea. He dipped it twice, took a bite and then let out a sigh.

'Today Samant sir came to enquire about the baby...' he said without any preamble. He was referring to his section engineer who had a soft corner for his hardworking junior who had on numerous occasions displayed an enterprising spirit.

He looked at his wife as he spoke, smiling at her innocent face full of questions. He knew she was patiently waiting to listen to him speak.

Ramya is the perfect wife in all senses of the term. Ganesh thought. An introvert by nature, what had attracted him was her simplicity. He had taken one look at her pretty face, quite fair for a Maharashtrian girl and had nodded his yes. But over the years her kindness had bowled him over. Very soft spoken she would rarely be seen getting angry on her own kids.

She had developed a great understanding of Ganesh's likes and limited dislikes and made herself a pillar of strength for him. Though she was not educated, her conduct, open and liberal mind would often make him think that she was years ahead of the educated memsahibs he would run into often when dropping Shruti off at school.

'He said these things happen sometimes and there is nothing to worry. Except for the eye our baby will grow up to be a fine woman.'

'What about the society? I can't bear to answer their sympathetic glances.' Ramya said letting out a sigh as she shifted her weight slightly to sit down closer to her husband.

He smiled and said, 'Our Jaya is a strong girl. She has accepted her situation. She is not sympathetic to herself. She looks beyond her this God given limitation. She is meant to do some magic in this world.'

Ramya nodded her head with a sad smile. But Ganesh knew his wife wouldn't need a lot to throw out her melancholy and nurture Jaya, the way she had brought up their elder daughters.

'Samant sir has told me, he will help out.' Ganesh replied changing the topic.

'He tells me there is a merit in my business idea and would like to sponsor me to get it started.'

Ramya didn't know much about business and kept quiet nodding her head at her husband's words.

But then another thought struck her.

'But what about the colour television you promised the girls?'

Ganesh shook his head. He didn't know whether to give into the girls' clamour for a television or to think of securing the family's future given the sudden turn of events. There were talks of people on contract being asked to leave.

'Shruti is very excited. I heard her proclaim yesterday to her friends that her father would be getting a colour TV home.' Ramya said.

Ganesh knew even Ramya was excited about the prospective of being the only family in their immediate vicinity to own a TV.

It had all started with the Independence Day parade being telecast on television for the entire country to watch. The children had been to the housewarming pooja at Mr Samant's new house. His cousin had gifted him a TV from Hong Kong and Ganesh had seen the children's enthusiasm at watching the 'box of magic' as they called it.

Everybody would stare at the box clothed in and kept spic and span even when it was switched off.

Mr Samant had laughed at the enthusiasm of Shruti and Mrunali and had told Ganesh to get one for the family.

He said, 'It remains shut most of the day but springs to life twice a day for the news and other things like agriculture and family planning. See the children can learn so much from it. It is also a status symbol eh!'

Ramya had rubbed her hands then and had pleaded with Ganesh to get a television set. A colour TV back then would cost anywhere between Rs.8000 to Rs.15000, and for a contractual worker like Ganesh it was a gargantuan task. Mr Samant told him that he didn't have to buy the imported one. There was a local shop he knew which would supply him a brand-new BPL or Philips television at a lower price.

The couple had started saving and had waited patiently for the day they would be able to show off their television to the world.

'We have to think of our finances now.' Ganesh spoke more to himself than Ramya. 'The girls are growing up faster than my salary and all their schooling and studies would be burning a hole in my pocket.'

Ramya nodded again, 'We will manage. But don't break the children's hearts.'

Ganesh shook his head again as he got up. 'Let me go, take a bath. It might help clear things.' He smiled to himself. He had set up the surprise perfectly.

As he took his evening bath, he remembered Mr Samant's words. During a late-night shift Samant had found Ganesh sitting at the canteen table calculating the monthly expenses. Clapping his hand on Ganesh's back he had said, 'Don't let these petty things get to you Ganesh. These are the entrapments of the lower class. Dream big! Don't you see the change India is going through?'

When Ganesh had countered it with his problems, Mr Samant had held up a hand with a slight smile. 'Who doesn't have problems my friend? But not a lot of people are adept at the solutions. The way you had sprung to action to avert that major disaster and help your colleague was inspiring.' Mr Samant said, recalling the event which had made him respect his junior employee. 'I see you are innovative and are not someone who should be tied down with these mundane tasks. I see a bright future for you and for that you have to dream big…'

Ganesh had taken those words to heart and had begun in earnest to change his circumstances. He had begun dreaming big and the television was one such small step towards a higher status.

Last week he had told Mr Samant that he was now ready to buy the TV and he had enough money. Mr Samant had put him in touch with the electronics shop and had exhorted the shop keeper to put an affordable price on the TV.

Ganesh had made the arrangements with his known electrician Dinesh, who had a brother drove a taxi. The television set would be delivered home later that evening by Dinesh's brother. He had been worried about the baby and hadn't found the time to break the news to his family.

But this latest conversation about the baby with Mr Samant had eased his mind and now he wanted his family members to also share his happiness.

2c. First TV, And Then Refrigerator

As promised Dinesh's brother brought the television set, a black CRT set in a packed carton carefully tied down on car roof. As the taxi neared the entrance to their chawl, the driver rang the car horn, two short hoots. The signal which would let Ganesh know his TV was here.

Ganesh came out on hearing the horn and so did Bhagwat kaka, a retired Head teacher at the neighbouring Municipal school. Ganesh quickly put on his blue and white pair of rubber slippers and hurried outside. Rarely would a car stop near their chawl.

Children who had been playing pakda-pakdi had stopped their bickering when the car had stopped and honked. Among them was Shruti. On seeing her father carry the big box to their home, she shouted out loudly to everyone within earshot, 'Aey…we got TV!'

Ramya broke into a laugh. Ganesh and Bhagwat kaka heaved and huffed and puffed their way through the narrow doorway inside and placed the box on the foldable table usually reserved for keeping washed utensils near the kitchen door.

Ganesh opened the box and all the children who had trooped in to see the TV let out a collective gasp in wonderment. There stood a beautiful black box with about two radials one for power and one for the lone channel that would go onto enthral audiences of all ages in the days to come. BPL, it proudly proclaimed.

Mr and Mrs Mhatre joined in. 'Ganesh, this is the best thing you did.' They were joyous, and happy for Tamhankars.

It was like a carnival at their home. Ramya changed into a nice saree, as more people came in to wish them on their latest acquisition and to see for themselves how a TV looked. They did a small aarti and Ramya put a tikka in the top middle portion of the TV where ideally its forehead should have been.

Everybody in the chawl had come in to look at the newest member of the Tamhankar's family and by the time 8-year-old Bunty, the last of their neighbours went home only because his mother had called out a warning that she would thrash him left right and centre as it was quite late in the day.

They hadn't switched the TV on. That would happen on Sunday, three days from then because, Ganesh had to go get the aluminium antennae and wire which would ensure that they would be able to watch Ramayana for the first time in all its glory in the chawl.

That night Ramya couldn't sleep, and she was sure from all the whispering she heard from the loft that the two girls were also super excited. Especially Shruti who could be heard telling Mrunali what she would be watching on TV.

***

On Saturday, Ganesh went with Dinesh and brought home a pair of aluminium antennae and a GI pipe frame and a long coil of wire. The next morning, which was a Sunday, Dinesh came early in the morning and climbed up onto the roof, stepping precariously on the asbestos sheets with the antenna.

Ganesh was inside the house twirling the thin wire fiddling at the back of the TV. Children from the whole chawl had gathered to watch the spectacle and slowly as the sun began to climb upwards, adults too came out, some brushing their teeth while some held newspapers and half-drunk glass of tea. All of them were gawking at the commotion happening outside Ganesh's residence.

As Dinesh finally managed to screw in the antennae and other contraptions firmly in place, he called out to Ganesh to turn the TV on. Jaya was amused with so much fanfare, with all the shouting and bickering that was going on around her, but Ramya hardly noticed. She rocked Jaya in her arms as Ganesh switched on the TV and almost everybody tried to get in to see what was happening. When the TV came on, again like last night there was a collective gasp of awe as people took in the grainy static in wonderment.

'Can you see anything?' Dinesh shouted from the roof.

'Not yet…uncle,' Bunty answered back, making a few of the mothers laugh.

Dinesh twisted the antenna slightly to the left and then rotated it some more and suddenly there was a break in the static on the TV and a first sighting of someone came on screen. There was a sudden burst of joy amongst the crowd with some teenagers even whistling.

Ganesh called out, 'Whatever you are doing, continue with that Dinesh.'

Dinesh could be seen fiddling with the metallic frame and then with one final twist he adjusted the antenna and suddenly Arun Govil appeared on TV screen in all his glory as Shri Ram and everybody went silent.

Some old women began to sing the praise of God under their breath, folding their palms and bowing their heads. They came in and sat down wherever they could find a space and let Ramayana wash through them that morning. Mrunali had Jaya and was sitting next to Shruti who had her mouth open as she sat there watching the show. Ramya and Ganesh surveyed the gathering with a sense of pride as they saw there were all age groups of people from the chawl watching Ramayana in rapt attention- on their TV and they were suddenly filled with a sense of joy. Mrs Mhatre brought tea for all the elders at home, this was an occasion of celebration. Well, some things are special. This was one such occasion. This would continue for a few years on most Sundays at the Tamhankar residence.

***

While TV became the centre of attention for many in the neighbourhood, it brought a new issue to Tamhankar family, specially Shruti. More, and more boys started coming to their house to watch TV for serials, movies, and cricket matches. Shruti started developing friendship with many of those. There were many boys elder to her, who liked her, fond of her beauty. Whenever they got a chance, they played with her, and touched her, in-appropriately at times. Shruti was not grown enough to understand the intentions, recognize the bad ones.

One day, Ajit came into the house. He knew that nobody is in the house except Shruti. She knew him and let him come in.

'Let us watch a movie,' he initiated. Shruti looked at him, and thought he is not requesting for it; but demanding it.

She started surfing the channels. 'Aha, this is 'Nagin', nice movie.'

'Yeah, you look like a Nagin.'

'Why?'

'Your cloths, like a Nagin,' he said, touching her cloths. Banter continued between them.

'I am Sapera, will catch you Nagin,' he suddenly got around her back, and caught her in his arms. He slowly grabbed her breasts. Shruti was noticing all of these, however ignored in the spontaneity of it happening. And, then he planted a strong kiss on her cheek.

Shruti realised in an instant that it is wrong. She applied all her power to come out of his hands and shouted very loudly. Ajit tried to calm her down. But Shruti was upset. He had to leave the house.

Shruti was not sure, whether to inform the parents or not. She kept on thinking about it, the pros, and cons of it. There will be lot of questions, lot of controls put on her. What if her parents confront Ajit or his family, it may come out in public? It can have disastrous side-effects. She decided to keep it low for now. But she was sure, she will be more careful with the boys, restrain them at a distance. She will be more selective on who to befriend. She did not tell her parents or share this incident with Mrunali.

***

Ganesh's business venture has kicked-of well. He has hired a contractor to work for him, and he was running this business between himself and his contractor. He was content with what he was making each week. Ultimately, he was the owner, and can manage his schedule per his wishes.

Summers in Mumbai have always been troublesome. When the refrigerator was invented, it was widely adopted, and most of the affluent Mumbaikars also welcomed a 'fridge' into their homes. Those who didn't have any cooling system would borrow some space in their neighbour's refrigerator and it was an accepted practice that those with fridge would help others in their time of need for ice or to cool their milk or occasionally prepared sweet dishes.

It was a surprise for Ramya one Sunday afternoon when Mrunali came back empty handed and in one hell raising rage.

'Where is the ice? And why are you angry?' Ramya enquired off her eldest daughter.

Shruti who had been outside playing with her gang, had entered the house right behind Mrunali answered, 'Tai and Kulkarni kaaku had a fight.'

Ganesh on hearing this perked his head up on his palm from where he was lying down on the sleeping mat.

'What is it?' he looked at Mrunali, 'Mrunali? What happened?'

Mrunali wiped some of the hair on her forehead with the back of the hand, but Ganesh couldn't help noticing, she had wiped the corner of her eye too. She didn't want her parents to see her crying.

'Did Kulkarni kaaku say something again?'

Mrunali kept mum, looking down at the empty container she was carrying.

Shruti tugged at her mother's saree and in an audible whisper said, 'Aai, Kulkarni kaaku was shouting at tai…'

'Shruti, keep quiet…' Mrunali had broken her silence, 'don't talk about things you don't understand…'

'So, you tell us…' Ramya prodded, taking the container gently from her hands.

'Parasite…' Mrunali burst out.

Ganesh sat up from his stupor and asked, 'What?'

'She called us parasites…' Mrunali said, tears welling up in her eyes now.

'She had one of her friends with her and made a big show and tell of how she helps the neighbourhood as the only member who has a fridge.'

'Did she tell you anything directly?' Ramya quizzed

Ganesh looked from his wife to his eldest daughter, who shook her head.

'She was referring to us. I was right there. I told her we rarely bother her. It's only that we would be having guests over.'

'Were you rude to Kulkarni Kaaku?' Ramya asked.

Ganesh marvelled at his wife. Teaching her children social etiquettes would remain priority number one for her. She didn't want them to grow up picking up all the negative traits usually children from chawls bound to pick up. She always spoke to them of outgrowing their surroundings and being the better person.

Mrunali looked at her mother. 'Aai, she was calling us…you a parasite…'

'But were you rude with her?' Ramya replied firmly but kindly.

'I…I don't remember, I said something that came to my mouth and then left that woman's house…'

'Tai told her off Aai…' Shruti began but one look from Mrunali silenced her.

Ganesh smiled, and then said, 'When we live in such close quarters, we shouldn't pick fights with people who we have to meet regularly. It becomes awkward.'

'I didn't like what she said, and I have made up my mind. I won't apologize to her and I won't go back to her house for anything…' Mrunali went upstairs without another word.

Ramya was about to tell her something when Ganesh gently shook his head and asked Shruti to go out and play. They could hear Mrunali crying silently, and both gently shook their heads, as if marvelling at the lack of patience of this generation.

That night Shruti would see her mother scouting for something amidst her cloths in her trunk in torchlight and would hear the ruffling sounds of money being counted.

This event caused the Tamhankars to have their biggest possession, a brand-new refrigerator. Ramya had saved some money from her household money, that was a big help to Ganesh.

Again, the people of the chawl converged at their home and someone even overheard Kulkarni kaaku proudly saying how she had prodded the Tamhankars to buy a 'fridge'.

2d. Mrunali's College And First Job

Ramya waited for her eldest one to return. It had been quite a while since Mrunali had gone to school with her friends. The SSC results (10th standard, board exams) were being declared that day. Like every parent she waited with bated breath for her daughter to come back with her results.

Ganesh had left for work saying he would return in the afternoon by taking a half day leave. Ramya kept looking at the Ajanta wall clock ticking away and stood at the door looking towards the entrance of the chawl.

Jaya was aware of the situation of anxiety and impatience in the house. She knew that it was a big day for her sister and family overall. She knew that it will be alright for her sister. She said to her Mom, 'Aai, don't worry. Tai will do the best.'

Ramya smiled to herself. How children grow up. It seemed like last week they had shifted their home to this chawl with a tiny Mrunali tightly clutched in her arms. And today they were waiting for the first milestone of her adulthood.

Mrs Mhatre, came asking for some spare sugar and looking at her taut face, laughed at her.

'kay ga...kashala ugach ghabarte?' she asked Ramya. (What happened? Don't bother so much).

'I am not afraid Tai...' Ramya replied with a sigh, 'this girl has been gone a while now. I hope everything is alright.'

'What will go wrong? Mruni is a smart kid, Ramya...' Mrs Mhatre very proudly said taking back her cup, filled with sugar, 'I am sure your girl will make both of you proud...' This is very common in the community to own up to your neighbour's kids and families. There is a sense of pride that one takes from the achievements of neighbours. And Mrs Mhatre's love for Mrunali never faded.

Some of her fears allayed, Ramya went back to her chores. Shruti came back from school and told her that the SSC students were being counselled by the Principal and Mrunali looked happy when she met her some time back.

Saying a silent prayer, Ramya continued with her work waiting for the arrival of both her husband and daughter.

***

It was late afternoon before Mrunali returned. Ganesh had finished eating his chapati and bhaji and some varan bhaat and was reading the Marathi newspaper borrowed from Mr Samant's office.

Ramya was about to go out and continue her vigil when Mrunali entered and touched her father's feet.

'Finally.' Ramya sighed. She didn't ask her about the results, the mother in her was just happy that her daughter had returned home safe and sound.

Mrunali gave the mark sheet to her father and took a sip of water from the steel tumbler her mother had handed her.

'Maa…I scored 62 percent…' she said after taking a sip.

Ganesh knew how significant this achievement was. His daughter scoring 62% and more, being a first-class; it has created a special place for himself and his family in the chawl society. Afterall it was a brave decision that he and Ramya had taken to continue to pursue his daughter's studies. This is a landmark event in her family, relatives and chawl community in general, and potentially paving a way for many more girls in the community to attend school and further studies. His heart was pumping with joy.

Ganesh peered into the piece of paper, which held the power to draft the future of an individual. He looked confused. The miniscule figures next to names of subjects were difficult to decipher for him. He had begun working when he had turned ten.

Ramya who understood the importance of a first-class degree smiled proudly, her vision going partly blurry from the tears forming in them. She ran her right hand over her daughter's head and mumbled a part prayer and part blessing.

Mrunali helped her father understand the mark sheet. She pointed out the subjects with their adjacent marks. She further said, 'Baba, teacher says I should take Science. I have scored the highest in both Maths and Science…'

Ramya looked worried now. Before she could say anything Mrs Mhatre and a few women from the neighbourhood came in joking about something loudly. Ganesh invited them in and indicated to Ramya to offer them the peda sweets he had brought.

The women turned their attention to Mrunali and boisterously congratulated her on her achievement.

Mrs Mhatre reached for the box of peda, Ramya held and said, 'See Ramya, I told you, your girl is intelligent. And here you were worried that she would do something to herself if her results were bad.'

Ramya wiped away the tears and laughed along with the other women as Mrunali slowly encircled her waist from behind.

'Kay tai…anything you say.' Ramya replied playfully admonishing the elder woman.

'What have you decided child?' asked another woman from the group now that everyone had received their sweets.

Mrunali turned to look at her parents and Ganesh nodded with his eyes closed as if to say we will see.

'It is not every day that we hear of a first-class degree, Ganesh bhau…' Dipti kaaku pitched in, 'You must allow the girl to study further…' Then turning to Shruti who had sidled in from behind, she added, 'Look at your elder sister. You have some huge shoes to fill little ones.'

Ramya replied, 'We also want that kaaku... it's just that college would put our finances in turmoil.' She saw Mrunali look despondent and hurriedly added, 'But we want her to study further.'

Once the group had left and Shruti and Jaya helped themselves to a palm full of pedas despite the strict instructions from Ramya to wash their hands before touching the sweets. Ganesh sat Mrunali down and beckoned to Ramya also to sit down.

'Beta...I would want you to be an educated woman...' he began looking here and there trying to find the right words. 'Scoring such good marks, now that I have heard these women describing your marks as an achievement, I have no doubt you will do well for yourself.'

Mrunali sat listening to her father and kept looking between her parents.

***

That night Mrunali could not sleep. Her mind kept pulling her along back to the discussion they all had, that evening. She knew her parents were extremely proud of her for scoring a first-class. Given their circumstances of living in a chawl where anyone could just walk in unannounced and sit for hours talking with the family and neighbours watching TV in her home with loud noise, Mrunali had scored well.

But now the question was about her future. What did she want to do? She wanted to tell her father that she wanted to be an architect. She wanted to design homes. She wanted to build them a house and move them out of this matchbox they called home. She had begun to think ambitiously after visiting Mr Samant's new flat in Chembur. How spacious the rooms were. How well planned it was. There was ample space for kids like Shruti to run around and play without the fear of falling into open gutters.

But her father that evening had snapped her dream. He told her, 'Mrunali, my child I want to educate you further. But I also have to think of Shruti and Jaya and your future.'

Ramya had nodded looking at her eldest daughter as if agreeing with her husband. Ramya knew about her aspirations.

Ganesh continued, 'Getting a seat in the college for pursuing...' he had paused trying to get the name properly, '...architect course won't be easy.'

Seeing the look of realisation on his daughter's face as to where this discussion was going, Ganesh said, 'Mruni... I am not going to stop your studies. But I won't be able to afford the college fees for the next few years.'

'It's okay papa...' Mrunali replied, putting a lid on her dreams, 'I will do commerce and start working. I want to work and help with the finances.'

Ganesh looked at her daughter, his heart wept. Emotionally he was hurt, he knew that this is not right. But this was not the time to indulge in further conversation.

Ganesh was equally taken aback by how mature his eldest daughter sounded and looked at Ramya. His wife had tears in her eyes but nodded her head in affirmation. He had at that time not paid attention to the part where Mrunali had said she wanted to work.

Mrunali had excused herself after that and gone up. She had buried her head into the pillow and cried.

Now lying there staring at the ceiling she realised that her parents weren't against her dreams. But being born into a lower middle-class family, sometimes you had to let go off many of your hopes and aspirations. She had learnt this at a very young age.

***

Ganesh had accompanied Mrunali to college on the first day. He hadn't entered the gates though and had waved his goodbye a few feet away from the gates.

The local Municipal Corporator had been instrumental in securing the college seat. A few days after the family had decided that Mrunali would pursue commerce, Ganesh had taken her to meet the Corporator, Mr Dewade. Ganesh handed over the box of sweets to him. The politician was mighty impressed by the young girl who looked intelligent. He had promised Mrunali that she would study commerce in one of Mumbai's best colleges and true to his words, had secured her a seat in Chinai

College of Commerce; one of the well-known commerce colleges in the city.

Mrunali had realised on the very first day that college would be an altogether different thing. Gone were the friends, she had studied with all through school. Gone was the unity of the school uniforms they used to wear. Instead, she was surrounded by youngsters who had been brought up in some of the posh localities sprinkled around Mumbai.

She realised in the first week that she would be judged for who she was and not for her mettle. The realisation that she was so below them in stature and status dawned on her and gave her many sleepless nights.

She made a friend in another girl living in the chawl in the other area, who had got into the college purely on her merit. A girl named Surbhi. Mrunali would spend most of her college hours with Surbhi. Both realised that they would be social outcasts for these rich brats coming in their parent's cars. They decided to stick together.

It was Surbhi who introduced Mrunali to the job at a coffee shop. Mumbai was undergoing a renaissance of sorts. Rich Mumbaikars who had a taste of foreign shores had returned to the city of birth and had begun investing in properties in and around the city. Slowly but surely the traditional land belonging to the mill owners were changing hands and were in the throes of being designed into some form of supermarkets- only richer and more snobbish.

Coffee shops were being opened to serve the ultra-rich, and youngsters like Surbhi were in high demand. They needed people who would work for long hours without complaining and whose many needs would be satiated by the meagre salary they would receive during the end of the month.

Mrunali decided to inform her parents of her decision to join the coffee shop her friend worked for.

Ganesh and Ramya initially didn't understand the concept of a coffee shop and thought she was going to work as a waitress in some restaurant.

Mrunali explained to them how it would help her earn a few extra rupees and contribute to both her studies and home expenses.

Ganesh said, 'Mruni, why do you need to work? I told you that even though finances are tight, I will do everything to satisfy your needs…'

Ramya added, 'What will the community say? That the Tamhankars are sending their daughter out to work.' This was the big deal. It was never meant to be an easy decision. While on one side, their minds and souls did not allow their daughter to go for work; on the other end there is society that they have to explain.

Mrunali listened to her parents intently. She understood they were afraid of the social implications and she decided to try a new tact. She replied, 'Aai, ask baba…what age did he start working?'

Ganesh looked quizzically at his wife. He didn't understand what relevance his age had, to this new obsession of Mrunali. He scratched his greying beard as he said, 'Beta, I am a man and I do have to fend for our family…'

But even before he could finish Mrunali had jumped at his statement, '…and I am the daughter of the same man, baba…'

Ramya looked at her daughter and replied, 'But you don't have to, Mruni. As long as your father and I are alive, we don't want you to work.'

'Then why educate me?' Mrunali asked her mother

'Mrunali,' Ganesh called out his daughter's name. 'What your mother wants you to understand is, we are not against you working. But right now, we want you to study. When you are a suitable age, ready to take your own decisions we won't stop you…'

Mrunali wasn't going to let it go so easily. 'How will I learn to be independent if you keep protecting me like this? I am going to college. I am doing the course you want me to do. Am I not? Can't you allow me to work? I want to earn some money, so I don't have to ask you for all my small needs.'

Ganesh and Ramya listened to their daughter in silence and wondered if there were some hidden reasons why she was being so adamant. They hadn't been to college and wouldn't know the dynamics of the college. The pressures of the youth would be an alien concept to them. But Mrunali hadn't demanded anything from them so vehemently and at last they decided to grant her, her wish. But they made her promise them that her studies won't suffer, and she would be back home before seven in the evening.

The next day Mrunali gave Surbhi the happy news and went with her to the coffee shop to submit her hurriedly prepared biodata.

2e. One Diwali And Shruti's Trouble

Mrunali wanted to celebrate the Diwali festival this year at another scale. She brought in a lot of crackers, two days before Diwali.

Shruti and Jaya were over joyous, 'Tai, this is too much. We will have lot of fun this Diwali.'

Ganesh asked, 'Why so many? Now you all are grown up.'

'Baba, we will play with other kids in the chawl. We should at least celebrate now more comfortably.' Ganesh nodded. He noticed the sense of confidence in his daughter's voice.

The same night, Mrunali asked her mother, 'Aai, we never celebrate Bhaiduj.'

Each Bhaiduj, Ramya felt absence of something in her family, devoid of that happiness for her daughters. However, she never openly discussed it. This question from mature Mrunali put her in shock.

'What happened, Mrunali?' she asked, wiping her tears. 'Why are you talking like this? Its Lord Ganesha's wish to not give you brothers. So, what can we do?'

Mrunali said, 'Aai, this is nothing to do with God.' Ramya noticed some resolution in Mrunali's eyes.

'We don't have our own real brother. That is fine, it is God given. However, we need to have positivity in our minds. There are so many young brothers that we have in society. I want to celebrate this Diwali Bhaiduj with them.'

Ramya just could sigh, 'Are you saying?'

'Yes Maa, is that okay with you?'

'Beta, you are grown up. Your thinking has so much matured for the society. Absolutely, we would be fine.'

On the day of Bhaiduj, Ramya, Mrunali cooked lot of food. In the afternoon, they invited all the young boys from nearby to celebrate the festival.

While Mrunali was doing the rituals with her rakhi-brothers, Ramya had tears in her eyes. This was the time when she felt if her daughters needed a real brother. But at the same time, she was pleased that her daughter Mrunali has raised herself above the society rules.

***

India was playing South Africa today. Lot of people in the chawl would gather at Tamhankar's house, to watch the cricket match on TV. Mrunali wrapped up the Bhaiduj celebrations just in time. She was very excited with the festivities.

Shruti wouldn't enjoy the gatherings in the house. During those days, she would go out and join the Sharma family in the neighbourhood.

Mr Angad & Mrs Pooja Sharma are good looking couple. They moved in this neighbourhood barely a year ago. They both are working and earn enough to have a bit of extravagance.

Shruti felt, that they are nice souls, and cared for every human being. She had developed a strong bonding with the Sharma family, and would refer them as bhaiya (brother) and bhabhi (sister-in-law). She liked them; she cared for their new-born kid, Munna.

Pooja's brother Varun had arrived from his hometown Indore; to spend some time with his sister. It was his Diwali vacations. He also wanted to explore the city of Mumbai. Shruti and Varun quickly became friends. They started spending a lot of time. She used to feel safe in his presence, she liked his companionship.

Within a few weeks, they became very close friends. Varun would often touch her. When she would ask him to stop; he would grab her tightly. Shruti allowed all of this thinking that he is here only for a few weeks. Her own affection for him overwhelmed her own conscience.

Shruti came to Sharma's house, knocking the door with fuming head, jumping her legs. Varun enquired, 'What happened?'

'There is no place in the house. It is completely full, filled with everyone in the world. Why do they watch Cricket? They have only my house to watch it. I cannot even go to sleep.' Shruti was visibly upset, and angry with the situation.

Varun looked at her, and tried pacifying, 'Calm down, Shruti. You look so cute when you are angry.'

This made Shruti smile. 'Where is Bhaiya and Bhabhi?' She raised her eyes in question.

'They are out for Diwali shopping, should be back soon. They left me to watch Munna.' Varun said, and offered a little place next to him on the bed lying in the living room with baby Munna in between them.

'Ok, I'm going to get a bit of sleep. Wake me up when Bhabhi comes in.' She just jumped onto the bed, fetched Munna closer to her; and closed her eyes.

Shruti immediately went to sleep. After some time, she felt little pleasure and some weight on her. She opened her eyes; it was Varun intimately close to her. She was surprised with what was going on. He was playing with her top. She retaliated a bit, 'Varun, what are you doing? Stop.'

Varun did not stop, he instead asked 'What? You do not like it.' He continued to gently move his fingers around her body. Shruti experienced something, some joy, she could neither retaliate, nor control her excitement. She has never experienced this feeling earlier. Her heart was pumping very fast. She fetched him closer.

Varun started to kiss her all over her cheek, eyes, and ears with passion. Then, on her lips. Slowly eased her cloths to pull her tits out in his mouth. He removed his pants, and her lower cloths. Shruti tried to resist, but the temptation to get into this was high. Varun was continuously rubbing himself against her. She felt this pleasure for the first time. She experienced the divine sensation. She demanded, 'More. More.' Varun was completely immersed into it, and it happened. Both were one, into each other, lost into each other. Push, and pull. Lots of it. And finally, there was calmness.

Then they untied, and quickly wore their cloths. Shruti did not bother to look into Varun's eyes. She ran to her house in no time.

Shruti could not sleep that night. She kept thinking about it. 'What happened, is not right.' She exclaimed to herself, 'Oh my god, why did I commit this. It is a sin.' She knew that it is not accepted in the society. This is something that must be done after marriage. She was morally deteriorated deep inside. She was the villain in her mind, and herself the cause.

She fetched the pillow, and cried deep within 'Why did you do this, Varun, to me? Why did you? I trusted you. You defeated me.' Anger within her came out in tears. But she soon corrected herself, 'I could have stopped all of this. I could have just said, No. Why was I enjoying it? Why was it a pleasure? I did it. I am the one to be blamed.' This dilemma has killed her many a times that night.

She decided to not return to Sharma's home until Varun returned to his hometown.

***

Things became usual again with Varun returned to his home-down. Shruti again started visiting Sharma's family and taking care of their baby, Munna.

One day, Angad returned home little earlier than usual. Pooja was still at work. Shruti was present in their house, taking care of their baby Munna. Shruti was surprised, but happy to see Angad bhaiya at home. She brought a glass of water for him.

Angad asked Shruti, 'Come here,' signalling her to sit next to him. She placed herself there without hesitation. He enquired, 'Shruti, there was a long time, you did not come here. What had happened?' Angad looked concerned, and he wanted to know. Shruti shrugged her shoulders, 'Nothing.'

Angad pressed Shruti to open-up. After lot of persuasion, Shruti opened-up, and briefly mentioned about what occurred with Varun. She cautiously hid the part of deep intimacy.

Shruti started crying while talking about it. Angad fetched her tightly in his arms. It was more than trying to console her, it was inappropriate. He started tapping her back. Shruti was uncomfortable, she showed reluctance.

There was a knock. Mrs Pooja Sharma came in. Her eyes could not believe what she was seeing. 'Whore' she threw the expletive at Shruti. Angad was shocked to see his wife, he released the control on Shruti. She swiftly came out of his arms. She got up and quickly adjusted her cloths keeping her eyes lower.

Pooja was seething in anger, she jumped onto Shruti. She threw another abuse, 'Kulta, you family spoiler. You call him Bhaiya and doing all this nonsense.' Angad trying to soothe, 'Pooja, listen. Leave it.' This only aggravated her further, 'you stay there.'

Shruti kept pleading that she did not do anything wrong. But Pooja kept dragging her by her hair and arms; and took her to Ramya.

Pooja shouted, hurled abuses, called Shruti a Slut, and slapped in front of her mother. She finally returned to her house. However, Tamhankar's were still in shock, absorbing what just happened. Shruti was sobbing, baffled, not aware of her fault.

3. Politics And Shree Party

3a. Ganesh Introduction To Shree Party

'Divide and Rule' is a common tactics of humankinds. Whenever a particular section of the society wants to rule; they resort to this ploy. They sow the seeds of divisions in the society into several groups to their advantage. It was done in the form of several castes in the beginning when human race was developing social paradigms. Later, kings, and colonists continued the trend. And now it has become an important weapon for political establishments. One sets-up the new political outfit and grows it into an empire simply by sowing hatred in the hearts of human beings against each other.

This is irony, that public falls prey to such political groups. There are hardly a few, who realize the power & impact of unity, which can bring tremendous difference to our lives. However, as rightly said in several religious scriptures; human race is faced with five evils – Kama (lust), Krodh (wrath), Lobh (greed), Moh (attachment), and Ahankar (pride). Political leaders play with these evils inside each one-of-us and do it to their advantage.

Since independence, there were several political parties born based on regionalism. Late eighties, one such party named 'Shree Party' was framing up and setting up its wings, which greatly influenced and affected the people of Mumbai and many parts of the Maharashtra state.

Shree Party aspired to grow its strength beyond limits. The head of Shree party, known as Shinde Bhao, his influence in general Marathi public was growing with each day.

Life On The Edge

At a public rally, the head of Shree party in his full form declared.

'Here is my right hand, on one side, and here is my left hand…You are either on the right side, or on the left side.' He was chewing each word deliberately.

'I am joining my left hand and right hand.' He brought his both hands together forward. 'Here.' 'You see this now. It is a thin line. You have to take a decision. Whether you want to be on this side of the path with me. Or you want to be on the other side.'

He declared again, on what it means to be on his side. 'If you are on my side, you are on the path of righteousness. You are on the path of truthfulness. You are supporting Devas on Asuras.'

'Remember, a lot of people died to secure the freedom for us in 1947. This is the time for us to secure freedom from 'Others'. Why should others' rule on us? Why should they take away our bread? Why should they take away our milk, vegetables, and many more things?'

'I see, several of our people from the ground, born here struggling to get their daily bread and butter.' Now he was melodramatic. 'Husband is not able to feed his wife. Father is not able to take good care of his children. Who is responsible?' Long pause.

Some in his party prodded. People roared in unison 'These Others.'

'Yes, these 'Others'. The politicians, who wants to serve these 'others', want to get their votes. What should we do?'

Public roared in unison, 'Bhagava, Niakala' 'Throw them out.'

'Enough of losing our own water, our own grains, our own wealth to the others. We cannot anymore see our own fathers, mothers, brothers, and sisters struggling, begging…We need to claim our right. Let us fight for it, fight for our right.'

Public responded to the ask 'You move ahead. We are with you.' It was unison, and it continued…It went on, and on. Louder, each time.

That was the charisma of Shinde Bhao!

There on the stage, Shinde Bhao was waving his hand, with eyes wide open, devoid of any emotion on the face; seeing such a large gathering as a ladder to reach to the top.

***

Ganesh and a few of his colleagues from the Railway had been inducted into the party around the time he had decided to quit his job and start his business.

Ganesh had begun looking up to the corporator Mr Dewade as an elder brother and would tag along for all the meetings of the newly formed party christened as 'Shree Party'.

Though Shinde himself was not a Railway worker, he had started working for the Rail Worker Welfare Committee, which had been an unofficial initiative of the General Manager of the Mumbai Division for Central Railway.

Shinde bhao had slowly gravitated to more issues plaguing the common Maharashtrian. He emphasized on regional pride in all his speeches and Ganesh would clap the loudest when he heard bhao's powerful rhetoric. Though Ganesh was a liberal at heart, he found himself agreeing with Shinde bhao on more than one occasion.

Ganesh had begun working earnestly for Shinde bhao around the time Mrunali had begun college. Shinde bhao was the real influence behind the corporator procuring a seat for Mrunali.

Ganesh and many others had joined the corporator to this public rally, which was completely full of people.

'The Maratha is an amiable human being and is always ready to help …' Shinde said.

'But the Maratha is also a fierce warrior. If needled beyond our tolerance, we won't stop ourselves from raising our sword once again in the name of Chhatrapati Shivaji Maharaj.'

Someone on cue had taken up the chant of 'Shivaji Maharaj chi jai' and Ganesh along with the crowd found himself joining in. He found he had goosebumps as he raised the slogan repeatedly.

Shinde bhao started, what he does his best. 'Go into any Marathi household; see what's cooking in their kitchens. You will only see dishes of pain and tears.'

He continued with the emotional monologue, 'Our brothers are finding it difficult to sustain their families. Our sisters are being forced to pledge their chastity, forget their dreams, and throw away their aspirations into the dustbin because they are not being given a fair chance by these outsiders.'

Shinde roared.

'Stop this drama of being Shivraya's followers and do something worthy of him. Take up your sword once again and like he had. Throw out these unworthy bastards, who are taking away your jobs, eating your food grains and living in homes meant for you...'

Shinde had thundered holding the microphone to the rousing chants of his fellow party members. 'Bhagawa, Nikaalaa.'

He had brought out the inner most torment the common middle-class man suffered from and had in that instance exhorted the listeners to get up and fight against the injustice. He had chided them for having the great Maratha blood in their veins and yet being meek in the face of this modern-day invasion by the 'outsiders'.

Shinde bhao held evening meetings for his blue collared worker brothers in one of Mumbai's biggest playgrounds, the Shivaji Park. Though the gathering was small, it had the potential to grow into a humongous organism. Ganesh had sworn allegiance then and there to the causes of Marathi manus.

Ganesh was in awe of the kurta clad, gentle faced Shinde bhao. He wondered how this man could look so peaceful and yet shatter all illusions of propriety with his words.

He was a lean man with wavy hair that occasionally would tumble onto his forehead during his many fiery speeches. He had a voice and a way with words which could summon your attention to the powerful arguments he made and make you want to agree with him.

The more Ganesh heard him, the more he became enamoured by his ideologies. He wanted to know more about this man. One such evening, while coming back from a political rally Ganesh started talking to Shinde bhao's man, Gangadhar. He had been with bhao from the time he had taken his first steps in politics. Gangadhar started narrating bhao's story.

3b. Shinde Bhao

Born in a poor household, Damodar Shinde had known what poverty was, right from a very young age.

His father had been a mill worker and had been laid off when a freak accident at the workplace amputated his legs. Even though the family of five received a compensation of fifty thousand rupees from the mill owner, his father would never be able to earn another single rupee all his remaining limbless lifetime. The money was spent on medication and tiding the family through the rough few months after the incident.

Damodar was too young then to replace him in the factory and Meena and Radha his elder sisters would be misfits in a male dominated space. They were asked to help around the house. He continued with his schooling as everyone said he was their last hope.

His mother went out to work as house maid and would blame his father every night as she massaged her chapped feet and made the children apply some medicated oil on her back to soothe her stiff spinal cord. The family continued to struggle for a few years to make ends meet.

Then one fine day his mother did not come back home. Some of the neighbours said they had seen her with the 'Madrasi', a Southern who delivered food to the colony residents nearby. That was earth shattering for Damodar. He did not go back to school again.

At the age of 15, he started accompanying one of their neighbours to the newspaper office and began delivering the Marathi newspaper. Though his schooling was unceremoniously stopped, his learning continued. He had a keen eye for societal problems and the various social reform movements that sprung up from time to time.

Damodar would slog the whole day, first at the newspaper office and then at the tea stall opposite the nearby railway station that served tea and piping hot vada pavs.

He would observe the tonnes of wide-eyed migrants getting down from the trains with looks of determination, wanting a slice of the city for themselves. He would smirk to himself as he cleaned the steel tumblers with the used water and wipe it off the last remnants of muck. He knew it would take about two weeks for the eyes to lose their sheen as the city would suck out the soul from these imposters.

The newspaper office and the tea stall became his school. He would keep his ears open at the newspaper office plugging into everything that was being spoken by the journalists who critiqued everything that the politician said and did. And he would keep his eyes open and watch the politicians as they milled around the tea stall for their daily fix and thrashed everything that the journalists wrote about.

He realised that the society was run by these factions - the politicians and the media. And he also learnt one of the biggest secrets they guard; that they might throw themselves at each other every minute of the day, but when night came, they would all sleep in the same bed, the politician and the journalist. They knew they needed each other.

Shinde defined himself and his thoughts with his day-to-day work, and he continued the path of becoming a socially responsible young man. He participated in all relevant social debates and started taking up political activities aimed at the creation of a separate State in western India with Bombay touted to be its capital city. He would read about all the prominent leaders who worked tirelessly towards Samyukt Maharashtra and then listen to their heated debates in the evenings.

***

In his earnest focus on the external society, he had forgotten to see what was happening with his family. His father had become a miserable relic and would whine away the time lying on the single bed next to the tiny window lamenting his misfortune, perennially drunk out of his wits.

'Meena…' he would call out to his elder daughter. He had started asking her to fetch his quarter of daroo from the tadi-madi vikri kendra. Meena met someone there during her daily sojourns and like any girl had begun dreaming a life of joy for herself. She was tired of the daily wretched grind and wanted to break free. So, she did. She grabbed whatever was valuable and worth grabbing and in the middle of the night, abandoned her family to their fate.

'Followed her mother's path...' the neighbours taunted while her father shook his head dully. Damodar ground his teeth but refused to offer anything.

His focus began to grow more towards the social causes as he began to realise this was his way out. He would go home whenever he had a handful of money but that became farther and farther apart.

His father had stopped drinking, choosing to cry himself hoarse during the waking hours or cry himself to sleep.

On one such visits home Damodar heard from Bunty, his childhood schoolmate who worked in a Gujarati Seth's garage that he had seen Radha at one of the gambling dens. He told Damodar that Radha had been in an objectionable situation.

All hell broke loose that night in the Shinde kholi when Radha returned and found Damodar waiting for her.

With a look of contempt, she crossed the small box of a room and fetched herself a glass of water from an earthen pot. Damodar realised suddenly that Radha resembled the decked-up prostitutes he would encounter near the Kamathipura lane while returning from the political rallies.

He got up and strode up to his elder sister and grabbing her by the shoulder spun her around and slapped her with the back of his hands. She reeled and crashed into the utensils lined up on a cement storage unit and sat down. More from shock than pain, she took a moment to register what had happened, then got up and grabbed his collar and started hitting him on his chest while beginning to cry.

Their father lay there soundlessly mouthing words urging them to stop hurting each other. But the hurt was far deeper than just physical.

'We had to eat, and he needed to be fed...' Radha gestured towards the bed casually without looking at their father.

'But how could you become this...this cheap...' Damodar searched for words.

'Cheap?' Radha looked at him, eyes ablaze. 'You know what is cheap?'

'What?' Damodar asked angrily. 'What was this compulsion that you could not help yourself from exposing your body parts like this to strange men and visiting such shady places?'

Radha wiped her tears, and hurled at Damodar, 'Have you tried to find out how your father eats? How we are able to survive with the pittance you used to throw into our hands?'

Damodar's eyes were wide open, he did not utter anything. He had been unable to visit his house and provide them any money. He had been so engrossed in his social activities, he realised he had neglected his family.

Radha continued venom spitting out with each word, as if she blamed her younger brother for the situation, they found themselves in. 'The ration that comes from the Desai stores comes because I have to go to his shop in the evening after he shuts the front shutters. That is how I manage to get the grocery.'

'I have to warm his bed. But you don't have to know anything about how we are surviving...'

She was in tears, but still speaking 'And the electricity officer who comes every month to threaten us with cutting the connection only goes away after he spends some time with the helpless woman who would do anything to avoid that. I wonder how he goes home to his children and wife after...after...'

Radha stopped, unable to put her feelings into words. But then what she spoke has hit him the hardest.

'And Bunty, your best friend has the audacity to ask your sister for some private service just to keep mum about the news of what I do from spreading in this colony, from ruining your political career. He is like my brother, isn't he? I had to draw the line somewhere.' Radha broke down now, completely dissolving into tears.

Life On The Edge

Damodar sat their listening to his sister unable to say anything, do anything. He was too shocked to react. He got up and went out, just to never return to that kholi.

That night was not yet over. They say light is at the end of the tunnel. But life can get worst, and more-worst. It is on the edge, from where it is not retractable. Radha hanged herself after poisoning her father.

'It was probably the shame.' Gangadhar stopped speaking abruptly. He was shivering. Ganesh let out a long sigh, 'Oh My God. Tough, very tough.'

***

Ganesh went home, his head in a tizzy. He could not even think of his own daughters going through whatever bhao's family had gone through.

Ramya opened the door and let him come in. She made a disapproving noise as she looked at the clock. Ganesh ignored it as he was in no mood to have an argument. He quickly washed his feet and lied to his wife that he had eaten outside with bhao.

He checked on his children, Jaya was fast asleep. Mrunali, who had woken up when Ganesh walked in, had a protective arm around Shruti, as the younger one snored away in bliss. He smiled at her and gestured to go back to sleep. She smiled back and closed her eyes.

Ganesh said a silent prayer and laid himself down on the sleeping mat. He promised himself as he went to sleep, he would do anything to secure his children's future.

To protect his family, he now realised he would have a greater role to play along with Shinde bhao. He would fight for every Maharashtrian who faced injustice. Yes, he would take up his sword like Shivaji.

3c. Ganesh And Politics

Ganesh had started treading the path of politics every evening after work. He would often be found engrossed in going through the party manifesto on most occasions in the tiny Party office that Shinde bhao had procured from a money lender after muscling out the poor immigrants, who had originally stayed there. When the money lender approached Shinde bhao to complain about the squatters, he hadn't realised he was inviting bigger trouble.

Soon the place was resplendent with Party emblems and party flags and flyers proclaiming their motto to anyone and everyone. The party was growing and needed foot soldiers and Shinde bhao had grand visions for everyone who would trust him and walk with him. He was showing them a tomorrow of fulfilment. Everyone was ready to do whatever it would take to make the dreams of Shinde bhao a reality. He towered over them and churned out philosophies and thoughts that had rarely ever sprouted in their seldom greased minds. Shinde bhao knew the pulse of his foot workers. He had seen the same days they were seeing and knew what to say and how to say it to spur them on. And he would sell the same two stories over and over again to every newcomer - Future and Money!

The future is the biggest lie told to mankind to keep him toiling away at tasks he hates. Keep feeding them with pictures of beauty and paradise and they will suffer silently and die keeping the picture in their hearts. Some would, but most wouldn't realise that it was all a big sham. A beautiful future doesn't exist. Even when it comes, you will not be enjoying it. You will continue to live your miserable lives, relieved that you don't have to think of another big question, money!

Money or the thought of money would fuel people onwards. They would do whatever was asked of them. People would even part with money they currently have if they are told about transforming it into bigger returns. They are all the same. The rich, the poor; the haves and the have nots

Life On The Edge

everybody wants to multiply their wealth. Shinde bhao knew it all. He had seen them at close quarters. The rich politicians coming to have a cup of chai at his stall to the beggar on the footpath who came for the crumbs, they all wanted more. They were all greedy for more.

***

One afternoon while Ganesh was sitting at his shop, Gangadhar came by. Ganesh was surprised as they had planned to meet later that evening at the Party office.

'Shinde bhao convened an immediate meeting and wants you there,' Gangadhar told matter-of-factly.

'Gangadhar dada I haven't done any business today and customers are complaining that I am not available when they want something urgently.' Ganesh replied and added, 'but tell bhao that I will come by in the evening and will be there right through the night if needed.'

'He told me you might be busy with work and asked me not to disturb you. But I know you are one of his most trusted allies and he would need all his close men when he is about to make this very important announcement, Ganesh.' Gangadhar could sound incredibly earnest when he wanted to.

He saw Ganesh thinking over what he had heard and then he saw a change of expression as he made his decision. Shinde bhao had told him exactly what to tell Ganesh. That afternoon, yet again Ganesh closed his business early and joined Gangadhar.

Ganesh would listen to all the talks bhao would give to his party members. The party was slowly moving forward, it had gathered momentum to stop with all the ideating and begin acting. He recognized that the agenda for this meeting was something different.

He saw Shinde bhao deep in thought. He went up to him and stooped to touch his feet. Bhao without breaking his thoughts, passed his hand over Ganesh's back. Ganesh went and stood at his customary spot on the right-hand side corner of the room from where he had a vantage point of seeing both outside the window and survey the entire room and the corridor outside.

Ganesh looked around the room. What he saw was burning Marathi pride written clearly on each face. Their shirts had lost their sheen long back. Of course, they were all poor. But they carried themselves with pride. They spoke to each other as if they had just finished conquering their kingdoms. Bhao had promised them all, the fruits of their labour would be sweeter than any nectar they had tasted in life and today they had all accumulated to be part of the first step towards that journey.

People had already started trickling in, loudly chatting, and laughing and thumping each other's backs and the voice levels in the tiny premise rose in crescendo. When everyone had assembled, Gangadhar slowly stood up and cleared his throat loudly. The crowd quietened.

'My brothers,' Gangadhar began without any preamble. 'Shinde bhao has something very important to tell us and he wouldn't have called you here urgently if it wasn't this important...' he trailed away when he heard Shinde bhao clear his throat mildly, indicating that he was ready to talk.

Gangadhar spoke into the microphone holding the stand with both his hands, 'Bhau will address you now.' He bowed himself back and Shinde bhao walked up to the microphone and faced the crowd.

The men looked at him keenly.

'It is time...' bhao spoke, then stopped and shook his head. 'I must correct. It is overdue now. They have kept thrusting themselves into our lives for years and we have remained silent, enduring them and this injustice all our lives.'

Ganesh was surprised at the acid in bhao's words. Someone from behind interrupted, 'What are you talking about bhao...We don't understand...'

Bhao raised his hands to silence the enquirer. 'You have always been clueless. You have never opened your eyes to see the things happening around you. And now you stand there and question me.'

The men collectively looked down. 'Why do you look down now?' bhao thundered, 'Since when have you known shame...? We have been converging here every day for the past so many months and never, not once have any of you taken any initiative to change your circumstances. Every day goes in eating someone's leftovers.'

'Bhao, why are you saying such hurtful things? What have we done?' someone spoke out again.

'Nothing. Absolutely nothing. And there lies the problem.' Bhao retorted. 'You haven't moved even your little finger to correct the wrongs in your own life. And I, like a fool, have been dreaming of a happy future, a secure future for each one of you. But what have you given in return? You come here like you came here today and indulge in banter and talks and go home, only to forget and return to your miserable flea-bitten lives as if nothing wrong has ever happened to you.'

Ganesh spoke, 'Bhao we are sorry. We all are. Please tell us what our mistake is, and we will correct it.'

Bhao glanced slightly towards Ganesh's direction but then went back to looking over the heads of the men in front of him. 'I am not your headmaster to teach you. I am just another man like you, who might have suffered more injustice than all of you combined.'

He looked over at Ganesh now. 'You all have your families to go back to and forget about the greater good. Keep doing that. I am shutting down this party. You are not worthy of any sacrifice…'

Bhao paused and took out a handkerchief and made as if to wipe a tear. Ganesh moved forward from where he was and held bhao's hand.

'Bhao, I promise you this. We are in this together with you. We look up to you as an elder brother. Just tell us what to do and we will do it for you.'

Shinde bhao shook his head slowly as if he had already made up his decision. But spoke clearly into the microphone, 'the path I suggest is too tough.'

'Bhao, we are ready to give our lives for you. Just tell us what to do…' someone shouted from behind. Ganesh didn't see Gangadhar at his usual spot and recognized his voice. But that statement had lit a spark in the men. Someone else picked it up from there and shouted his assertion. The air was filled with men raising the slogan of Shree Party and shouting out their allegiance to their leader.

Ganesh joined in and in that moment swore his priorities towards the man whose hands he had held. For him from that moment on it would only be Shree Party.

That evening an important change had been inducted into Shree Party. Shinde bhao had created an army of soldiers who would do all his biddings with no questions asked.

That evening Shree Party had its first action plan. They would be protesting the new appointment of a BMC head. Alok Shukla had been appointed and it hadn't gone down well with Shinde bhao. His acquaintance had approached him at this gross violation of his own right as son of the soil. Shinde bhao knew this was what he was waiting for, but he needed to spur his men out of their lethargy.

***

The next morning Ganesh and Gangadhar led the men to the BMC headquarters with hastily created banners made from white bed sheets. They began the picketing at 9 am and continued to shout slogans against the new head. As the car carrying the BMC head made its way towards the sprawling gate, Shree Party workers stormed towards it and started banging on the bonnet and the window. Ganesh and Gangadhar were busying throwing slogans at Shukla who sat inside the car petrified. Ganesh felt bad for the man, but quickly realigned his thinking. The man sitting inside was symbolic of everything that was wrong with the system.

Suddenly Gangadhar took hold of Ganesh by his arms and pulled him out of the chaos and moved towards the nearby alley. Ganesh was surprised but followed with a surprising glance at Gangadhar.

In answer to his enquiring look, Gangadhar beckoned to the approaching police vans.

'Our work is done. Bhao had asked both of us to report back to the office in case of any police interference.' Gangadhar spoke over his shoulder as he started hurrying down the alley far away from the protest.

Ganesh followed him walking fast to keep up with Gangadhar. 'What about our men?' he asked.

'They will all take care of themselves. Shinde bhao has said each man for himself. They know what they are getting into. It is all for the greater good…' Gangadhar trailed away looking behind to make sure they weren't being followed.

Gangadhar asked him to go home for the day and said he would come around the next day to discuss their future plans. Ganesh went home, a lot of questions in his mind.

***

Ganesh was coming home late more and more. What he hadn't realised was that his household was going quieter and quieter and was growing more distant from him. It began very slowly but the fabric of his happy family was coming undone. Ramya, the thread that bound the family members of his household was not talking anymore. He didn't realise it for quite a long time.

Shree Party and its daily work kept him away from the family quite often. Ganesh realised that his savings were dwindling and the money from business was getting lesser and lesser.

He had begun his business after severing ties from his old employer – The Indian Railways. He had rented a store near one of the proposed Industrial Estate Areas. The Sixth Five Year Plan aided industrial activities had begun with gusto and Ganesh had opened a small workshop that dealt with manufacturing of spare parts for small machinery items. He had dreamt of getting orders from neighbouring electrical and automobile industries which he knew would thrive once the Government blessing was received. He had staked out the plant managers who would come in occasionally to take stock of the facility layout. He would chat them up, offer them tea and initiate what according to him was business talks. They loved the affable man that had a smile on his face and who knew his machines well. He had started positively but his hard work was being threatened with his growing focus on Shree Party. Shree Party activities took up majority of his time and he couldn't dedicate time towards the venture.

Mhatre used to ask him 'Tamhankar, where are you now a days. You have become a moon of Eid.' He used to extend 'You are a right man, not made for politics. Tamhankar, you are wasting your time.'

Ganesh didn't know how his family was getting through the days. Without his knowledge Ramya had breached their savings, something they had been saving for a rainy day to get her through the daily needs. The younger children had to be sent to school and Mrunali had just started college. Ramya hadn't uttered a word to him and was waiting for him to discover the 'theft'. But he seemed to care lesser and lesser nowadays.

***

Ganesh had altered his schedule now to accommodate the growing demands from Shree Party. Their hastily aborted mission to protest Alok Shukla's appointment at BMC was followed by some more minor skirmishes by Shree Party workers. Some of the extremely vocal factions in the party who thought they weren't doing enough to get the message across, were indulging in what can be called as muscle flexing to do exactly that. Being power drunk on Shinde bhao's growing clout had indulged themselves in burning a few auto rickshaws and some carts belonging to migrant class.

Ganesh didn't like these activities and would spend his time advocating against creating a negative image. He would see Shinde bhao also trying to talk sense into the workers. But he had that rare instinctual feeling that Shinde bhao secretly loved these overindulgences.

Whenever he would complain to bhao, he would be met with a shake of head and a rhetoric question, 'What can one do about these rascals?'

Gangadhar had been elevated to second in command and had been anointed as the party treasurer. All the funds that were flowing into the party coffers were strictly monitored by him. He had started carrying a leather-bound diary with the insignia of a growing industrial giant which had entered most of the business sectors in India. The Company was apparently run by this middle-class man from Gujarat and anybody who came away after interacting with him brought stories of extreme passion and 'jugaad' characteristic of the Gujaratis.

He would also brush aside the objections Ganesh would raise as negligible things in the grander scheme of bhao's vision.

***

One evening he reached home early from the party office. The discussions were not going anywhere, and Ganesh wasn't keen on participating in any decisions of further violence being planned and perpetrated by Shree Party workers. On reaching home he realised that he was home earlier than usual. Yet the lights were all switched off and everyone seemed to be asleep. He opened the front door with his spare keys and entered his home silently. He could see all his children were fast asleep. Ramya on seeing him wordlessly got up and as had become practice, served him his dinner on the makeshift kitchen desk and went back to lie down next to Jaya.

He went about his routine. Cleaned and freshened up a bit and then sat down to have dinner. His eyes fell on a marksheet kept on the desk. He picked it up and saw it was Shruti's term end examination marksheet. He realised, somewhat surprised with himself that he wasn't aware of the exams getting over or hadn't seen the children sit and study in a long time.

Another big shock was awaiting him as he looked through the marksheet. There was a small table lamp that threw a tiny light – enough to cover the surface of the table and its contents. He held the marksheet close to the light and studied it. He was jolted when he saw that all the subject marks are emblazoned with a red pen. But these marks looked like somebody else's. Shruti who was a little naughty, otherwise was a good student. She would go out and play the whole day before exam and still give a good examination. Which would only mean Shruti had not just scored poorly in a subject, she had failed in all her subjects.

He heard a small sob and looked up from the marksheet. He saw that Shruti was awake and was sheepishly standing at some distance away from him. She looked morose almost as if she had cried herself to sleep. He beckoned her to come forward and gave an encouraging smile. He wanted to understand what had happened and didn't want the child to withdraw into a shell. Shruti slowly walked up to him and stood at an arms distance from him. Though he had never raised a hand on any of his children, the fear that Shruti and her siblings had for both their parents was born out of respect. Both Ramya and Ganesh didn't believe in blindly thrashing their children.

He placed an arm on Shruti's shoulders and made her sit on the small stool next to him. Raising the marksheet high he asked her, 'Shruti? What is this?'

She didn't answer immediately.

'Beta, why have you flunked all your subjects?' he asked her again, being careful to keep his tone rational. He was a calm man and though there was a volcano waiting to erupt inside, he controlled it.

Shruti looked up at him and he was surprised to see that his otherwise happy go lucky daughter had tears brimming in her eyes. She looked as if she would cry any moment.

'I study a lot papa…' she began but then stopped on seeing that her mother was sitting up and looking at her. 'I do study papa, but I don't know I am not understanding anything, and I am finding it difficult to remember what I have studied.'

'Why have you not come to me with your doubts? We would have set down and figured out something,' said Ganesh, he noticed out of the corner of his eye that his wife had given a subtle shake of her head. He knew he had not actually had time to sit with his children in a long time. Jaya coughed up, and that caught Ganesh's attention towards her. She was still asleep. He realised with a jolt in his heart that Jaya looked grown up.

And Shruti's next sentence just asserted his sudden realization. 'Where do we get to see you papa?' Ramya made a coughing sound and Ganesh thought she had stifled a cry.

'I don't get to talk to you anymore...' Shruti concluded. The simple statement innocently made had a powerful impact on Ganesh. He realised suddenly that his political journey had made him venture farther and farther from his family.

He returned her marksheet to her and told her to go to sleep and that he would sit with her from the next day onwards.

'Papa? Promise?' He smiled back at her and said simply, 'Promise.' He could see that had cheered up his daughter.

Jaya woke up from her sleep with a start and began to cry. Ganesh hurriedly went over and picked up Jaya and kissed her cheek. The child impatiently wiped her cheek where his moustache might have scratched her and struggled to go to her mother. Ramya got up from her place and took Jaya without looking at Ganesh. The family started settling down for the night.

That night Ganesh sat looking at his family. It looked darker to him.

'This is my world.' He thought to himself. 'Oh my gosh, what am I doing. Is this what I intended to do with my family?'

He wanted so much to be there for them. He had dreamt of a happy future for them, but his present was at a risk of destroying his future with them.

He looked at Jaya as she drifted off to sleep and realised his youngest daughter who wouldn't stay away from him, just a few months back had become used to being without him. 'She is growing up so fast.' he fondly remembered the childish games they used to play - be it akkad bakkad or hide and seek and he longed for those days. He ached for the days when Mrunali would tag along on his way to the market or when he would walk her back from college and he couldn't remember the last time he had been to her college.

He suddenly realised that Ramya had not pestered him for the monthly fees for their elder daughters and was suddenly becoming aware of the growing discord between them. Ramya had become aloof. It all made sense now. They would rarely ever have their evening tea. Talk was almost negligent as he would be pouring over the party literature even at home and would reply in monosyllables. He had alienated his wife and she had drifted apart from him.

He now knew that whatever financial constraints his family was facing, he was to be blamed but he also realised he wasn't aware of the finances anymore. Had he become inconsequential to them?

He decided to have a heart to heart with his wife first thing next morning and begin putting more time for his family.

3d. Disenchant With The Party

The next morning Ganesh woke up earlier than usual and decided he would make some changes around the house. Ramya was shaken out of her sleep by the banging of cutlery in the kitchen. She initially thought that a rat might have found its way in from all the barricading. Rat menace was a common problem in the chawls, and the residents had gotten used to it.

She was surprised to see the slouching back of Ganesh humming to himself as he made tea. She saw two steaming steel glasses of tea being poured out by her husband. Some of the tea bounced out and landed on the platform and she could almost make out his sheepish expression even though she couldn't see his face. She suppressed a smile as she saw him turn around. He winced as the hot tumbler must have scalded him. But he smiled at her when he saw she was awake.

Ramya couldn't remember the last time her husband had made tea for her. Though he was a loving man, his adventures in the kitchen had in the past been limited to applying some butter on bread loaves on the rare occasions the children had to be fed and Ramya had come down with the flu and was in no condition to get up and cook.

Those days were quite few and far in between. Ramya didn't return the smile. She got up and went to wash her face but came back and sat near her husband. Ganesh kept looking at the side profile of his wife who continued to stare into the distance. He remembered how they had met. His father had arranged for him to meet a 'sundar, susheel' girl from the neighbouring village and he had been adamant about not going. He had just got a big job in with the railways in the city and he didn't want to be tied down in a marriage so early in his career.

His father had looked at him with his weather-beaten face and said, 'Son, we will all be gone soon. The earth beckons me every time I plough the land. We will all be beneath this land soon and you will be left without anyone. Your late mother would be so proud of seeing her son settle down with a family and raise healthy children like we did.' He had let out a sigh and then as an after-thought added, 'Just come with me and Jadhav kaka and meet the girl. If you don't like her, I won't force you.'

Ganesh had agreed begrudgingly and had set out to meet, Ramya who, he didn't know then would become his wife and the mother of his three children. The house was again the kutcha types, with thatched roof and a piece of land attached, all reined in by a wall made of sticks and coconut tree leaves.

The elders had all conspired together and had nudged Ganesh to go meet Ramya who was shyly standing inside the doorway of the hut.

He had walked into the hut, straightening his shirt and had been taken aback by the beautiful girl who had a plaited, well-oiled hair which ran all the way down to her knees. She stood there demurely, and he cleared his throat. But as he was about to talk, his voice came out in a croak and he stopped abruptly as she burst into a laughter so merry that the entire house seemed to come alive.

He had fallen for her then and there and had nodded his agreement when his father had enquired with a raise of his greying eyebrow.

The elders had solemnized the wedding three months later in the presence of a priest. Ganesh and his bride, who had never been to the city had packed their belongings and travelled on the train to Mumbai, which would become their permanent residence. Ramya's big eyes would take in every sight, every sound greedily and would look towards Ganesh in excitement. That zest for life in her eyes had never dulled and she had only matured to enjoy life's smallest pleasures.

Ganesh was always impressed by the level-headed woman his village bred wife had become. She had adapted to the city like a fish taking to the water and had stood by him, taking charge of the household while he toiled away at the railway factory. He had never heard her complain and sadly today as she sat right next to him, she seemed to be miles away from him, both emotionally and mentally.

Life On The Edge

'Don't you like the tea?' Ganesh began by way of breaking the ice. She nodded taking a tiny sip from her steel tumbler.

'Are you angry with me?' Ganesh decided to hit that nail straight on its head.

'Should I be?' Ramya asked, her voice betraying a slight edge.

'I have not actually been around, you know…' Ganesh trailed of, but kept looking at his wife and now he saw her eyebrows furrowing and knew he had ticked a raw nerve.

'Hmmm…' she acknowledged that statement but didn't offer anything in return.

He tried another tact, 'I was thinking, I should start helping Shruti and Mrunali with their studies more.' He saw Ramya smiling as she took another small sip of tea.

'But do you know anything they teach these days in Commerce colleges?' she asked snidely.

He guffawed, beginning to feel the thaw and knew his wife couldn't hold a grudge for a long time.

'Ramya, I am sorry for not being there for you. I will sort out everything. I will tell Shinde bhao that I won't be able to put in late night hours at the Shree Party office.'

Ramya frowned at this, 'Can't you please stay away? I don't like that man; my gut feeling says there is something sinister about that Gangadhar too.' 'Please, let's just focus on our family…' She pleaded.

Ganesh replied carefully, 'Ramya, I am doing this for our family…' He paused, gave some more thought into what he was going to say next and then continued, 'Mumbai has become un-inhabitable because these elements and I want our girls to live a happy and fulfilling life here…'

Ramya shook her head as she tried to get up and Ganesh held her palm. When she looked at him, he merely said, 'Trust me…please.'

She nodded and got up to do her chores so that her family would troop out to tackle the world. Mrunali had finished her early morning chores and was getting ready to leave for college and after that the cafe she had begun working at. She called out to her mom that she would be late and waved a bye to her father, who smiled back at his eldest.

***

The day had begun normally like any other day, only happier for Ganesh because the situation at home had resolved itself. Ganesh left home little late today.

He had gone to his place of business only to see all the neighbouring stores were being shut. He went up to the Marwari businessman next to his premise and asked what happened.

The Marwari businessman gave him a sour look and then asked enigmatically, 'as if you don't know? Why are you people kicking us on our stomachs. We are also trying to eke out a living, you know.' Saying thus he locked his steel shutters and walked away in a huff.

Ganesh didn't understand. Soon however he realised what was happening, and what the Marwari had said to him became clear. He saw a small mob heading in his direction and recognized a few people. They were waving Shree Party insignia and were chanting in Marathi, 'Down down, outsiders. Take down the outsiders.'

He walked out of his establishment and called out to Chandu, the friendly porter he had known from his days in the Railway. 'Ganesh dada, Shinde bhao has called out to us to put our plans into motion. We missed you last night. Why did you leave so hastily? Mumbai will remember this day. We will throw out the imposters taking our places.'

Ganesh was irritated. He didn't know the urgency of this action. 'Why did Shinde bhao make this movement so hurried?' he thought to himself. The importance of what they were doing would all be destroyed. They had already drawn flak over the Shukla episode, and whatever bhao claimed, the judicial system would not take kindly to thuggery. He decided he wouldn't be a party to it and told Chandu to carry on.

As he got busy in his workshop, he lost track of time. He was happy to be back amongst his machines and he knew it would take only a small amount of time for him to tidy his business back. He was surprised when in the afternoon, he saw his neighbour Jaywant Surve hurrying to his shop. Jaywant was a tiny man, who worked in the nearby textile store, who had once offered to help Mrunali get placed in the college. Their families knew each other since the time they had set base in the chawl and would often come in handy for each other.

'What happened Surve anna?' Ganesh asked, wiping away the sweat on a piece of rag.

'Please come with me…' Surve said, the urgency in his voice palpable.

Ganesh knew that if it wasn't serious, Surve would never make this trip to this part of the neighbourhood. He quickly dressed, praying in his mind that it be a non-issue.

As he shut the shop, he saw Surve look at his watch, and then nervously look around.

'What happened?' Ganesh asked, 'Why are you sweating? Everything alright at home?'

Surve shrugged, his gesture non-committal. He didn't want the unpleasant task of breaking the news to Ganesh.

'There…there has been an incident,' he paused again and as Ganesh opened his mouth to ask him for details he continued, 'it's at Mrunali's place of work.'

Ganesh felt his heart falling out of his chest. It was as if someone had delivered a powerful kick to the pit of his stomach. No, he hadn't heard it right.

'What…did you just say?' he stopped Surve, and the tiny man pulled at Ganesh's arms to make him continue walking.

'Please, the city is burning, and the police have just declared a curfew. They are rounding up Shree Party workers.'

Ganesh stopped dead in his tracks for the second time as Surve realised it and returned to grab hold of his forearms.

'I will explain. Please walk fast. We need to get to the hospital. Ramya is inconsolable.'

'How's my daughter?' Ganesh hurried behind Surve. 'Is she fine?' he didn't want to think anything else.

'She was brought in unconscious, but the doctors have asked for more time to assess her condition.' The words were like barbs tearing into his being. He hastened his pace further.

Only three words Surve had said seemed to register in his hazy mind- Shree Party, Mrunali and Hospital. They reached the hospital and Ganesh took the stairs climbing rapidly to the general ward.

Mhatre was already there, he came up-to Ganesh. 'Go that side.'

He could see Ramya in the distance and when she saw him, clutched the edge of her saree, and muffled the sob escaping out of her mouth.

Ganesh walked up to her and tried to hold her hands and ask about their daughter, but she simply yanked her hand out of his grip and went over to where Mrs Mhatre and Surve tai (Jaywant's wife) were standing. He decided this was not the time for any clarifications.

He caught hold of a passing nurse and introduced himself as Mrunali's father. He asked about his daughter's condition. She shrugged her shoulders and continued down the alley clutching her steel tray laden with medicines.

***

Ganesh walked into the ward, where his daughter lay on a white bedspread breathing with the help of an oxygen mask. Her eyes were partly open as she stared outside the window, where the evening was announcing its arrival. He sat down next to his eldest daughter and was suddenly reminded of the day when Ramya had handed over his eldest new-born into his waiting arms. Lying on the bed, Mrunali looked as vulnerable and tiny, as that day when she was handed over to him for the first time.

Life On The Edge

It was only after couple of hours, doctors declared her in a stable condition, and she was off oxygen support.

Ganesh placed his hands on her head, as a tear drop gently rolled down from the corner of her left eye. He tenderly wiped it away and asked, 'Beta, tell me how this happened?'

Mrunali looked like she was recollecting the incident. 'I don't know how it happened...' she began, then curbing a sob, she said, 'it all happened so fast...'

'Tell me what happened?' Ganesh prodded again.

'You know Sanjay, my colleague?' Mrunali asked then continued without waiting for a reply said, 'Sanjay is from Uttar Pradesh. He comes from a poor family; his father was a farmer who died, and he had to come to Mumbai. A distant relative got him this job.'

Mrunali had begun to cry inconsolably. Ganesh patted her arms gently and asked, 'then what happened?' He wanted to get to the bottom of it. He wanted to know how his daughter had come in harm's way.

'Some of your friends came shouting slogans of Shree party and asked if we had hired any outsiders.' Mrunali continued, her voice wavering, unsteady. But she kept talking. 'Sanjay confronted them and requested them to not create a ruckus. But some of them began taunting him, calling him by names. Bhaiyya. Um. Outsiders.'

'Then...then without any reason they began to beat him. I was nearby and I saw some familiar faces standing watching. I ran to them and pleaded them to stop it. They merely laughed.'

She took a long breathe. 'I had no other option. Sanjay is a friend. He is a good person. It is because of his situation that he came over to this dreadful city. I tried to pull back one of the workers. Someone slapped me. I fell and banged my head against a steel container. Then everything went black.'

Ganesh was just about to open his mouth to defend Shree party's motto when the next statement from Mrunali stopped him dead in his tracks. 'We all are Indians, human beings first. Why is your party doing this to us? Why are they dividing us?' His daughter was blaming him as much as she was blaming Shree party. She had just spoken with a clarity beyond her age and that was enough for Ganesh to realise the poison that Shree party was becoming. He took a decision then and there.

***

In the evening Gangadhar, came to the hospital to ask about Mrunali. Though Ganesh was seething from within, the middle-class man in him didn't vent his frustration. But he had got a clear indication about his standing in the party. It didn't amount too much. Bhao had sent Gangadhar as an emissary.

Gangadhar summarized what Shinde bhao had asked him, to convey his regrets at what had happened. 'Such small things happen in big battles.'

Ganesh repeated a lone word 'small' over and over in his mind as the rest of what Gangadhar said just failed to register. It finally began to make sense. For Shree Party and bhao, battles were to be fought and he and countless others were supposed to be pawns in it. Dispensable soldiers who were supposed to sacrifice their lives, families, and happiness so bhao would have his victories.

Ganesh decided then and there standing in the drab hospital ward, that he didn't want to be part of bhao's grand vision. He would go back to his family and take care of them from coming in harm's way. Once Mrunali was discharged, Ganesh made a vow to Ramya that he would only think about them and nothing else.

Shree Party workers did come home and even to his shop to convince him to return. He said his health wasn't allowing him to make it for party work. They left after he convinced them to give him a few months to take care of his health.

Though he made it a point to keep tabs on Shree Party, Ganesh went back to his work with vengeance, never venturing back into politics, steering clear of any kind of rallies or party work. He was done. Finally.

4. Riots, Family, And Society

4a. Structure Demolished

Ganesh went through his business with renewed vigour. He was seeing a change in Ramya too. As the kids were growing up, he realised Ramya was shedding a lot of her inhibitions, she was taking tailoring classes, teaching rangoli designs, giving baking lessons to women and children in the neighbourhood. He realised there was a hidden entrepreneur in her and really didn't mind as long as it didn't hamper with her household work and their children's schedule. He didn't want her to do too many things and stress herself out.

'Ramya I don't want you to get bogged down with all these activities. Why don't you take it slowly? One at a time. I see you are running around all day, teaching so many things, I don't want you to be tired.'

Ramya smiled back and replied, 'Aho I am not doing it alone. Mrunali is helping me out occasionally. And rangoli and baking lessons are mostly for children. I don't do them as regular activities; I just do it around holidays or vacations. I am only doing tailoring and that is not a bother at all.' She seemed pretty gung-ho about her entrepreneurial streak.

Ganesh laughed at this. Not only was his wife planning out her activities perfectly, but she also had thought for contingencies. And he knew she was making some money out of these little ventures. He was content with what life was giving them.

Mrunali had shrugged of the trauma and had become more extrovertish. Shruti was the same naughty tom boy, Ganesh had always loved. He would look at her and be reminded of his childhood. Jaya's kindness and helping nature was appreciated by people in the chawls.

He would go to work, to his industrial parts workshop early in the morning, slog there through the afternoon, eat lunch, take a nap at the workplace some days, complete the work for the day and then return home by evening six. It had become a schedule for him. Ganesh and Ramya had gone back to their old habits of sitting at the doorsteps discussing the daily reports and ruminating about earlier times.

Ganesh did occasionally see some of his colleagues from Shree Party and would keep an eye out for the activities of the party. But he ensured, no politics entered his happy home. Everything was looking wonderful, and no one could have foreseen that a tragedy was waiting to unfold just like that.

***

Society is a weird creature. Most days it's merely a sleeping monster waiting to wake up, till one day it's not and then it rears its ugly head up and inflicts self-harm and destroys anything that stands in its path. Ganesh would have never guessed going by the undercurrents the magnitude of unrest that was to descend on Mumbai, due to events being unleased in other parts of the country. The unrest simmers till a point in time, when like hot molten lava it spills out and devours everything in its path.

The initial murmurs and whispers became more pronounced. Someone said something. There would be counter arguments against that. Someone would be hit; someone would get hurt. All would be forgotten for the time being till it all began again. This started happening at regular interval.

The tremors began before the actual earthquake. It was initially too tiny to be even given a thought, but families in the chawl were waking up to a situation where a possible unrest was becoming a distinct reality.

Ganesh came home that evening slightly early, and he saw Mhatre waving his hand calling out to him to come over for a chat.

He waved back to Mhatre, went over to him. He was standing with a smile, 'Kasa Aahas?' (how are you).

Mhatre said, 'All is well here. But you know what is going on after what they did in Ayodhya? It did happen in some part of India.' He said in a

Life On The Edge

conspiring tone and then as an afterthought continued, 'far, very far away from Bombay.'

'Some said that it had to happen. When you torment a structure to frame a new one, it must regain its own self at some point of time in 'Time'. This is destiny.' 'They justified, that one symbol was demolished to reclaim the prestige of originality.'

Mhatre continued 'Some could argue that it was a political move. But a political move would not take such a shape, if it is not backed by a strong social chord, a move epitomized by masses.'

'But there are other voices as well. There is a section of people who feel alienated, their sentiments are hurt. They have the right to raise their voices, and objections. This is the beauty of democracy.'

'There are rumours that this unrest is going to spread all over the country and communal elements want to fan the fire even here, in Bombay...' Mhatre trailed off.

'Oh my gosh, I did not know that so much was going on,' Ganesh was caught off-guard. 'Where did you hear this?'

'My brother in-law called in the morning today. In Bombay downtown, Muslims arranged a massive parade opposing the demolition the other day. It was meant to be a peaceful demonstration. However, it took a sudden turn of drastic events. The act has polarized the atmosphere further. There were anti-Hindu slogans raised vehemently. Some even attacked the policemen.'

'Really?' Ganesh asked, incredulity writ large on his face.

'Police had to use tear gases and lathi-charge to disperse the crowd. Then, the sequence of reaction-and-action just caused havoc. The impact was felt all-across. In fact, just yesterday, there was really an unfortunate incident occurred, rather an act of cowardice. You know, that chawl in Jogeshwari? In the middle of night, when the families were deep in sleep; their doors were locked from outside; and their houses were put on fire. Families died. Some who got saved, have severe burns...'

Mhatre stopped for a quick breath, then continued, 'Allah-U-Akbar' was heard loudly and clearly amidst voices of kids, women and men crying for help. They were burning inside, and outside there were men with beards celebrating it. How could they be so cruel? How would they face their God after such a menacing act? This was the tragic face of humanity. Where is all of this heading?'

Ganesh was shocked and speechless. 'Lord Ganesha. What is going on? Where have been I?'

Mhatre concluded, his forehead wrinkles stretched with stress, 'In our chawls, people were unaware of the after-effects for a long time. But we will also have to face the heat sooner or later.'

With a heavy heart and mind, Ganesh stepped into his house.

***

The next morning, it was the usual routine in the house. Ramya woke up and turned off the alarm. She started her day by first trying to wake the children up. She failed the first couple of times. The children didn't usually get up this early.

Ramya knew this. She just didn't want the kids to wake up all of a sudden from sleep. She preferred that they warm up to the day before their final wake-up call.

Ramya called out to her husband Ganesh only to put her typical dialogue 'Aho, it is already 6.00am. Why don't you get the milk packets?'

With a mischievous smile, Ramya gave him the bag and began her other chores. Ganesh left to fetch the milk packets and the newspaper. She was already in the middle of preparing food for the children's breakfast and lunch when Ganesh returned. He struck up a conversation with her as she began to boil milk.

Ramya observed that her husband was not his usual self. She was a bit puzzled and wondered as to what could possibly be bothering him.

Ganesh had slept restlessly during the night as his mind kept wandering to the conversation, he had with Mhatre. He decided to share his concern with Ramya about the recent occurrences so she would be alert.

'There has been quite a chaos in the surroundings,' said Ganesh, looking at Ramya, 'and am sure you are not aware of what is happening in the community, are you?'

Ramya, amused a bit, replied, 'No, I am not aware of anything around.' She added 'Nor am I left with so much of time to bother about anything around except about our home. But why? What happened? Is there anything that I must know?'

She could sense a kind of concern from her husband's expressions. She asked again 'Would you please tell me if there is anything you might want to share?'

Ganesh with a lot of fear opened-up. 'I am certain, you have not heard or seen on the television about the unfortunate events ever since the incident in Ayodhya.' He narrated the entire conversation he had with Mhatre and saw Ramya's expression change as she began to understand what was bothering her husband.

Ganesh concluded by saying, 'Our country is not in peace and harmony anymore. The temples are being attacked every now and then. The policemen are being brutally attacked. The Hindus are being burnt alive in their homes.'

He took a deep breath, 'I was scanning through the morning newspaper and the scenario looks bad. It is chaos everywhere. There are protests and rallies taken out by the Muslim community to provoke the people which went haywire. A few policemen who were apparently Hindus were beaten up in the whole melee. There are reports coming that the entire Hindu community was put on fire at one place in Bombay. 50 or so Hindu families were burnt in the rooms, locked from outside. There were women, there with kids. None could be saved.'

Ganesh turned the pages of the newspaper. It held a blazing headline with the familiar face of Shinde bhao looking extremely animated. He was drawn towards the article and wanted to know what is that bhao had said now. The news article was a reportage of some of the activities of Shree Party had done the previous day and held details of the press conference bhao had held supporting the views of the workers. Ramya joined him, giving his cup of tea.

She peered over his shoulder reading the details in the newspaper and let out an involuntary gasp. She pointed her finger at the part where she had read the disturbing remarks of the party leader and asked, 'But how is he allowed to make such statement?'

'Why?' added Ganesh, 'is he making such a statement?'

They both continued to read the article and saw that Shinde bhao was making his usual tall proclamations. He had made numerous controversial statements about what Muslims were capable of and what he would like to do with them. He had spared neither the women nor the children; everyone had come under his scathing acid insinuations. For Shinde bhao, this is just another opportunity to expand his national aspirations. He concluded his statements with the wish that he wanted to personally tour the country and personally lead the destruction of all their places of worship. He likened them to unwelcome cockroaches who were just multiplying and eating up the resources of the unconcerned Hindus. 'It is time that the Hindus wake up from the deep slumber and react.' He had concluded.

Ganesh looked at Ramya, 'We live in this society where all the religions stay in peace and harmony. We all happily invite each other during our festivals. What is the reason for such turmoil?'

He continued, 'Shinde bhao is flaring up the sentiments of people. The families residing in the same locality will be horrified with such statements. This one unfortunate incident is not sparing anyone. I am really petrified with the current situation and concerned about the kind of safety here in the chawls as we have so many Hindu as well as Muslim families residing.' Ganesh was worried.

Ramya nodded her head. They were both unaware of what lay waiting in the days to come.

4b. It Hit Chawls

Situation quickly deteriorated.

The violence took off to the next level. If one side was doing heinous crimes on the name of 'Allah U Akbar'; the other side picked up on the name of 'Jai Bhavani, Jai Shankar.'

Shinde bhao from Shree party just capitalized on this for his own gain. He ignited the sentiments of Hindus. But there were many who empathized with Shinde bhao. If not for him, who would have taken the cause of Hindus? Someone would have to take the baton for the wellbeing of Hindus.

It is a scary sight altogether as these people started picking up a fight for no apparent reason. Many masjids were burnt; countless temples were broken. People were killed on the name of religion. Lots of them. It was havoc everywhere.

The scale of the conflict only inflated with the news on TV showing the flames of fire. The flames which were put on the houses, when the people were sleeping inside, when the women were locked inside. People were crying and asking for help. However, there was no-one to save them, no-one to listen to their cries.

There were riots all-across the country, making this the one of the most tragic chapters of Indian societal history. Bombay, an epitome of social harmony for people all-across India, witnessed a mayhem. It was burning everywhere. People of Bombay lived those dreadful days, when minds and hearts were filled with terror, a deep-within fear. Temples were broken one side to burnt masjids on the other side. There was bloodshed in every corner, and innumerable deaths.

City was mourning, not only for the losses of many lives; but it has lost its true character. The city has lost its own purpose. Harmony was affected deep into its roots of religious co-existence. A sense of mistrust has deepened.

***

On being served dal once again, Ganesh made a face and turned to Ramya and asked her, 'Aga…why are you serving dal daily?'

Ramya made a scowl and nonchalantly replied, 'Aamir Kaka has not come with his vegetable cart since the past four days. He must have gone home to his family. I am not getting time here because of Jaya's school and Shruti's tuition.'

'See I told you not to overexert yourself with all these additional things that you do…' Ganesh began but was immediately cut short by Ramya, who said, 'Aho, why are you blaming my extra work. You know, it really brings home the money. Also have I told you about Shafia?'

'The little girl who is always the last one to leave from here?' Ganesh queried.

Shruti chipped in, 'She is Aai's favourite student, papa…' She wagged her tongue at her mother.

'I think, Shruti would be like her.' Ramya let out a dramatic sigh then continued, 'She helps me in the kitchen, she just likes being here and such a penchant she has for cooking…' Ramya hushed as there was an urgent knock on the door.

She could hear some commotion even as she reached up to unlatch the door. Ramya opened the door and found that there were a few men from the neighbourhood standing there with lathis and some cycle chains. One of them asked, 'Isn't Ganesh dada in?'

Ramya could only nod in apprehension and beckoned to Ganesh. He got up quickly as he too had heard the commotion outside.

***

'What happened?' Ganesh asked, 'What is wrong guys?'

'Haven't you heard?' Someone from behind shouted, incredulity writ clear in the question.

Ganesh couldn't make out who it was, peering at the men milling around his home, he repeated the question, 'What is wrong? What happened?'

'The Muslims have started showing their true colours...' the same voice from behind was heard again.

This time Ganesh identified the source. It was Raghu. He was the local miscreant known for causing trouble occasionally. He had a few charge sheets filed against him at several police chowkis across town and he was somewhat of a celebrity, in that he had a familiar face. You would see him smiling drunkenly at all functions, sitting around aimlessly probably plotting his next mischief. Cheating and armed robbery were his favourite sport, was the neighbourhood joke. He was often sought out by the political parties for exactly this.

Ganesh realised who was spreading panic. He addressed the men in front. They were more respectable and like Ganesh valued family and relationships.

'See, whatever you have heard, I am sure there is more to it. What are we doing armed with lathis, creating panic like that?'

He realised his entire family was now standing behind him and were latching on to every word that was being spoken. He quietly signalled to Ramya to take them inside and gently close the door.

Now that he was outside, he had a better view of the group. It was predominantly the men from the neighbourhood. They all had a scared but resilient expression. It meant we are all scared for lives, but we will die protecting our families from any harm.

They all decided to move towards the huge banyan tree next to the compound wall. Ganesh sidled along next to Mhatre and nudged him and whispered, 'Isn't all this a little too much?'

Mhatre shook his head and raised his arms as if invoking almighty, 'deva la maahit...' (only God knows).

Raghu seemed to have been given the status of the group leader. He did look like he relished the newly found 'responsibility'. Ganesh saw him stand as the head of the crowd with his hands on his hips and address the crowd, 'These mullahs don't know what is good for them. They come to us; we answer them in the same coin.'

The crowd nodded some looking like they knew what he was referring to. Ganesh was baffled. He didn't understand this power that Raghu held over a group of better placed men than him.

Raghu noticed Ganesh's expression and misunderstood it for something else. 'Some of you think they know everything. Well, they haven't seen the burnt bodies of our Hindu brothers. The expression of horror is still clear on their charred faces. They didn't spare even the little kids.'

'What is he talking about?' Ganesh asked the man standing next to him.

The man whispered in a conspiring tone 'They are not letting the news out. But somewhere in Malad area, in a village 4 or 5 Hindu family homes were torched by Muslims, when they were asleep. They came shouting 'Allah U Akbar' with swords and mercilessly killed those 5 families. The only saviour is that they did not kill the women in the house. Otherwise, in Jogeshwari, they burnt the entire family, men, women, and kids. Heinous.'

Ganesh was horrified. He understood the charged atmosphere. It is coming close to their place.

'They were one of us a few days ago. Now they want to be Muslims. They want to take away our lives. What is going on?' Pandey made a point.

Raghu snatched the moment, 'Forget what happened in Malad and Jogeshwari. I heard they are moving outside in gangs murdering Hindus who they find alone. Tomorrow they will come into your homes and rape your daughters and wives. They won't even spare your mothers. It is best to be prepared for any eventuality.'

Ganesh knew Raghu was just playing on all the whispers to scare the already scared men.

But the next statement from Raghu hit him harder, 'We don't want any Muslims near us. That means Yakub has to go.'

Yakub was Shafia's father. He grasped, Yakub was not part of this group of men.

'What does Yakub have to do with all this?' Ganesh raised his voice. 'We have known him for a long period of time. He is a respectable man. His family is no threat to us.'

He was surprised by the words of 'us' versus 'them' he had used. How easy it was for human beings to segregate themselves. The British had thrived on divide and rule, now someone else was using the same strategy.

'When it comes to their blood thirst, they will forget all sorts of respectability.' Someone else joined in from the other side of the crowd. Ganesh couldn't make out whose voice it was. But whoever it was, it seemed their conjecture did ring true with the crowd. Ganesh found that he was the lone voice of protest.

Everyone was scared. Fear makes human beings irrational.

'But this is being misused by politicians. See what Shree party is doing. Just today morning, the Muslim shops were looted in the nearby community. This was done by the goons of Shree party.' Mhatre inserted.

'But there will be a reaction for every action. Someone has to take a lead, and Shree party has to be at the forefront for saving our lives.' Raghu was clearly putting the narrative of Shree party.

'Leave that aside. Let us think about how to save our lives. Our wives and kids. Lives of our families. Let us safeguard ourselves.' Mhatre inserted himself again.

Worried faces. Men, who earn their daily livelihood by going to work each day; were prioritizing the lives of their families.

Raghu had a finality in his voice. 'It would be better for everyone to be together. We don't want unwanted incidences like the one that happened at other places to happen here.'

'What do we do?' someone asked from the crowd.

'We do patrols. We can't depend on the police. We should remain cautious. All these gaddars should be thrown out from amongst us.'

Ganesh felt Raghu's eyes linger on him for a second more than was needed. He continued, 'Everyone who supports gaddars also should be identified and thrown out.'

Ganesh was about to retort, but he felt Mhatre's restraining hands on him. Mhatre gave a gentle shake of his head as if asking him to remain silent.

Raghu was giving out orders, playing every bit the pseudo leader of scared men. 'I will protect you all. Nothing will happen to our families. But it is best for us to keep our loved ones close to us for a while. Don't venture out alone to any new places. Stop sending your children to school for some time.'

'And be vagrants like you?' Ganesh muttered under his breath. Someone standing ahead heard it and turned and glared at Ganesh and whispered back, 'Better to be illiterate than be dead…'

Ganesh realised that Raghu had touched a chord with the men in his society. He wondered where it would all end up going.

The meeting went on for a some more time and then the men dispersed. Some being given the duty of guarding the community. The men decided to curtail their movement as much as possible which meant going out of their homes only when needed.

***

It was quite late in the night by the time Ganesh finished discussing about the meeting with Mhatre and a few of the sober ones. Ganesh realised he wasn't after all the only one who had apprehensions about the sudden escalation of situation. The others had just thought it was prudent to keep their silence.

Ramya was still lying awake when Ganesh entered the house trying to make as little noise as possible. He changed into his pyjama and lay down next to Ramya.

Ramya placed a hand on his chest and gently asked him, 'What was all that?'

Ganesh let out a sigh. He didn't know where to begin. He didn't want to bother her unnecessarily. But it was equally important that she be aware of the changing winds.

'Ramya, I want you to listen carefully to what I am going to tell you.' Ganesh began, 'I don't want you to alarm the children and I don't want you to worry also...'

Just then they heard a couple of voices outside their home, talking loudly with each other.

'Who was that?' Ramya asked a little surprised that their chawl hadn't gone to sleep this late.

'Those are men from our chawl who have been assigned patrolling duty today. It has been decided that we have to be careful from now on to avoid any untoward incident. It makes sense with what is going on.'

'But why all this suddenly?' Ramya asked. Ganesh felt her surprise evident in her voice now.

He replied, 'That is exactly what I was coming to...' he paused for a second, 'Everything will be fine. But we all need to be careful. There are certain kinds of people out there who want to flame this communal fire and create terror.'

'But...' Ramya began to speak, but Ganesh stopped her, 'Listen. Don't ask me any questions. Just listen. Things are beyond our understanding right now. All we need to do right now is be careful. What we do? Where we go? People are watching. We are going to maintain the utmost level of vigilance.'

'Okay, so what do we do?' asked Ramya, hints of fear in her voice evident.

'It means I might not be able to go back to the workshop in the industrial area.' Ganesh said grimly. Then almost as an afterthought added, 'Only for a few days, till all this cools down...'

'What about the girls?' Ramya asked, the thought coming suddenly to her, 'they pass through that sweetmeat corridor. There are a lot of Muslims living in that colony behind the lane.'

Ganesh thought for a while, thoughts cloudy, sleep was beckoning. In the meeting he had been strongly against stopping the children from going to school. He knew within that no harm would come to the children, but the father in him urged rather be safe than sorry.

'Ramya I don't like it, but don't send Shruti and Jaya to school. Mrunali should avoid going to college till things are sorted.'

'I hope it does soon…' Ramya trailed off as she heard Ganesh grunt in sleep.

***

The men in chawls started taking turns in guarding the community. In each round, they were awake the whole night. All these men were armed with whatever possible weapons that are available in their homes. This looked like an age-old drama with such household artillery. The men were all alert and their presence of mind at best to deal with the circumstances that may arise.

They devised a way to communicate with the other members as an alarm if something serious happens or there is a sign. It was like a round-the-clock duty to safeguard themselves from the ruthless acts.

Nobody had any clue about when the things might settle. All they could do was to pray and be vigilant in groups.

4c. Yakub Being Questioned

The man held on to his son as he darted into the dark alley. The child continued to enjoy the late-night sprint unaware of the lurking danger. The man breathed easy for a second, the alley comforted him. He was out of the spotlight. He could hear them. All he wanted to do was take his baby to safety. The occasional barking of dogs would follow the rest of the cacophony, night throws out.

The child was thankfully not making any noise, taking the man's anguished breathing on his neck as some sort of game, he sucked his thumb continuing to make tiny babbling sounds. The man shushed the child, patting his back as he listened for any signs of the pursuers.

The group of men couldn't find the man. They thought he had run into one of the houses and were going about their search thoroughly. They had seen he was holding a child. They knew they would be able to locate their prey by tracking the sound of the child. As he heard them near the alley, the man prayed to his god for the child's safety, if not his. He held the child closer and shrank back into the darkest corner he could find there.

Two men from the group forked out and entered the alley.

'How do these bastards hide so quickly? They are like cockroaches, switch on the lights and you see them scatter.' He rasped. The taunt was menacing.

The other man chuckled, 'Yeah, when I get them, I am going to squish them under my boots, and see their juice squirt out,' he laughed at his own joke, or cruel face.

The man tried to shrink back more, hoping, and praying fervently that the pursuers would exit the alleyway. The men gave the alley a customary glance and turned to search somewhere else. The toddler however was now bored with the game. He wanted his father to run and play. He let out an angry growl and scratched his father's face. And arched his back to get his father to get up and play with him. The father held him tighter and was about to cover the toddler's mouth when the boy turned his head and let out a full-blown wail of frustration.

Too late!

The man groaned to himself, he would have to move quickly. He hoped against hope that the men had left the scene.

Just as he reached the entrance of the alley, he stumbled upon a few stragglers from the group. They immediately caught hold him and slapped him. Someone called out to the others loudly as the child, now scared at the violence being unravelled began to cry. Hands took hold of the child and brutally pulled the child out of the man's protective grasp.

There was a celebratory tone to the pack of men who resembled vultures as they circled back smelling the stench of death, of humanity.

They took hold of both man and child and pushed them back into the darkness of the alley.

***

A few kilometres away, Ganesh woke with a start. He was soaked with sweat. Was it a bad dream? Or had he heard something?

Next to him, Ramya continued to sleep soundly. He didn't want to disturb her. He gently eased himself away and went and stood next to the window. He could see a couple of people roaming around outside, guarding the community.

He wondered how long this unrest would continue. Men turning against men. Animals had so much more dignity. They killed when they were hungry. Men killed at will. There need be no motive either. He let out a sigh as someone went past his window with a baton. Human beings were at the top of the food chain and yet so many things about them enforced his opinion that they didn't even deserve a place at the bottom of it.

***

Life On The Edge

The next morning on his way to work, Ganesh heard some commotion. On following the noise, he encountered a large mass of humanity standing as a few policemen assisted a couple of white dressed hospital staff to carry out a stretcher covered in white cloth. As he approached the onlookers, he saw a hand jutting out of the stretcher motionlessly moving as the hospital attendants loaded the stretcher into the waiting ambulance. He was about to resume his journey when he saw a second stretcher being brought.

With a sharp pinch in his chest, he realised the stretcher seemed light. It seemed the occupant wasn't very heavy or old. The white sheet had been folded into half and only covered the middle of the stretcher.

Abruptly his eyes clouded. Tears began to stream out even before he realised, he was crying. He had the sudden urge to see Jaya. Hold her tightly in his arms.

As he turned to return home, he saw Mhatre a few feet away plucking himself out of the crowd and walking towards him.

'They didn't even spare the child!' Mhatre narrated without any prelude. Ganesh didn't reply as he quickly wiped his eyes on his shirt sleeve.

'Which religion teaches such brutality?' Mhatre continued, 'Looks like they cornered the father and son and thrashed the father mercilessly.' Ganesh merely shook his head looking down as they walked together.

'The police aren't revealing which religion the victims belong to…' Mhatre let out a sigh.

Ganesh stopped in his tracks, turned, and looked at Mhatre and his voice quivering with emotion blurted out, 'Mhatre, how does it matter?'

Mhatre didn't know how to respond to that. They continued walking in silence.

Another commotion seemed to emanate from their colony. Raghu and his gang could be seen arguing with someone.

Both the men hurried their steps towards the commotion.

Yakub could be seen trying to placate Raghu and his henchmen and he seemed to be outnumbered and spoken down by the bigger group.

Ganesh saw Shafia and her mother standing a few feet away, sobbing as Yakub was being accosted by some of the men in Raghu's group.

'What is happening here?' Ganesh asked as they approached the gathering.

'He and his family have to move out.' Raghu thundered for everyone to hear. Ganesh noticed that he was making it a show for everyone.

He approached Raghu and whispered, 'Raghu, let's not do this. Stop it. Yakub and his family have been with us since the beginning. Don't bring religious animosity into our colony.'

Raghu gently thrust out a palm and placed it on Ganesh's chest. And even though he didn't push him, his look conveyed the fact that he would be rough if anyone asked for it.

He continued to address the crowd, 'Why should someone who doesn't belong to our religion continue to stay near our holy place.' He meant the temple. 'Who knows what all they eat and then desecrate out place of worship with their unworthy presence?'

Ganesh looked at Shafia, whose eyes had reddened with the incessant tears. She kept holding tightly to the hem of her mother's salwar kameez and was visibly going into shock.

Ganesh went to her and picked her up. She let out a loud cry thinking he was going to hurt her. Ganesh shushed her, trying to calm her and addressed the crowd. 'Look at this tiny heart. Have we all suddenly turned into stones?'

A murmur went through the crowd. Some of them quietened a bit. Ganesh continued, 'Shafia is almost the age of my second daughter, and I haven't seen a more pious girl than her.' He looked directly at Raghu. 'I do not mean the kind of religion which evaporates when the lid of a beer bottle is opened.'

Raghu looked livid, he looked ready to retort, when Ganesh continued loudly, 'I mean the kind of religious beliefs one can only get from their god-fearing parents. We have all known Yakub and Tahira.'

He gave Shafia back to her mother, the child looked relieved to be reunited with her mother.

He walked forward and placed an arm on Yakub's shoulder. 'Have any of you ever heard any harsh words from this man's mouth? Have you ever seen him with anything other than a smiling face? Today you see tears in his eyes and the Hindus in you want his blood?'

'Is that what you want to do? Murder him and his family in cold blood?' He didn't stop. He pushed out all his frustrations. This was not impromptu; this volcano was waiting to lash out since the past few days. Seeing the dead body of the child had somehow triggered him.

'Let their blood be in your arms. But remember tomorrow you will be where Yakub is today, surrounded by men baying for your blood and no one will speak for you. No one will plead for mercy. Those who live by the sword, die by it.'

He now looked squarely at Raghu, 'And some of us have a lot of experience.'

Raghu looked back at him sourly. He realised he had lost his hold over the crowd. Ganesh's outburst seemed to have turned their favour towards the Mohammedian.

'No one wants to kill or hurt anyone. We are issuing a fair warning. Better to pack up and leave, or we will be forced to do it for you.' He started walking away, spitting savagely.

Mhatre now spoke up, 'Come-on, lets disperse. Everyone, please go back to your homes. Beta Tahira, take Yakub and the child and go home…'

Yakub turned to Ganesh and raised his arms as if to thank him but started crying. Ganesh drew him into a tight embrace. He turned to Mhatre and said, 'I am taking Yakub over to my house for some chai.' Then addressing Tahira, he said, 'You also come. Shafia can do with some garam garam batata vada.' He smiled at the child, who was now rubbing her eyes giving a grudging smile.

***

Once the men had settled down on the chairs and Ramya had gestured Tahira to follow her into the tiny kitchen, Ganesh heard Shruti enthusiastically shouting out some rules to Shafia. 'Kids and their games…' he smiled at Yakub, who continued to look downcast.

'It's the games played by grownups that are weird.' He clearly was exhausted, shaking his head still looking down.

'Raghu is a mischief monger, and you will have to be careful. I don't know why he wants you to vacate your house. It is a tense atmosphere anyways.' Ganesh replied scratching his chin.

'Must be something to do with this broker, who had come to our house a few months ago, before all this problem started. That guy looked like a suspicious person. He told me, a brahmin family wants to move in next to the temple and he would get me a good price for my house.'

Ganesh seemed surprised, 'Hmmm…and what did you say?'

'Nothing I politely turned down the offer and said this was our family home.' 'My father before me had stayed here and died here. He used to take care of the temple premise. That is why Tahira till date washes and cleans the temple compound and walls. And on the days, she enters the temple we make it a point not to cook any non-veg.'

Ganesh nodded. He felt sorry for Yakub. 'There is no need to explain these things to me Yakub.'

Yakub shook his head as a new thought came into his mind, 'I think I have seen that broker with Raghu a few days back. They want to usurp my property cheaply. I am sure there is no Brahmin family, they just want to run their nefarious activities next to the temple so that Police won't dare to touch them due to religious sentiments.'

Ganesh replied, 'I think you might have something there Yakub. But we can't prove it.'

Ramya returned with chai and Tahira stood near the kitchen door sipping from a steel tumbler.

Yakub said 'thanks' as he accepted the chai and taking a sip he said, 'Suddenly I feel I don't belong here. I fear for my family. We feel we are surrounded by strangers. I have been uneasy for the past few days. The stares, the whispers I have tried to ignore for a while. But now I guess people are no longer worried about being inappropriate.'

He finished his chai and nodded to Tahira as he got up. Tahira called to her daughter and as the couple made to leave, Yakub turned towards Ganesh and said, 'it was a brave thing you did back there. You are a true brother. I won't ever forget what you did for me and my family.'

The couple left, and Ganesh let out a sigh. Even basic and simple things such as standing up for another human being was now being appreciated as something extraordinary.

4d. Yakub's Family Under Threat

It was a total chaos. The army forces were deployed at many places to take control of the horrible situation.

The government declared curfew in many places. The schools and other institutions declared an indefinite shutdown.

Ganesh said 'People are simply raging a war; they don't even know who they are fighting with and for what cause. People attacking each other in a very violent manner is an unaccepted thing.'

Ramya just overheard a news that the near-by Muslim chawl has been evacuated over-night. She calls out to Ganesh and says 'what happened to the people, where could they have gone in one night? The people who made this mess have gone to a safe place possibly, and what about the many Hindu families staying here since so many years?' Ramya is worried with lot of thoughts.

The army forces were asked to separate the Muslims from the Hindu dominant areas and vice-versa. It was important to keep human lives safe and allow the calm and common sense to prevail.

***

Mhatre would often come over and share tea and discuss the politics of these incidents which had stopped being stray and were happening more regularly. Though the army and police had taken harsh measures to control the situation, sporadic incidents were getting reported almost daily with alarming frequency. Even though Ganesh didn't relish those conversations, he didn't want to antagonize his friend who was himself a devout Hindu. He had never exhibited any animosity towards the Muslims till the Yakub incident happened. Ganesh could sense a disquiet fermenting inside Mhatre that wasn't exactly visible.

Something that looked like a tumour seemed to grow inside Mhatre, just under the surface. Nowadays, Mhatre often indicated that Yakub and his family should leave for their safety and to safeguard their part of town from any bloodshed.

'If anything happens to a Muslim amidst us, the mullahs will torch us all…' he had mused reading another incident in the Marathi newspaper. Ganesh had absentmindedly nodded, wondering what Mhatre would say and do, if it was his family who was the odd one out. He hadn't voiced his opinion though.

One such day, Mhatre had hurried over to the veranda, he indicated Ganesh to follow him behind the colony wall. Some children sped past them making a ruckus and Ganesh sidestepped them poking playfully at the youngest boy trying to catch up with his friends.

Mhatre, beckoned him and caught his elbow and steered him close to the wall. Throwing a worried look here and there, he whispered to Ganesh, that the Hindus had made up their mind to answer the Muslims in the same coin.

'You remember what happened in Ramojiwadi?' he asked, reminding Ganesh of the Hindu temple sacking by unknown people. The chief priest had been beaten to death near a rural town in Maharashtra and the young temple cleaner, who had the presence of mind to hide on the roof top; saw how the arsonists stole the sacred ornaments, beat the priest to death and desecrated the temple premise by spitting and urinating in the sacrosanct space. He was found mumbling in shock when the devotees hearing the commotion rushed to the temple only to find many parts of it in flames and destroyed by fanatics. No Hindu would do this, they proclaimed and concluded. The temple sweeper reaffirmed their beliefs that though the vandals had covered their faces, the flowing beard and their tawaiz (referring to the sacred amulet worn by Muslims) couldn't be hidden. This was the final straw and the Hindus spurred by many political patrons like Shree Party had decided to take up the cudgels.

Ganesh was growing impatient but also worried, he didn't like the direction this was going. Why was Mhatre talking about this?

'What happened Mhatre?' he asked touching his forehead and feeling the glistening sweat droplets forming there.

'I overheard Raghu…' Mhatre mumbled, still not making any sense, 'they are going to do it later tonight, or tomorrow first thing in the early hours of morning.'

'What are you talking about?' he asked

'Yakub, you have to warn him to take his family and go away…' Mhatre left it there. Realization dawned on Ganesh.

'Mhatre, please tell me clearly what you heard…' he took Mhatre's palm trying to calm down the older gent. 'How did you come to know about this?'

'I told you… I overheard it…' Mhatre almost sounded like he was party to the conspiracy. 'I am sorry Ganesh. Don't ask me anything. I just thought it was not the right thing to do.'

'Hmmm, why not go tell Yakub directly. Why me?' Ganesh suddenly doubted his older neighbour.

'Ganesh, trust me if they see me going to him, they will know. I will be the target. This way we would be able to save Yakub and I will not be suspected.' Ganesh bit his lower lips, unsure what to do. He decided to trust Mhatre.

He went home and called for Shruti. He hurriedly wrote a note and folded it and told her to take it to Yakub's house. As she turned to leave, he stopped her, 'Pori, only give this to Yakub uncle. Do not stop anywhere. Do not talk to anyone. Do you understand?'

Shruti folded the note one more time and put it deep into her skirt pocket, nodded once and left. She returned after a while as Ganesh kept watch at the windowsill. He worried for his family, but he thought what he was about to do was of paramount importance.

A little while later, Yakub nonchalantly left his home and walked out of the colony. Ganesh and Mhatre looked at each other and wondered if everything would be alright.

***

Later in the evening, Ganesh found a few notorious men loitering around the compound wall near the temple. The back of Yakub's house and temple was quite close to the compound wall and the space behind it was used by people to wash their utensils or to hang their clothes to dry. Ganesh's kitchen window also overlooked the same compound wall. Beyond the wall there was a thick cover of trees.

The Yakub residence was being watched, as Ganesh had foreseen. And that is exactly what had happened.

A while later Ganesh returned with a bag. He went into his house and the door closed. He told Ramya to do exactly what they had planned. The children were forbidden from venturing out. Mrunali was given the task of making 'arrangements' upstairs. Everything was silent. The sun had set and children and a few elders who were playing had begun to thin out. The colony was exceptionally quiet.

Suddenly the calm was shattered by someone shouting at the top of the voice. Even without going over to the source of voice, Ganesh guessed who it would have been. And he was proven right. Raghu had magically presented himself. He was standing inside the temple compound and was holding up a headless chicken, warm blood still flowing from where its decapitated head was missing.

Ganesh joined the crowd that had come running to find out what had happened.

'Once again our holy place of worship has been desecrated.' Raghu shouted at the crowd, every single word spitting venom.

'They do not respect our deities and think this is a dumping ground for their black magic practices.' 'Enough is enough. Time to teach the mullah Yakub a lesson…' someone from the crowd, probably Raghu's minions thundered.

The crowd was wonder stuck and still trying to make sense of everything that was happening. No one rationalized how did the headless chicken and Yakub were connected. No one questioned how they had arrived at this conclusion. Their deity had been disrespected. Their religion was disrobed. The consensus was clear. Yakub and his family must pay for this.

Ganesh wondered how he would have taken it if he hadn't been aware of the backstory. Would he have raised these questions? Would the crowd be willing to listen to his protests? Would he have protested this direct attack on his faith? The crowd headed over to Yakub's house, which wasn't lit from inside. Raghu gestured to one of his henchmen to knock. The thug started beating the door with both his fists.

'Yakub come out…' Raghu called out, 'now you cannot hide. We do not want to break open your door. But we will if you and your family do not come out this instance.'

Ganesh found a few in the crowd inching forward. They were all well-rounded like the thug pounding the door. They also carried sticks and at least two of them held choppers. Ganesh shivered involuntarily.

Raghu stepped closer to the door and indicated that they should put their shoulder to it. Together they heaved and thrust themselves at the door as the crowd continued to watch. Ganesh felt a hand at the small of his back and turned to find Mhatre standing there sweating profusely. All this was too much for the man.

Raghu called for two more of his men and together the four took turns to break open the door. But it looked like Yakub had barricaded the door from inside.

Then someone from the crowd had a brainwave to go check the back. Two men rushed around the house and returned. They quietly went up to Raghu and whispered something in his ears. The expression on his face was worth watching. That was what Ganesh was waiting for. He smiled to himself despite the fear that was building up.

Someone from the crowd asked, 'Raghu what happened?' Raghu didn't answer.

Someone else separated from the crowd and went around the house, a few followed.

Ganesh followed the crowd as he saw Raghu throw the chicken with an angry yell.

Behind the house, the window stood still, a few sarees that had been drawn on both sides now were lying down on the ground probably flung aside by the thugs. The window stood bare. The entire wooden frame with the iron bars was missing. It had been removed completely. A bedsheet could be seen thrown across the compound wall. It looked like Yakub's family had escaped from the back wall in time.

Raghu came striding and edged his way through the crowd. 'Go find them...' he growled, 'They wouldn't have gone far. Find them and bring them all back here...'

There was a sound of an approaching police van. Raghu looked at the crowd and thundered, 'what are you looking at?' he looked like he wanted to make himself scarce before the police party came.

The crowd began to murmur, and a few turned to leave. Mhatre held Ganesh again by his shirt and tugged at it. Ganesh turned and walked away. He didn't want to turn around again and find Raghu looking at him. He wasn't sure whether his face would betray the secret. He continued walking all the way to his home and nodded sideways at Mhatre.

He closed the door as he heard thick boots marching past their homes towards the temple.

Ganesh drew the curtains and called for his family. 'The next few days will be crucial.' He told them as Ramya held Jaya, who was constantly trying to get out of her arms and make her way to the stairs.

'We have to go about our business as naturally as possible.' He stopped, trying to find the right words. 'Our guests will continue to stay hidden upstairs and no action from our part should tell people that they are here.' Mrunali nodded.

Upstairs Yakub said a silent prayer. He clutched at the note, Ganesh had sent with Shruti. It just held three statements. 'Your life is in danger. Remove the window at the back and come to my house. Bring family.' Ganesh knew the window frame could be removed with minimum noise as they themselves had to remove theirs as part of a small renovation job he did long back.

Yakub had shown the presence of mind of slinging the bedsheet tied together across the compound wall to mislead anyone who wanted to target them. He had gone for walk, cut back double speed on the other side of the wall, and had tied the bedsheet to a sturdy tree branch and then strolled back home with a bag containing the tools he would need to remove the window frame. The family had smuggled out of the window and had entered Ganesh's house just when the dusk had blazed off.

Yakub knew the personal risk Ganesh was taking by letting them in. He prayed for their safety as well. He wouldn't know how many days this would go on. He wished to go back to the old days. Harmony and peace were commodities that were in rare demand nowadays. But he remembered a verse in the Quran which said in such times of conflict, some God sent Samaritans would rise out of the ashes and protect the downtrodden and the hurt. Ganesh was one such Samaritan.

5. Vivek, The First Love

5a: Mrunali Found Someone

Mrunali was waiting at the bus stop. Today the bus was unusually late. 'Frustrating', she muttered to herself and tapped the pillar of the bus stand. 'Calm down, Mrunali. This happens,' she said to herself and came to posture.

'Did I just see, Vivek,' she turned in the same direction, and quickly glanced at him. He was looking at her. She thought 'it may be a coincidence,' though her inner voice was in joy that Vivek was actually looking at her.

She knew that Vivek lives in a nearby chawl. 'There are too many pluses for him,' this statement from her friend flashed in her head. 'He is a good-looking guy with fair complexion and six feet height. He followed the rituals of going to temples each day. He greets elders by going on his knees. Something he may have learnt from his Brahmin parents.'

Mrunali gave another glance at Vivek, he was now looking somewhere else. She exclaimed. 'No doubt, why girls in the neighbourhood have a crush on him. And why would his name be thrown as a wish list.' She paused for a moment.

Her friend's words brought smile to her face, 'He would never be found roaming or goofing with his friends. He is a shy and an introvert person. He is very hardworking, always surrounded by his books.' Mrunali knew that Vivek completed his master's in science and started his career as a teacher in a coaching class where he taught kids various subjects. He was a role-model for many in the nearby chawls community.

Mrunali understood that probably he takes the bus to his coaching centre. From there on, she could see him almost every day at the bus stand, however it was limited to casual glances at each other. No smiles exchanged; no conversation started.

***

Vivek & one of his students went to the counter to place an order.

'Hey, you?' Vivek was surprised to see Mrunali.

'Hi' Mrunali was pleasantly surprised. 'How come, here?' Mrunali asked, and she was not sure if that was the right question.

'My coaching centre is nearby only. It is Teacher's day today. My students wanted to celebrate. So, we are here.' Vivek said, waiting for the next question.

Mrunali smiled, 'it is nice.' 'What do you want?'

Vivek was not sure, if he understood the question 'Means?'

'What do you want?' Mrunali with her eyes raised, repeated the question.

Vivek was not sure yet, he was confused and said to himself 'isn't it going too fast?' Then, Vivek's student interrupted, '7 Cappuccino, please.'

Vivek was ashamed, 'Sorry.' Mrunali took the order but could not take away her eyes from him. While his students indulged in Cappuccino and pastries; Vivek was lost in the thought of having his first conversation with Mrunali.

***

It was a difficult wait for Vivek. The next day at the bus stand, he finally made a move and talked to Mrunali. 'Hi, I am Vivek. We met yesterday at the cafe, remember?' he asked.

'Yeah, I do,' she said, looking into his eyes.

'By the way, we also meet every day at the bus stop,' he said and smiled. She looked down, with a smile on her face, 'So, what you do, apart from that cafe?' he asked.

Vivek was doing his best to seem confident, internally he was nervous. He was making effort to get the conversation going.

'I am doing master's in economics and work at a cafe as a part-time job.' she replied.

'Ah, that's great, I mean studying and working together is superb.' he said enthusiastically.

'Yes, I earn for my studies and don't want to be a burden on parents.' she shook her head.

'By the way, what you do, as I saw you yesterday with so many kids over there?' she knew the answer but acted ignorant.

'I am a teacher at a coaching centre. Those were my students who celebrated teacher's day yesterday.'

Before they could talk more, Mrunali's bus arrived, she waved her hand and left for her college.

***

Vivek was very keen to blossom this relationship. He never missed any chance to talk to her, either at the bus stop or in the market, or sometimes at the cafe. He was trying his best to convert those short talks into a friendship. Mrunali was least interested. She had closed all the windows to avoid Vivek's hands of friendship. She was looking for ways to escape every time they met.

Vivek continued making efforts. One day he waited outside her cafe. At the end of day, she came out of the cafe. She walked towards the bus stop, casually ignoring him.

Vivek quickly followed and halted her.

'Oh, hi, I didn't see you,' she said with an absent smile.

'No, you saw me.' he said with a red face.

'What happened, Vivek? You are behaving strange today,' she asked.

'Rather, what has happened to you? You are acting bizarre from past few days,' he asked back.

'No, nothing of that sort. Everything is alright,' she calmy said.

'No, it is not. You are running away from me.' Vivek seemed agitated.

'No Vivek. It is not that.' Mrunali was calm again.

'Then what is it? Is there any problem? Have I done something wrong?' He asked all questions at once.

She stood quietly, without uttering a word to his questions. Vivek asked again with impatience, he begged her to provide the reason for avoiding him.

'Vivek, there is no reason for this. I am like this only; I don't believe in friendship. I was just maintaining some distance.' She was trying to bring in a bit of rudeness but was failing to do so.

'I know, there is something else. I just want to know the reason. After that, I will never show you my face.' Vivek sounded adamant.

He continued to persist, wanting to hear more from her. She finally spoke, 'Vivek, all this is going in some wrong direction. Right now, you want friendship. Later you will want to take this to the next level. That will make us fall into a well of troubles.'

'Troubles, what troubles?' he asked confusingly.

'You are an upper-caste Brahmin, and we are Kshatriyas. We are financially poor and won't be able to match your status.' She said all this in one go.

He started laughing after listening to her. Puzzled seeing him, she asked, 'Why are you laughing?'

'You are mad, you are completely mad,' he laughed out loud.

'Tell me what happened? Did I say something wrong?' she asked.

'Yes, you did. It is difficult to believe that these words are coming from a girl like you, who believes that girls should study and work; so that they can support their family. I did not know that your thinking is so small. You believe in this caste system and status thing?' he said bringing taunt and disappointment all at once.

'Everyone believes in it.' Mrunali reasoned.

'I don't. And I feel you should not believe it too,' said he, waving his hands in air. 'Moreover, Mrunali, I have asked for an innocent friendship. Look, I am an introvert person and I do not feel comfortable with everyone. I talked to you and saw a friend in you, with whom I can speak, I can share my feelings and preferences. And you. You are talking about this entire stupid caste thing.'

'I don't know what to say?' she said.

'I know you don't believe in all this. You are just scared of this society. I am not forcing you for anything. Just be yourself.' He said, with a calm demeanour this time. He left immediately.

She stood there for ten more minutes, thinking about what just occurred. How long can she avoid him, she liked him deep in her heart.

The next day Mrunali waited for Vivek at the bus stand. He was a bit late than his usual time. He noticed her but did not bother to acknowledge. Mrunali grinned at this. She went near him, 'What happened? You late today?'

'I woke up late in the morning,' he responded, but looking at the opposite side.

'Why are you acting bizarre today? Is there any problem, you can tell me?' she said and gave a witty smile. Vivek too smiled. Finally, they crossed the first step of becoming friends.

***

This was a special relationship, blossoming. Vivek and Mrunali started spending a lot of time together, they talked about their families, their likes, and dislikes, and almost everything. They would go for lunches, outings, and shopping. But somewhere inside, Mrunali was still conscious as this caste and status issues were troubling her deep inside. She used to stare at Vivek while thinking about how far this would go, but she never showed it to him.

Days passed, and by the passing days, their bond became stronger. Vivek has developed feelings for her. It only became stronger seeing how independent Mrunali is, and how she carries herself. Her perspectives were aligned to how he used to think.

Vivek had thought about expressing his feelings to Mrunali many a times; he was scared of her disapproval. He was afraid of losing her friendship. Every night he would gather the courage to propose her, the very next day. But the inner himself would acquire him with numerous questions, 'Will she get upset?', 'Will she break the friendship too?', or 'How will she react?', and many more. Every day he fraught for the answers, but he could only end up with sleepless nights.

Finally, he decided to consult his close friend, Babu.

After hearing the entire narration, Babu declared, 'It would not go well in the society. Your parents would have lot better options as you are educated and doing well.'

But Babu soon understood that his friend is really serious about this relationship. He suggested, 'Please think through this very well, and then decide.' 'Do not hurry up.'

This discussion did not help Vivek conclude. The indecisiveness was killing him inside. Mrunali noticed his confusion and strange behaviour. She asked him a few times, but he avoided further discussion saying that it is work related stress.

***

Finally, he decided to convey his feelings to Mrunali. It has already been a long wait, tormented between the possibilities. His appetite for patience has hit the sealing. Moreover, his stronger feelings for her, gave him the courage to open up to her.

Proposing Mrunali was again a challenging task for him. This time he has decided to not let his energy down. He wanted to make his best efforts. He gave a thought to Mrunali's likes and dislikes.

Life On The Edge

He bought a pair of beautiful earrings, he knew that Mrunali would like it. He also prepared a card, filled with his feelings. His heart has essayed a touching piece.

A new cafe was open in that area, so he asked Mrunali to come over there at five in the evening. She agreed.

Mrunali reached at the cafe sharp at five. She looked for Vivek, but she couldn't find him. A waiter came and made her settle down. She was looking here and there, waiting for Vivek. But there was no sign of him.

She made a few calls to him, but he was not picking up. 'This is frustrating. Vivek has never made me wait for so long ever.' She put her phone down. 'What is going on?'

The same waiter came and gave her a card with a red rose, and a gift-wrapped box. She was confused; before she could ask him anything, he left. She saw the gift-wrap, her name was there over it, so it was not misplaced for sure. She started unwrapping it. A big smile just appeared on her face. These earrings are beautiful.

Vivek was gazing at her, from the corner. He smiled, 'She liked it.'

She opened the card; and started reading. At the end of the card, it said, 'Lots of love, Vivek.' She was in tears while reading. As soon as she dropped the card, she found Vivek standing next to her. She was at loss of words; did not know how to react, what to say. She wiped her eyes.

Vivek with a big smile was waiting for her answer. 'So,' he asked inquisitively with all the enthusiasm, raising his eyeballs. 'Do you like the surprise?' he further prodded her. She was quiet, looking shocked and tensed.

'What happened, Mrunali?' he asked again, but with a missing smile and an equally tensed face.

'Why did you do this to me?' she finally asked.

He got nervous, 'What happened? What have I done?'

'Vivek, I knew this will happen, I had warned you before that this will not end up with a mere friendship.'

'I like you Mrunali, and I know that you do have feelings for me. Then why are you denying it?' he asked.

Mrunali gave a stare at Vivek, 'Because I know what the consequences of all this will be.' She said in a frustrated and sad tone.

'What consequences? What are you talking? Why are you thinking like this?' he said.

'Our relationship will not be acceptable, not in our families, and not in the society.'

'And how do you know all this? Are you some astrologer?' he said with anger.

'Because of this caste system…,' before she could complete her sentence, Vivek interrupted.

'Please, Mrunali.' 'I don't want this caste system thing again. You know I don't believe in all this.'

'You don't, but others do. They will not accept our relationship. They will not accept it.' Her eyes were moist again, with tears rolling through them.

'Why do we care about this society, hun? And I know that our love will convince our parents.' He held her hand.

'This is not easy,' she looked into his eyes, and gently took her hand away.

'I know this won't be easy, and there will be hurdles in our way. But we will together solve them.' 'Do you love me?' he further asked.

She did not speak. 'Answer me, Mrunali,' he asked again.

'Yes, I love you.' Mrunali was surprised with her own bluntness. She had feelings for Vivek, but it would come out so easily; she did not know.

'Thank you, thank you. Thank you so much Mrunali, for these words, I love you too. I will be there with you every time, no matter what.'

They walked back home, Vivek was very happy, Mrunali was happy too, but at the same time, she was tensed about convincing her parents about them.

5b. Parents Do Not Always Agree

Love between people cannot be hidden for long. It is like, fragrance that one enjoys little more each time until that little more reaches a point when it becomes difficult to breathe.

Mrunali and Vivek were enjoying their time of being together. As they say, love was in the air. There was excitement in choosing the new locations to meet. Be it Gorai beach, or be it the Bandstand, or Powai's lake, these were beautiful when they were together. It was fun to explore different tapris. Rains were so soaking. Bollywood songs were more meaningful. Traveling in auto was never this lovely. The company of each other, made them forget the world, forget all the pains of their lives. They could get solace in each other.

Mrunali often had tense moments, with the thoughts of talking to parents about this relationship. She was afraid, as she was a bit aware of her parent's reaction. She was enjoying this phase and never wanted it to end. She always wished that this time would pause, and their fairy-tale will never end. But the time comes with wings, and it flies away soon.

It was getting tough for Vivek to wait, he wanted Mrunali to meet his parents at the earliest, and soon for them to get married. He asked her many a times to announce their relationship, make it official and inform their parents. But Mrunali held up every time, she wanted to finish her studies first. Vivek agreed to her, as he knew how passionate she was towards her studies; she wanted to get a decent job.

***

Mrunali was very nervous today. Vivek consoled her, that she should not worry. He teased her, 'after all, I taught you.' Vivek joined Mrunali to her college today. Her results were going to get announced. She was excited, and nervous together.

'Hey, I passed,' Mrunali came out running after seeing her results, 'I'm really happy.'

'Congratulations Mam,' 'where do we have the party?' Vivek asked mischievously and opening his arms, with a hint to Mrunali.

She smiled, 'Wow, what an actor is here,' and put his hands down. 'Now, I'll have to get to the next steps.'

'What is it?'

'You know it. I have applied for jobs for teacher post at colleges. I have to make it to at least one.' Mrunali sighs heavily. She was happy, and ready for the next phase of her life. Vivek nodded, he knew that she has worked very hard to achieve this.

They caught an auto. Vivek first dropped Mrunali off to her house, and then he left for his home.

Ramya and Mrs Mhatre were waiting at home. They got excited when they saw Mrunali entering home.

'Aai and aunty, I passed; and not only passed, but did really well.' Mrunali touched her mother's feet and then Mrs Mhatre's.

Mrs Mhatre hugged her, 'Oh my pori, we are proud of you. We want all the daughters in our chawl to follow you. You have set an example for them.'

Ramya was elated at the news. She bought a glass of milk with saffron in it. 'Laado, you do well. Proud of you. Do well in your life ahead.'

'Now I need to get a teacher's job. Praying that it happens soon.' Mrunali put her head into Ramya's arms. Mrs Mhatre concluded, 'Beta, you will achieve, what you set out to. Our blessings are always with you.'

Ramya and Ganesh were on the moon that day. They could not express much to Mrunali, but their heart was pounding with happiness. Their daughter has given them several moments of pride. 'She worked hard for this. She created path for herself. She has decided her own destiny.' Ganesh said, while holding Ramya's hand. 'May God bless every father and mother with such a daughter.'

Shruti and Jaya knew that her sister has laid the foundation for them to follow.

***

Vivek was waiting outside the Paikar college. Mrunali has gone inside for a job interview. She was happy that she is shortlisted for the final round. She had prepared a lot for this interview. She looked very confident before she went inside. He just hoped that all goes smoothly for her.

Vivek's wait was finally over. Mrunali came out from the gate. His eyes blinked after seeing that smile on her face.

'So, you did it,' he flashed a high-five; and she responded.

'Yes, finally.' 'I'm so happy.'

'Let's celebrate your success and go to the cafe,' he said in a cheerful tone.

'Firstly, let me call Aai and Baba. They must be waiting for me,' she said.

'Call them from the cafe,' he insisted. She agreed.

They reached the nearby cafe. While Vivek went inside to secure a place, Mrunali called her parents.

'So, what did they say? How was their reaction?' Vivek asked.

'They are very happy. They have worked really hard to get me here. It was easy for them to not do it, like other parents. Today I gave them the biggest happiness.' She was emotional.

'You are a good daughter. They are proud of you,' said he, holding her hand. 'And I am sure, you will be a very good daughter-in-law,' he grinned to cheer her up. She smiled.

In the meantime, the waiter came with a black forest pastry, French fries and two cups of cold coffee, all were Mrunali's choice. He always knew, how to make her happy, and succeeded this time too. A big and bubbly smile came on her face, looking at the order. She couldn't wait and started eating French fries.

Vivek looked at her eating for a while and then said, 'Mrunali, I think, it's the time now. We should inform our parents. Time to make our relationship official.' The spoon fell from Mrunali's hand and her face too.

'What happened Mrunali?' He got nervous on seeing her. 'Are you not excited to talk about us to your parents?' 'Don't you want us to get married?'

'I want all this to happen. I want that,' she closed her eyes briefly.

'Then, what is the problem? You have completed your studies. You got a good job. Everything is all set now.'

'I am just afraid of the consequences if our parents don't agree with our relationship? Then what we will do.' She opened up with her concern.

'I know Mrunali. It is going to be tough to convince them.' 'They may not be happy. They may get angry. They may scold us. But we will face them. We will show them our true love.'

'I am too scared, Vivek. Don't know what will happen?'

'Don't worry. I am there with you always, we will fight all this together,' he said convincingly.

They both left the cafe, while Vivek was escorting her home; every step was looking so hard. He too was nervous.

***

She reached home. Ganesh and Ramya were ecstatic. Ramya has made her favourite food, and they both gave her blessings and showered her with all the love. All this made her more nervous. Finally, after the food, she collected enough strength to tell them about Vivek.

'Aai, Baba, I want to tell you something.' She was sweating.

'What happened, Mrunali. I could see, you looked tense, since you entered home. It is your best day, and happy occasion.' 'Is there any problem?' Ganesh was worried, thinking it may be about further studies, or any specific needs at the college that is bothering her elder.

'Baba, I want to tell you something.'

'Tell me, what is troubling my daughter?' Ganesh asked.

'Aai, Baba. You know, Vivek. I mentioned to you about him, Aai.' Ramya looked at her.

'We know each other for a long time. We like each other.' she said in a low and scared tone.

Her parents didn't say anything, it was a piece of huge and shocking news for them.

'Who is he?' Ganesh asked after a minute pause. Ramya was still quiet, puzzled at what she just heard from her elder daughter.

'Vivek lives nearby. He teaches in a coaching centre, well settled. He is good, really cultured. Respects elders, women.' She said all this without a pause.

'I know; it is all your decision. You have the right to decide your life partner. But I think our opinion also matters to you. That much right we must have.' Ganesh said with a heavy tone.

Ganesh has always supported Mrunali. But he was not sure what he should do this time. He knew, she is smart, and she would never make a wrong decision.

'Of course, baba, you have all the rights. I want your happiness, and your approval too.'

'Ok, I want to meet the boy and his family too.' he said after a long pause. His eyes met Ramya and could see an approval from her end.

'Thank you. Thank you, Baba.' She said. This was a bit relief for her. But she has not yet mentioned the major thing.

Her father was about to leave. 'Baba,' she stopped him.

'Now what?' he plainly asked.

'There is something more. About Vivek.' she said.

'What is it?'

'He is an upper-caste Brahmin. His family is one of the well-beings in the society.'

'Are you in your senses, Mruni? This won't be possible. It is not acceptable in the society, and I am sure his family will not accept you.' Ganesh was visibly upset. 'You kids have made all this a joke.'

'But baba, we want to be together. We love…love each other,' she said, with her eyes gazing at Ganesh's legs.

'Mruni, this love will end soon and then you have to face the real life. That will be tough. They will taunt you for your caste and other things. You won't be able to adjust over there.' He tried to be rational.

'Vivek is a nice boy. He has said, he will take care of his parents, convince them. He loves me very much, and I am sure he will take care of me and all the other things. Baba, you please meet him once. And then decide for him.' She pleaded.

'I don't know about him, but I am not sure about this relationship. Is his family ready for this marriage?' Ganesh shot back.

'Today, he will also speak to his parents. After that, he will arrange a meeting for all of us.'

'Ok, let him first talk to his parents. We will decide after that.' he said and left the room. Ramya was in the corner listening to their conversation. Her heart was pumping with what is happening, and what will happen next.

Mrunali's hopes were now on Vivek's conversation with his parents. He has always mentioned how his father believes in the religion and rituals. So, it looked the difficult part. But Vivek always seemed confident, that it will work out well with his Aai and Baba.

5c. The Other Side

Vivek and his parents were having dinner. He was quiet. But inner somewhere, he was preparing himself to talk to them. He has all the questions and answers ready in his mind. He was getting ready to face them. Vivek knew that they love him very much, as he was the only child, and was an obedient one. His father was happy to see him living a healthy life, focusing on career and future. Vivek found it difficult to strike the initial conversation, but he knew once initiated, it will be concluded smoothly.

After dinner, he went to his parents' room and sat next to them. His mother sensed that he wants to say something. She asked him, 'What is it, Vivek?'

'Nothing, Ma. Just that, it is something important, I want to tell you.' he said and grabbed their attention.

'What happened, do you need something?' his father asked and waved his hand on his head.

'No, papa, it is something else,' he replied.

'What? Tell us.' His mother asked him.

'I know this girl. I think, I like her. I mean, I like her.' He quickly muttered.

'What? Who is she?' His father's voice was louder this time. That got Vivek scared, but he gathered the courage to continue.

'Mrunali. Her name.'

'I am not asking her name. Who is she? Where she lives? About family? Religion? Caste?' Strain on his father's forehead was visible.

Vivek was aware that these questions would come, but it was not easy for him to now put the answers across. His all the prior preparation now seems to have gone for a toss.

'She lives in a chawl nearby. She is a Tamhankar.' He said in an inaudible voice without looking up.

'Say it, loudly,' said his father, lifting his chin. His mother put her hand on his father's shoulder to calm him down. But his father showed his finger with eyes wide open, indicating his mother to stay out of this.

Vivek breathed heavy, and persisted, 'Pa, she is a Tamhankar. So what?'

His father was about to slap him. But his mother stopped him, 'Aaho, what are you going to do. Please calm down.'

'How can I control my anger? After his words? I don't allow the lower community people to enter in our house. He wants me to bring a non-brahmin girl as my daughter-in-law.'

Vivek was quietly listening to his father. The sudden news has made his father irate.

'Vivek, I don't want this kind of rubbish in my house. How can you even think of this?'

'Papa. She is a nice girl. She is a professor in a college. I am sure she will take care of you both.'

'I don't want any care. I don't even care how good she is. I just don't want this to happen.'

'But Papa, I love her. I can't live without her. I want to spend my life with her.' Vivek could not resist himself to talk openly.

'Look at this shameless boy. Talking like this in front of us. If you have decided everything, then what you are waiting for? Inviting for the wedding.'

'I am not inviting. Papa, I am here for your blessings. I want you to meet her and her family. At least once.'

'I am not going to meet those people. They don't belong to our society, and I will not go beyond our system.'

'You will ignore your son's happiness for this society? Who is more important to you, Papa? The society or me.' Vivek sounded adamant.

'Don't teach me all this, and don't try to throw these kinds of tantrums at me. I know who and what is more important. But I can't leave the society and my rituals for your stupid affair.' his father was decisive.

'Baba, this is not some infatuation. We both love each other.'

'This is not love; that girl has trapped you, for your money and possession.'

'She is not like that, I know her.'

'I don't know whether she is good or not. And I don't want to get into that, but this will not happen. That is final.' His father emphatically concluded.

'But papa,' before Vivek could say more, his father interrupted him by showing him the hand.

'No more discussion,' his father said, and asked him to leave.

Vivek's mother tried to talk to his father but he did not listen. Then she went to Vivek, but he too was not willing to talk.

The whole night, Vivek was not able to sleep. Mrunali on the other side was restless. She was strained thinking about how Vivek's parents would have reacted. And what will happen after both the families meet.

***

The next morning, Mrunali got ready for her college. It was her first day. She was nervous. Not for the first day at college but thinking about what might have happened at Vivek's house the previous night. Her mother made her eat sweet curd and blessed her. She reached the bus stop but could not find Vivek. She was now stressed.

Vivek did not go to coaching centre that day. His mother decided to talk to him, so she went to his room.

'Are you not going to coaching today?' she asked. Vivek did not respond, he was still in abysmal state.

She sat next to him, held his hand, 'Don't be upset.'

Vivek broke down. He needed his mother's touch the most now. He hugged his mother tightly and cried like a baby.

'Maa. I love her very much. I cannot live without her. Please help me.'

He continued, 'She is a nice girl. She will take care of both of you. Please tell papa. Please make him understand.' He begged to his mother.

'You know, how your father is? He is rigid in all these matters. He will not understand.' She reasoned it out.

'Then, I won't be able to live. I will die. I can't live without her.' He again started crying.

Her mother hugged him tightly and stopped him from saying all this. She consoled him and agreed to talk to his father in the night.

***

Vivek was not at the dinner table. His father enquired, but his mother kept mum. It was unusually very quiet on the table.

After the dinner, when Vivek's father was resting in his room, his mother initiated a talk. 'Aaho. Why are you so rigid?'

'Aata kaay, why are you troubling? We discussed this topic enough.'

'Vivek is grown up. He can take drastic steps.'

'What steps will he take? Will he run away? He should better behave. We have to live in the society.'

'Please think about this. Vivek loves that girl a lot. He is crying like a baby. He can play with his life. I am really afraid.'

His father got visibly upset, and shouted, 'Vivek, come here…Vivek, can you hear me? Come here fast.'

As soon as Vivek was in front of him, his father showered him with abuses.

'I explained to you yesterday that this girl will not fit in our society, in our home. Can't you understand this simple thing?' he was forceful.

'But papa,' before he completes his sentence, his father interrupted him.

'I don't want to hear anything,' he continued, 'and, if that girl becomes your wife, I will die instead of showing my face to the world.' He delivered and left his room.

Vivek held his mother's hand. Their eyes met; his mother could only give compassion. He cried, cried a lot, 'what should I do, Ma?'

'Don't worry, it will be over.'

'Ma, what should I do…' Vivek cried.

'No, Beta. Don't…Don't cry, you are man, it does not look good.'

'But Ma…Do I have no option? Can I not choose my future?'

It continued for long. Mother's heart wept for her only child. Alas, she could not offer any help.

5d. Calmness, Takes Aggression!

Vivek broke down after his father's vigorous reaction. That painful night turned him into a stone, devoid of emotions. He secluded himself into his room and stopped talking to anyone. He did not go to the coaching centre after that day. He indeed did not speak to Mrunali since then.

His mother tried to find out ways to talk to him. But there was no reaction from him. Vivek was finding it difficult to handle it. The days were emotional, and the nights were painful for him. He was somewhere crushed in between the thoughts of Mrunali and the decision by his father. It was not easy for him to choose one over the other. The stress was taking a toll on his health. He did not eat properly, and with busy mind he did not get enough sleep.

He was quickly falling into depression zone with his condition becoming vulnerable each day. His mother was getting very concerned. She talked to his father many a times, but he did not shy away from his rigidity. His father would convince her that this is just childish act, and Vivek will get over this soon. But his mother, being a mother remained concerned and looked for ways to cheer up her son.

***

Mrunali was becoming tense each day. There was no contact with Vivek for a week. She called at his coaching centre, but they did not have any information. She tried to call at his house too. Many a times no-one picked up the phone. A few times it said 'hello'; it seemed to be his father's voice, and she had to promptly disconnect it. Her restless wait for him continued every day at the bus stop, only to meet with disappointment at the end of the day.

After all the failed phone calls, she again decided to attempt one more time. With a hope she visited the phone booth. She dialled his number, with every ring she prayed for Vivek to pick up the phone. But God was not with her as yet.

'Hello,' his mother was on the line.

A silence. 'Hi, I'm Mrunali.'

His mother did not speak for some time. She fell into thoughts of how to react. Should she be angry? Or should she simply cut the call? She regained her composure.

'Wait…' She put the phone on hold. 'Vivek, there is a phone call for you.'

There was no response.

'This is from someone, Mrunali. She is here waiting on the call.'

Mrunali's name generated energy in him, it's just like life came in a dead body. Vivek ran to the phone. 'Hi…hello Mrunali,' he said those words after a long time.

'Vivek, where are you? Why are you not coming to the coaching centre?' 'I mean, what happened? You doing okay? You didn't call me?' She asked non-stop questions to him. He was listening quietly. Those words from Mrunali were like flower petals falling on him, and he was enjoying the fragrance and celebration of it.

'Vivek, answer me. Please.' She asked again.

He came back to consciousness. 'No, I just want to hear your voice,' he said with running tears.

Mrunali could hear that he was sobbing. Her tears started falling as well, 'Vivek, please no'.

Vivek's mother standing in the corner, could see the state of her son. She could hear Mrunali's crying as well. Her heart wrenched; she could not stop herself from crying. She grasped conclusively that Mrunali is very important for her son, and they both love each other.

'Vivek, I want to meet you. I want to see you. I want to feel you.' Mrunali said.

'I also want all this. I am sorry. I made you wait these many days.' Vivek took pause, 'I am coming tomorrow. You wait for me at the bus stand in the morning.' He finally said.

***

Vivek was filled with new energy. Mrunali's call has breathed new life in him. He was happy. He was super excited to meet her the next day.

His eyes were repeatedly looking at the wall clock, as it felt to him that the time has stopped, the clock was not moving. His mother was happy to see him like this. In the past week he was like a detached person, but today he was back to himself.

Vivek came to the dinner table after a long time. His father taunted 'Saheb is here.'

His mother has cooked his favourite palak paneer. His father noticed that Vivek had a smile on his face.

'You are looking fresh today. Is something special?' his father asked looking at him and his mother.

'I am meeting Mrunali, tomorrow,' he said in an excitement, without noticing the fact that he was talking in front of his father.

'Still, you are with that girl.' His father got angry and tapped the table hard. The angry voice of his father made him realize the present. The smile and happiness from his face waved away.

'Don't be angry, look how happy he is today.' Mother interrupted.

'I don't want this happiness. Nothing is more important to me than my pride.'

'Vivek, listen carefully. I don't want any drama. Don't want to listen to that girl's name again in my house,' his father said and left the dining table without having his dinner.

Vivek was shivering. There was anger, frustration, and outcry; all within himself. It was all black in front of him. He somehow could compose himself and left the dining table.

5e. Unthinkable Happened

The short-lived excitement being suppressed, turned into an aggression. Vivek started throwing things, walking restlessly in the room. He held a pillow and cried bitterly. He took out the greeting cards and all the gifts given by Mrunali. Those were his soothing pills. One after another, one memory and the second one, and the next one…and so on. He kept on looking at them for a long time. Tears were his companion. This was joy, this was celebration of love. He was remembering all the beautiful memories of them being together.

But then the harsh words of his father struck him; it overpowered the memories, and his emotions. The soother feelings vanished away, and it again turned into sorrow and rage. He has never embraced anger as much as he has in the last few days.

'I won't be able to live without Mrunali.' 'But what to do with baba. He won't agree to it. He won't allow this.' He murmured.

'It cannot go on like this.'

He was looking at this photograph with Mrunali and him, that they clicked in a studio. Mrunali was not willing for it; but he insisted for this picture.

He quickly scribbled something on a paper, wrapped up that photo with this letter. He was decisive.

He went into the kitchen, quickly scanned through the utensils. He picked a knife, with a thought in his mind. He got back to the room.

He relived the memories of past, his childhood with parents, his growing up memories, his friend Babu, and then the beautiful time with Mrunali. And then his heated exchanges with his father.

It was that moment. He slit his wrist with all the strength that he had. He watched his blood oozing through him, around him. He slightly went back, took the corner of the bed. It has started hurting him, it was blanking him. He kept saying, 'Mrunali, I love you.' It became black all over. But he could see, Mrunali everywhere.

Then, his body pumped a few times like a fish out of water. Then he fell for the peace.

***

Few hours later, Vivek's mother came to his room. 'Oh, re deva,' she shouted and ran to him. Took Vivek in her arms. But he was not responding.

'Aaika ho, come here…come here. This is disaster.' She shouted for his father. He came running to the room. His mother kept shaking his son, but he was unconsciously lying on the floor, with a bleeding wrist.

His father quickly called the ambulance and took him to the hospital. Doctors mentioned that his condition is critical, and directly admitted him to ICU. Vivek's parents waited restlessly outside the ICU.

After some time, the doctor came outside. Vivek's father ran up to him.

'Is he ok?' he asked the doctor.

'There is a lot of bleeding. He is unconscious. We will have to pray, that he wakes up. Next 24-48 hours are critical.' The doctor replied.

'Now, what will happen? In how much time, will he be ok?' his father was not able to speak. He was stammering.

'We can't say anything right now. But as said earlier, his condition is still critical,' the doctor said and left.

His father was shaking, he fell on the floor. His mother came forward and held him from the back. She made him sit on the chair. They both are crying. Their only child, only son now is fighting for his life.

***

In the morning, Mrunali excitedly went to the bus stop. She wore the suit gifted by Vivek. She reached the bus stop, waiting for him. She could not see Vivek anywhere. She waited for him for over an hour, but then she left. The whole day, she was thinking of him. She had so many questions running around in her head, almost in the state of panic. She could not resist waiting for the next morning.

In the evening, she called his home from the cafe. His mother picked the phone.

'Hello, aunty…' a pause, 'Is Vivek at home?' she asked.

His mother did not say a word. She was just crying.

This made Mrunali more worried. 'What happened aunty? Is everything Ok?'

'Nothing is fine.' She said in a sobbed voice. 'Vivek tried to kill himself. He is unconscious since morning.'

'What….' the shock made Mrunali speechless. 'How? Why? How is he now?' she could finally ask this. After a brief pause, her own frightening thoughts got interrupted when she heard his mother's shout-out cry.

'What should I say? He is our support system, and now he is on the hospital bed.' It took a while, before she attained composure.

'Aunty, can I meet him?' Mrunali asked fearfully.

'Yes, you can come and meet him. He is admitted to Swastik hospital.'

'Thank you, aunty.' she said before placing the phone.

'Why you gave her permission?' Vivek's father shouted on his mother. His mother just showed her hand 'Gappa basa' indicating his father to shut up. Her husband was shocked, but he empathised her reaction. They both didn't say anything further.

Mrunali came home walking, with lot of fear in her mind, scary thoughts, not knowing exactly what happened and how is Vivek now. She was sweating, her inner self crying.

She took a corner of her bed and cried out a lot. This was tough for her. Ramya came near her, 'Beta, what happened?'

'He should have waited for me. He should have talked to me. Why did he?'

Shruti and Jaya were in shock, seeing her Tai, what happened to her. They just watched, as her sister cried ruthlessly.

'But what happened?' Ramya put her hands on Mrunali's head. She has never seen her elder daughter being so emotional.

'Ma, Vivek attempted a suicide.'

'What? Why?'

'Aai, I don't know. He is unconscious. He is in the hospital.' Mrunali's crying was profound.

'Don't cry. Don't worry. He will be fine.' 'We'll go and visit him in the morning.' Ramya embraced her elder tightly.

Ganesh too joined in to calm her down. It was only after a few hours; she could console herself.

Mrunali's thoughts jumped from one to another, all conveying horror, scare, sadness, and sorrow. She kept turning from one side to another. Sleep was elusive, her heart and mind kept asking for the well-being of Vivek. Ramya's eyes were wide awake, thinking about her inconsolable daughter.

***

In the morning, Ganesh and Ramya accompanied Mrunali to the hospital. Mrunali has never met Vivek's parents earlier. But she could figure out his mother. She greeted them, 'Namaste'. His mother signalled her to go to the room. Mrunali slowly entered the room.

Each step was getting difficult for her. Vivek was lying unconscious on the bed. She sluggishly moved to his bed; tears betrayed her again, they found the way through her eyes.

'Vivek, See I am here. Open your eyes, Talk to me.'

'I don't like this, to see you like this. Please get up for me, for everyone.' she said, crying, holding his hand.

Mrunali is watching Vivek and remembering all the memories of them being together.

'Vivek, didn't you say, you will be there with me. Always. We will together convince our parents. Then why you are not here, now?'

'Please get up, please don't leave me alone, I need you. I need you in my life.'

Listening to her crying voice, Vivek's mother came in and consoled her.

'He will be all right. You don't worry.'

The mother only wanted her son to get well soon and get back to his happy and healthy living.

***

That night, Vivek's pulse rate got down, oxygen level was continuously dropping. His mother was sitting next to him, she immediately called the doctor.

The doctor checked, injects him with some medicines, put on the oxygen mask and tried to control the situation. His parents were watching them doing all these and praying for everything to get normal.

Then a silence generated after this huge storm. His body lay silent; the computer screen was showing linear motion. Doctor's looked hopeless. They started removing the instruments.

Vivek was no more.

The news broke both the parents. They had lost their only treasure of their life.

The doctor shook the father by his arm, 'Please come, and do all the formalities. Then they can discharge the body.'

His father came to his senses, he controlled his emotions with a heavy heart. His mother was crying her heart out. But the father has a job to do.

His mother remembered about Mrunali and phoned her, 'Beta, Vivek is no more.' In a shivering tone, she could quickly mutter out.

'No,' Mrunali shouted aloud after hearing the news. Her thoughts of horror have come true. The news took away her soul. Vivek was her life, and she could not imagine herself without him.

'I want to see him, baba. Please take me over there.' she cried to Ganesh.

All of them visited Vivek's house. His parents were crying and sobbing near his body. Mrunali was profusely crying, Ramya held her. She kept speaking to herself, 'How can you leave me, Vivek? How can you do that. You said, you will not leave me. Then why are you going? Please get up. Please, for our love. I cannot live without you.' She kept thinking, crying.

Mrunali and her family left for their house, while Vivek's parents and relatives performed all the rituals.

***

Mrunali had lost all her energy. She did not have any further desire.

Ramya and Ganesh watched her helplessly. Ganesh spoke to her a few times. But then allowed her some time to come out of it.

One evening, Ganesh gave a letter to Mrunali. 'Hold this. Vivek's father met me today morning at my shop. He asked me to give it to you.'

'Vivek's father?'

'Yes, that poor man has lost his entire life. Vivek was his earning, his savings, his only future.' Ganesh showed the soft corner for him. 'Indeed, both mother and father; their world is gone.'

'He insisted that I give this to you. He said that you only take this, Mrunali.'

Mrunali took it from Ganesh. But she heard her Baba, there was a message for her in the letter.

***

Hey Dear,

I Love you. Love you so much.

Want to be there with you always.

Not sure, if it can happen in this birth. Things are a bit difficult. But we will definitely meet during our next birth.

Till then, please remember me. But keep smiling. I get the world's happiness when I see you smiling.

Mruni, you have a long way ahead, here in this life. Love you!

Yours,

Vivek'

Mrunali fetched the picture. This was the same picture that they had clicked together in a studio, and Vivek had insisted for it. He had said, this will always remain as our long-lasting memory.

Mrunali cried. Cried a lot. Memories of living those moments with Vivek flooded her thoughts. They surfaced, made vibes, touched every corner of hers.

But then she was out of it. She decided to live. Live happily for the sake of Vivek. For the sake of her parents.

6. Shruti And Her Struggles

6a. Shruti Discovering Herself

Shruti stood transfixed before the mirror. Through the misty glass which shouldered the burden of old age and neglect, her face reflected a glow of freshness. Her cheeks looked a little brighter this morning. With affectionate hand Shruti touched her cheekbone. Against her soft palm, her cheek felt smooth. It was pretty-unlikely for a girl who lived in a chawl. Shruti knew it. The harsh weather and difficult life usually bruised the youthfulness. But Shruti bloomed with time. Her long, dark hair hung on her back. She liked to wear it lose. The touch of the silky mane made her feel like a fashion model.

Tune of a latest Hindi song floated inside Tamhankar's house. Someone was listening to a radio. She hummed along the song as she studied herself in the mirror. A smile played on her face as she caught a glimpse of a face peeking through the thin cotton curtain of her window. Ramu did this, every morning. He knew that she would be here before the mirror at this time.

'Shruti.' The stern voice broke the spell. Shruti turned to see her elder sister Mrunali staring at her with disapproving eyes.

'Are you done with your studies?' she asked.

Shruti flashed a dazzling grin at her sister. 'Yes, almost done.' She prayed that Mrunali did not delve deeper into the matter. Since the morning, she had not even touched her books.

Mrunali dragged a deep breath. She opened her mouth to say something. But then her eyes fell on the wall clock. It was nearing 9 am. Mrunali's shift time would begin soon. Teachers had a time off on Saturdays in her college, but she had picked up an early shift at cafe on those days.

'Okay, I am in a hurry,' said Mrunali. 'I will see you in the evening.' She turned to walk away but then something stopped her. 'Shruti, focus on your study. You are getting too attached to the other things.'

Shruti nodded like an obedient girl. In her head the Hindi song kept buzzing. She wanted to try out the dance move of the song. But for that Mrunali must leave the house. Jaya would be home from school soon. So, she had little time in her hand.

'I will, Tai,' said Shruti. 'You don't worry. I will score high in school.'

Mrunali nodded. Her hard eyes remain fixed on Shruti for a moment too long. Then the eldest daughter of Tamhankar family departed the house, leaving behind a beaming Shruti at the mirror.

The house quietened after Mrunali's departure. Jaya has already gone to school. Shruti wondered, how could someone, who spoke so little could bring such hush with their absence. Mrunali had that quality. Each time she stepped out of the house, a doom like silence settled in. It shrouded the entire house and clutched at the hearts of the residents. Life without Mrunali was an unimaginable tryst that Shruti did not even want to ponder in her mind. If only her elder sister let her live without poking. Mrunali had an in-depth disgust for self-adoration. She kept reminding Shruti that good looks alone would not serve the real purpose of life.

There were times when in the deeper space of her heart, Shruti wondered whether the rebukes emerged from suppressed jealousy. Though she had not ever voiced it or acted upon it, she had wondered, only once or twice. Each time her own face reflected beside Mrunali's plain one, the thought crept up like a reptile about to deliver a deadly blow. Like a warrior making a great sacrifice, Shruti battled the thought. But the contamination remained in her mind. Slowly, she started caring for Mrunali's advices less and less. Just a plain Jane trying to belittle the beautiful princess. Shruti shrugged everything Mrunali said with casual demeanour.

A last look at the mirror told her that she did look like a Bollywood star on the making. She ran her hand through her hair imitating the move of a shampoo model she admired. Sound coming from outside had started to fade. The afternoons usually rested in silence with people out for work. Noise rose again with the dusking sky as the residents started to come home.

Shruti looked at the wall clock. She was surprised to see that it was almost 11 in the morning. Time had lost its track as she looked at herself in the mirror. She thought of Vikas. No wonder the young boy acted like crazy for her. She loved the admiration in his eyes each time he saw her. Last night when she went down wearing a red dress that stopped at her calf, she saw something else in his eyes. The admiration had transformed into love. It churned something so feminine within her soul and she felt her skin erupting with goose bumps.

Would she be lucky enough to catch Vikas alone? The thought brought out a tinge of deeper pink on her cheeks. Maybe she should try to catch him. The apartment at the opposite side of the wall belonged to Vijita aunty. She worked in a primary school as a non-teaching staff. Vijita aunty was a risk, Shruti did not want to expose herself to. The woman reminded her of Mrunali. With stern eyes Vijita aunty kept an eye on Shruti.

Shruti tried to tip toe her way by the wide-open door of Vijita aunty's apartment. But to Shruti's utter disappointment, Vijita caught the hesitant movement. 'Shruti,' she called in her usual teacher like sternness.

Shruti halted at once on her track. She turned to look at the elderly woman standing in the narrow hall with a knife in one hand and a slice cabbage in another. Before Shruti had a chance to speak, Vijita asked. 'Where is Ramya and where are you going now?'

The same old chawl life, Shruti exhaled, a little enraged by the fact that everyone knew about everyone's life. In this chawl, nothing remained private. People even talk about the secret lives of the married couples with glee. Shruti's disgust with the place increased by the day. She looked down at her feet before coming up with the right reply.

'Mother went to fetch Jaya from school,' she said. 'I am going down to get notes from Asha.'

Vijita, satisfied with both the answers, went back to her chore of cabbage slicing. A terrifying vision arose before Shruti's eyes as she descended the stairs. In the vision she saw herself slicing vegetables to prepare lunch for her kids who were about to return home from their schools. She saw herself waiting for her husband in the evening to bring home meagre amount of money to run the household. A shiver of fright passed through her spine. She hurried down the steps to meet Vikas. He had been her hope to get away from the hell which grew deeper every day to engulf her. Vikas was a bright student with high prospect of making it big in life. She needed to create a path away from the life this chawl presented before her.

Vikas was sitting by the window of the tiny space beside the living room which affluent people in the chawl used as a guest room. The gloomy space was wide enough to accommodate a single bed. But so much narrower prohibiting freedom of movement. Vikas had shoved his suitcase under the bed to create a little space beside the old wooden bed.

The house was empty except for Vikas. He seemed delighted enough to see her. 'You look pretty,' said Vikas in his usual absent way which attracted Shruti so much. He appreciated her good looks. But at the same time, he appeared to be detached from it.

'Thank you,' she said, dropping herself beside him. 'You know…'

But Vikas hastened to speak before she did. 'Shruti, I like you,' he said in a voice which promised some heart break.

'But you know I cannot promise you anything right now. I am studying. You know that. With you around my studies are being affected. I cannot afford to fail at this point.' He looked at her. The usual warmth had left his demeanour. He did not even seem sorry to speak to her like this. 'I am going away tomorrow.'

With that Vikas shattered the hope of getting away from the chawl. Shruti made her way back to her apartment in a state of shock. The shock did not come from the breakup. She was shocked by the calm way she had taken the news. It seemed completely normal for a relationship to come to an end. Instead, she felt surprisingly alive about the prospect of meeting someone new.

***

The new interest came in the form of Rohit, Vikas's cousin and Shruti's neighbour. Rohit was a few years older than Shruti. His air of maturity attracted her from the beginning. But she had never expressed her interest in him with Vikas in the picture.

But now that the former love interest had departed, she had nothing to hold her back. Rohit's first hint came from a simple touch on her hand. He innocently touched her hand to catch her eyes that day. She reciprocated by catching his hand, with a bit of press; to find the familiar affection in them. She started thinking about Rohit a lot.

Ganesh went to his work early that morning. Ramya went out to fetch Jaya from school. And Mrunali was away to work. Thick clouds veiled the sky that morning. Without warning the downpour started. Wind hissed with madness and the smell of wet soil filled the air.

Rohit paid a visit to Shruti's apartment that noon. He knocked on her door using his knuckles. The rap made Shruti alert. She had been dancing to her favourite Bollywood song. She came to the door to find a smiling Rohit, standing at the threshold.

'Vikas has sent a message for you,' he said.

The mention of Vikas's name made Shruti draw sharp breath. Now that Vikas was gone, she felt a strange emptiness down her soul. It was as if he had taken away something utterly precious along with himself. Without it Shruti would never be complete. She stepped away from the door to allow Rohit inside.

Sound of thunder rambling outside sent a tremor to the chawl. The thin walls rattled under the impact. She gestured Rohit to sit on the bed. He did. 'Can I have a glass of water please?' he asked.

'Sure,' Shruti said, going inside to fetch the glass. When she came out, Rohit had already shut the door. It did not seem like an abnormal event given the fact that Rohit had come to her apartment many times.

'Come sit here,' invited Rohit. 'I need to talk to you.'

Shruti obeyed and occupied a space beside Rohit. He placed his hand on Shruti's shoulder. 'You see Vikas is a young man. He is studying. He will go to Pune to study.' His hand slid down her back in slow rhythmic motion. Shruti did not think much about it. The prospect of getting Vikas's message excited her in a way that she did not think anything extra ordinary about Rohit's hand or the lust in his touch.

The spell broke when Rohit took a step forward by inching closer to her. Shruti froze on the place. She was unable to get any word out of her throat. Everything blurred for a moment before her eyes. Fortunately, she found her sense back before the matter went out of her hands. She pushed Rohit away with all her strength. He did not try to force himself further. Without another word he pulled himself up from the bed and walked away from the apartment, leaving a flushed Shruti sitting on the bed.

The incident had brought a flurry of memories from the depth of her soul. The past had suddenly come forth like a raging storm, bringing back her past with Ajit, Varun and Sharma, which had marked her heart with shivers of frights. Shock had muted her for a long time in the past. However, this time with Rohit, she experienced a fusion of emotions. On one hand it frightened her, shocked her but on the other hand she felt goose bumps creeping all over her flesh. The sensation which passed through her nerves, left her in a state of longing. She discovered within herself a woman who wanted to feel alive.

6b. Deepak, Another Fling

Deepak drew a deep breath as sweat poured down his back. He had been standing at the entrance of the chawl for a long time. His friends had already started to complain about the long hour and heat. But Deepak did not budge. He wanted to have a glimpse of Shruti.

The tales of her beauty had surpassed the boundary of her chawl and reached Deepak's in no time. He had planned to visit her chawl many times. But the situation did not permit him the chance. Today, however, he did not allow anything to come between him and his desire.

He had taken his cycle and paddled half an hour straight to visit this chawl. Now he stood under the mid-day sun and waited for Shruti to come out. He wanted to see her just once, he told himself.

From his friends he had come to know about the location of her apartment. The information had helped him place himself near her house in the chawl. He wiped his face several times to get the sweaty feeling off. His back itched as he waited. The over-washed cotton shirt clung to his back like a second skin. Should he go away? Or should he wait a little longer?

In the moment of undecidedness, the door to Shruti's house opened, and a young girl walked out. Deepak coughed at the sight of her. One of his friends whistled in low tune and Deepak understood the excitement. He had no doubt in his mind who the girl was. She had long dark hair, flowing behind her narrow back. Her face glowed with youth and health. She wore a simple cotton salwar suit which accentuated her slender body.

She stood in the veranda with a lost expression, her eyes remained fixed on the sky. Then she looked down and their gazes met. Deepak wanted to smile. He wanted to give her a signal that he had noticed her. But her beauty had him transfixed. He could not move. A strange sensation passed through his spine. He felt a sudden tug between his legs. Before the feeling swept him over, he turned and left the chawl, knowing he would return soon.

On the way to his own chawl, Deepak thought of the young woman. His friends kept chattering, but he did not hear anything. nothing registered in his mind. Only the image of Shruti teased him. Her girlish looks and womanly body made him want to become a man. Did she know about the relationship between men and women? Or would he have to teach her that? The notion of taking her innocence forced out an eruption of heat. He would surely turn her into a woman. His paddling speed increased as he saw himself kissing her roughly.

He wanted her. He had no shame in admitting that she had awakened a part of him which he had not acknowledge for a long time. He had seen women. There were too many in his chawl. They came in all shapes and sizes. 'Yet, Shruti comes with a gift of perfection. She had the right body, the right face, and the right way of holding herself.' he exclaimed.

'Bhai, she is too good looking to pay attention to you,' said one of the boys in his group.

It evoked a male rage which Deepak had not experienced before. He turned towards the grinning boy. 'In two weeks, she would be moaning beneath me.'

That made the group laugh as if Deepak had made a joke of some kind. They had come to stand at the entrance of their own chawl. Deepak had dismounted the cycle. His head thudded with ache. The long paddling in the harsh summer, sun had its effect on him. But he disregarded the discomfort. His mind reeled with plans. He would have to meet her alone. He corrected immediately; he would have to get her alone.

'Bhai, leave it,' said another boy. 'She is really too good.'

Before Deepak could say anything, the group of boys walked inside the chawl. They all had their opinion about how Shruti would reject Deepak. The jeering voices followed Deepak as he made his way inside the chawl. A plan began to form in his mind as he walked.

The next day, Deepak crept out of his chawl unseen. He made sure his friends did not see him or else they would want to accompany him. With them tagging along Deepak would not be able to lure Shruti in his arms. As he paddled towards Shruti's chawl through midday traffic, he envisioned himself inching close to the young girl. He saw himself brushing against her soft body.

His paddling speed increased that moment. With effort he dragged a long breath. He must have her.

The journey did not appear to be laborious that day. Rather Deepak felt exhilarated at being able to see Shruti alone today. He did not want anyone else to take away the freedom of getting to know her.

He reached her chawl within half an hour. His mind reeled with possibilities. Should he climb up and go to her room? But the notion of scaring her into a tantrum made him scratch the plan entirely.

The chawl appeared to be deserted that day. Not many people loitered outside. Fortunately, Deepak noticed Shruti immediately. She had been fetching water in a bucket. Sweat had the thin material of her salwar suit cling to her delicious body. Deepak could not help noticing the roundness of her breasts. She must look stunning without her clothes.

Deepak situated himself at a corner in the shadow and watched Shruti struggle with the bucket. He rushed forward to lend her a hand, knowing he would not get the opportunity again. He needed to introduce himself.

'Please let me,' he said leaning forward to take the bucket from Shruti's hand.

She turned to face him, startled at the sudden appearance. Even if she had recognized him, she gave no impression. Instead, she allowed him to take the bucket from her hand. He carried it without effort. They climbed the stairs without speaking. Finally, when Shruti reached her room, she turned to thank him.

Deepak placed the bucket on the floor. 'I am Deepak.' He flashed a smile at her.

She nodded in an absent manner. Men were nothing special for her, Deepak noted with anger as she went inside her house and shut the door on his face.

Shruti stood by the door for a long time. Her senses were hyperactive, and heartbeat fast. She had seen the look on the young man who had introduced himself as Deepak to her. She had noticed him looking intently at her. With effort she had kept her face neutral. Her mind raced as she had visions of her and Deepak together, laughing and chatting over tea and chaats.

Footsteps echoing from outside told her that Deepak had left. She went over to the mirror for a quick scan of her face. Did she look as beautiful as before? Each day she lived in the fear of losing her beauty. But the reflection in the mirror assured her that she still looked the same, maybe a little more beautiful, she thought with joy.

That evening she met Deepak once again. He had been with two other boys. But to her dismay he did not look at her. When she tried to smile, he appeared to be nonchalant. Till now, no one had ignored her this way, Shruti fumed as she walked away, not noticing a smug smile playing on Deepak's face.

It was the same the next day. Deepak did not even notice Shruti as she passed by. A little taken aback by the behaviour of the young man, Shruti stood a little distance away and looked directly at him. But Deepak was deep in conversation with his friends who always tagged along with him.

6c. Developed An Interest

Two days later Shruti found Deepak alone near her chawl. It was her chance to talk to the young man to find out why he behaved so strangely with her. So, Shruti went over to talk to him.

'Deepak.' She came to stand before him. He appeared to be a little occupied. He did not look at her immediately. Shruti had to call his name again to get his attention, 'Deepak.'

This time he did look at her. 'Oh, hi. I did not notice you.'

'What do you do here in my chawl every day?' asked Shruti. She felt angry for being ignored for so many days.

'I like it here. The chaiwallah is good. He makes amazing masala chai,' said Deepak, still not looking directly at Shruti.

It gave her a horrible thought. Was she not good looking anymore? Why Deepak did not look at her? The thought delivered such a strong blow that Shruti had to blink her eyes to focus on what Deepak was saying.

Deepak went away that day, but the thought remained with her. Shruti could not get away from the fear of losing her beauty. Multiple times she went to stand before the mirror to check her appearance.

***

Shruti did not protest when Deepak touched her back for the first time. The insecurity that she is losing her beauty has crept in her. She was so overwhelmed by the way Deepak treated her earlier that she did not dare offend him.

'You study in school?' Deepak asked as he continued to explore Shruti's back. They stood at a corner of the chawl. It was a shady part where no one went because of the fear of insects and rats. But Deepak had urged Shruti to go there for a little chit chat.

'Yes,' Shruti said. Her skin crawled as the fingers played on the bare part of her back. But she could not move. It was as if some force kept her to that space with Deepak. 'I…it is getting dark.'

Deepak moved closer towards Shruti. 'I know it is getting dark.' He now placed his hand on her shoulders. 'I like it dark.' His hands slid down her front. Shruti breathed a protest but she did not tear herself away from Deepak for the fear of offending him and losing the attention he had been showering upon her.

It was an hour later, Shruti walked out of the shade with a flushed face. Her body trembled as she remembered the event that took place inside the shade. Deepak had refused to hear her protests and went ahead with his passion. He placed her against the wall and leaned over her with his full body weight.

Shruti did not allow herself to think further. She needed to take a bath and fast. The thought pushed her into a frenzied run towards her house. She did not even look back to see the grinning face of Deepak.

***

It was later that evening. Deepak sat with his friends in his own chawl. He had the expression of a man who had won a valuable prize. His friends looked at him with expectation of a little juicy details.

'You did it?' asked the boy who had said that Deepak was no match for Shruti earlier.

'Yes', said Deepak. 'She cried out in pleasure as I did it.' The satisfaction in his voice made the other boys go green with envy. 'And I did it inside a shade. I did not even have to take her to bed, you know.'

'How was she?' asked another boy.

Deepak grinned at the pimple erupted face of his friend. 'Find out yourself,' was his direct jab that hit the target hard.

'I will.' The resolution in the boy's voice made Deepak throw his head behind and laugh.

'Sure, go ahead and try.' He challenged his friend.

***

Next day Shruti felt a little feverish. Yet, she pulled herself up from the bed and got ready for the school. Her mother looked at her closely. 'You are looking a little strange today. Everything all right?'

Shruti looked at her mother. 'Yes, mother. I am fine.' Her voice sounded hoarse.

She walked out of the chawl in a derailed state. The event of the earlier evening kept playing in her mind. She should not have gone to the shade with Deepak, she thought for the thousandth time.

'Shruti.' The voice made her look back. A thin boy in his late teen stood looking at her. His face had the eruption of transition time pimple. Some of it left scars on the cheek.

'Yes?' she asked, already a bad feeling began to spread across her heart.

'I am Suresh. Deepak's friend,' he said. 'Haven't you seen me around Deepak?'

Shruti took a step backward looking around. She saw people turning to look at her and the boy she talked to. 'No, I have not noticed you.' With that she wanted to part from the strange looking young man.

But Suresh did not let the matter drop so easily. 'Deepak told, you and him in the shades.'

That halted Shruti on her track. She turned to look at Suresh with horrified gaze. 'Deepak told you about us?' she asked.

'Yes, he did.' Suresh flashed a smile at her. 'About the shade incident and others as well.'

Speechless at the blow, Shruti stood transfixed to the spot. Her face flushed at the thought of what else Deepak had told his friends about her.

'Would you like to be my friend as well?' asked Suresh with a leering smile.

That shattered the composure. Shruti turned and fled from the spot. She hurried towards her school, not wanting to be in public anymore. Deepak had succeeded in winning her heart. She could not believe he had betrayed her trust by discussing her with his friends.

***

When Shruti returned to her home, she could hear the muffled voices of her parents. They talked in urgency to each other. She did not want to walk inside when her parents were having an important discussion. Thus, she stopped at the doorstep.

Ganesh's voice floated out even though he had carefully guarded his tone. 'They are all talking about Shruti. You need to tell her to control her acts.'

Ramya, her mother, said in the similar guarded tone. 'I am not sure I would be able to talk to Shruti about this.'

Ganesh let out a deep breath. 'We need to do something. Her reputation has created a lot of problems for us. People are asking about her, and that loafer boy called Deepak. They say, they have seen Shruti with him.'

'Today, people saw her in the middle of the road, with another tapori. We will lose our hard-earned honour, and reputation; if she continues this nonsense.'

Ramya was quiet for a long time. Then she said, 'I would keep an eye on her from now on.'

Shruti was deeply embarrassed that her parents have to discuss about her. 'What if they ask some questions? What if they want to know about Deepak?' She thought to herself. She was red-faced and put into an awkward situation.

'Is there someone who has seen us in the shade?' that thought just raised her temperature.

6d. Shruti Shames Family

Shruti splashed cold water on her face. The harsh summer ray had damaged her skin a lot. She could see red patches on her cheeks. These horrified her. The marks needed to go before she started to go out again.

Ramya came to stand behind Shruti. 'I am going to the market to get groceries.'

Shruti looked back at her mother, a little ashamed after she eavesdropped their discussion about her. It took all her strength to look her parents in the eyes, even though they had not said anything to her.

'Yes, mother,' said Shruti. 'I will be studying now.'

Ramya did not make a move to leave the room yet. She stared at Shruti as if she wanted to say something serious. Then Ramya's expression changed. She drew a deep breath before retreating from the room. Shruti heard the sound of fading footsteps with relief. It was difficult to stay near her parents when she knew the agony that she has caused them.

She inhaled before settling down on the bed with her books. From now on, she would focus on studies and forget about her social life.

Her heart ached a little at the thought of Deepak. He had evoked a mature kind of dream inside her. She had begun to enjoy the time spent with him. Maybe with time she would have fallen in love with the young man. Yet, she could not understand why he would have to boast to his friends about their relationship.

***

While Shruti dwelled in the thick fog of her youthful misery, Deepak was reaching the front yard of her chawl. He had been in the state of lust filled daze for a few days. That low life Suresh had ruined his chance of a long-standing relationship with Shruti. It had been a week since he had seen her. It's been too long; he had not been able to touch her. The memory of her soft body beneath his hard one made him paddle his cycle in haste. Anyhow he needed to see her, for one last time. Even though he prepared himself for the last time, he knew that the last time would not come soon enough. He waited at the gate to guess the situation at Shruti's home. Fifteen minutes later, he watched Ramya hurrying out of the chawl. It was the time to make a move.

A knock on the front door got Shruti out of her daydream where everything was alright, where she had become a famous model, and everyone knew her. She looked at the wall clock, it had been only ten minutes since her mother left. She should not be back so soon. Another knock sounded on the thin wooden plank which served the purpose of the door. This time the knock came with a little impatience. Shruti got to her feet to open the door.

It was Deepak standing at the door with a grin. His face showed the arrogance of a man aware of his sexual abilities.

'Hi,' he said. 'Can I come in?'

Shruti shook her head. 'No, you cannot. You…'

Before she could finish the sentence, Deepak moved inside the house. He walked in even though Shruti stood guarding the door. To keep her falling on her back, he wrapped his arms around her narrow waist. With his right foot he shut the door.

'I need to talk to you,' said Deepak, setting her away on the floor to free his arm. Without waiting for her to recover from the shock of seeing him at her doorstep at this time of the morning, he stuck his hand inside her blouse. 'I missed you,' he said in a thick voice.

'Deepak don't,' Shruti protested in a weak voice. She felt her resolve dissolving as Deepak's hand found the most sensitive part of her body.

'Mother could come back anytime.' This time her voice dropped to the level of whisper.

But Deepak paid no attention to her protests. He continued to play with her softness. 'Don't you like it?' he asked, knowing well that she did. 'Oh

Shruti.' He moaned her name out, burying his face against the curve of her neck.

Before, he could pull her blouse down, before he could push her to the little cot which sat at the corner of the room, the door of the house swung open. Shruti heard a gasp from a distance. It felt the sound came from million miles away rather than from the room itself. Then came a shriek.

'Shruti' Ramya's voice, penetrated the haze into which Shruti almost plunged. She jumped and like struck by thunder, Deepak too jumped away from her. They looked around to see a wide eyed Ramya standing at the threshold of the door.

Shruti had no idea, how her mother came back before time. She had no idea how she had gotten herself into this mess. She did not know how to explain the situation to her mother.

Deepak did not wait for Ramya to say anything. He turned and swiftly walked out of the house, leaving behind a horrified Ramya and surprised Shruti to resolve the issue among themselves. His footsteps echoed in the corridor and then faded. Only a doom like silence settled now that the mother and daughter stood face to face.

Ramya erased the distance between her and Shruti quickly. Without saying a single word or giving warning, she raised her hand and slapped Shruti across her left cheek. One more. And one more. Ramya stopped, she was exhausted. She was crying her heart out, cursing her fate. The blow left a cruel reddish mark on the fair face of Shruti. She shrieked but did not cry, knowing that somehow, she had called the situation upon herself.

She was filled with shame. This is what she did not want to happen. How would she see her parents, elder sister, or younger sister in their eyes?

She has breached the trust in the family. She has broken all unwritten laws to sustain morale standards. Because of her, there are people to raise fingers on her family, on Baba and on Aai.

***

Ramya spoke to Ganesh. It agitated him, pained him beyond words. He could not imagine his daughter losing the path, not acting in conscience.

But he had to act sane now. He knew, that talking had never been one of Ramya's skills. She was a silent tower of strength, more like the walls of a house. People tend to forget they exist. Yet, after a hectic day, they always long to return to the safety of the walls. So, Ganesh did not hold it against Ramya that she did not fetch the matter of Deepak out in the open and talked to Shruti. Maybe as a father it should be him.

He found Shruti curled on the floor with a textbook in hand. From her eyes Ganesh could say that her mind drifted somewhere else.

His footsteps brought her out of the reverie. Shruti flashed a hesitant smile at Ganesh. It made him ache a little to see his beautiful daughter become too rigid. But he did not point that out just now.

'I met Purvi today,' said Ganesh. 'She asked whether you are free tomorrow.'

Shruti appeared to be thoughtful. 'Baba, what did she say?'

Ganesh shook his head. 'No, she wanted to drop by and study with you.' He paused. 'You two have studied together for a long time.' With a meaningful glance at Shruti, he said, 'You should meet your friends, Shruti.'

'Friends' Shruti thought with longing about the time, she used to be the centre of attraction in her friend circle. It was before Deepak appeared in her life. They used to adore Shruti. But after the incident with Deepak, she found it difficult to look her friends into their eyes. Something had gone missing. Though she could not point it out, she knew that they would not accept her the way they did before.

'Mrunali and Jaya, you too come here.' Ganesh has brought snacks while coming back home. He started pouring snacks on different plates and gave it to each one. Shruti picked up her plate, she was still keeping her eyes low. She did not have the courage to face her father yet.

One by one Mrunali and Jaya joined in. Ramya was in kitchen which they had separated with a thin curtain from the living room. She pushed the curtain aside to be announce her presence.

'Kids,' Ganesh said.

'My father and mother taught me that it takes years to build your respect and honour in the society. And it is just one moment, one mistake which can take away all your treasure that you have earned over the years.' He took a brief pause.

'See, they got lot of learnings from their parents, and grandparents. Then their own experiences of life taught them what is right and what is wrong. They passed on those learnings to me.'

'I have grown up on their learnings, their teachings, and obviously what life has taught me over the years.' Mrunali was curious, why is her father philosophical today.

'We have lived very difficult days. Back in the days of village, whenever due to heavy rains, or typhoons; we lose agriculture; we may not have the food to eat. But we did not lose our self-respect, our prestige.'

'We may have borrowed the money from people; but made sure that we return it at least one day before.'

'We were pushed, and destiny brought me to Mumbai. There were nights when I did not get dinner. But I kept my calm. I did not steal, did not beg, did not do any dirty act.' His voice has become husky.

'And hence one thing was for sure; I could go to sound sleep at the end of the day. I could go anywhere with my head and esteem held very high the very next day.' This brought tears to family. Ramya reminisced the principles and self-esteemed conduct that her husband has always adhered to.

'By God's grace, I got married to your mother. For the first time, I thought, I had the support system. Ramya and me have taken lot of pain in bringing you up.'

'When I could not feed all of us, she remained hungry to ensure that you all are fed. But we did not go outside and beg upon.'

'We are such, if we find even a twenty-five paise; we try to find the owner of that money; and give it back to them. We avoided all bad habits, which can affect our prestige. We always stayed away from any mistakes or sins, so that people on the road; in the neighbourhood, in the society can question us.'

'We live in a society. We align our actions so that we comply with the laws of the society. For each action of our conduct, we look for an affirmation in the society, right? We are human beings, we cannot live in isolation, and alone. Animals too live in their clans.'

'Duryadhan and Yudhistir both belonged to the same clan. But Yudhistir ended up wearing the crown because, he never exploited his right or acted irrationally or immorally. People hence supported him. Lord Krishna supported his righteousness.'

The room fell silent. Mrunali nodded, completely getting the point. Shruti recoiled a little inside herself. To Jaya it seemed like a story their father was telling them.

Ganesh looked at his daughters. 'We want only right thing to happen for you.'

'What we teach you, is out of our learnings, our parents', and our own successes and failures in the life.'

'If I or Ramya ever go against your wishes, it is not that we do not wish well for you. We want only good to happen to you in a long run.'

'For you the fallback mechanism is us; hence we want you all to be successful.'

'Your decision may be contrary to me. Your thinking may be different than ours. But we can speak, learn from each other and then take the right step.'

Ganesh took the corner of the wall to get the much-needed support to his back. His voice had gotten husky.

'My family is everything to me, my wife and my three daughters. I am proud of myself, and my family. When I go outside, I walk with my head up, chest upright. I face the sky with an open heart. I have nothing to hide. I have committed, no wrongs. Never. I've done no sins. Never. I have no shame. No guilt.' And a pause from Ganesh. Long one.

'But today, I'm in shame.' Tears moistened his eyes. 'I'm no more the same Ganesh.' He said, with a red face, and hoarse voice.

Shruti no longer had the strength in her heart to bear this. She started crying. She could not see her father like this.

Jaya was watching all of this, and just wished it had not happened.

Mrunali understood the moment.

Ramya has never seen her husband so weak. Her heart has come out. She pressed Ganesh's hands. Everyone cuddled together. The family got more united than ever.

Shruti, that night just kept thinking about what her father said. The pain in his eyes, the huskiness in his words, the stretched lines on his forehead. 'I'm no more the same Ganesh.' It hounded her.

She cannot be the reason to put her Baba into shame anymore.

7. Mrunali's Marriage

7a. Mrunali To Agree

Ganesh returned home with an unfocused expression on his face. His eyes spoke of million thoughts going on inside his head. Ramya narrowed her eyes at the sight of her husband. She stalled for a moment, lingering in the living room while Ganesh settled down on the tattered stool. She wanted to ask what bothered Ganesh. But then decided to bring a little refreshment first.

'Aaho, has something happened?' she asked after placing water and a cup of tea on the little plywood made coffee table. 'You look a little…' Ramya paused, groping for the right word. Then added, 'A little disturbed.'

In reply Ganesh drew a deep breath inside. His face contorted with worries unspoken and long suppressed. Then he forced a smile for Ramya's benefit. 'Nothing alarming.' He picked up the steaming cup in his right hand. Then decided to come out with the truth. 'You know the Kelkars, right?' he asked. 'Their daughter used to go to same school as Mrunali's.'

Ramya nodded. 'Yes, Sruvi.' She remembered the cumbersome girl with long hair and stupid eyes. 'She did not continue beyond seventh.'

Ganesh took a calculative sip from the cup. 'Yes, she is getting married this month. The guy has done ITI and earns well.' He dropped his gaze down at the floor. 'Kelkar bhau was at the shop. He looked happy now. All his worries have melted overnight.' Ganesh sighed. A dark curtain fell on his face then. 'He was worried man a few months ago. Sruvi was getting old and not married yet.'

Agitation creeped in, on his face, 'when will Mrunali settle?' A worried father in Ganesh spoke.

Ramya sat next to him. 'Aaho. I'm worried too.'

Not wanting to add to Ganeshs's stress, she quickly had some change of thoughts, 'but it will happen. Lord Ganesha is with us. With his blessings, we'll get her married soon.' Ramya continued. 'Now, she is promoted as a full-time teacher. Also, she is become the manager for that coffee shop.'

'Cafe, it is called Cafe.' Ganesh interrupted and smiled. 'But that is what worries me more. We will not get boys more qualified than her. On the top, boys do not want to marry a working girl.'

Disquiet looming large on his face, Ganesh continued, 'She has been rigid until now to not look for grooms. She was not ready for marriage. She earlier said, her teacher job is provisional. But now, there are no more excuses.'

'She is getting older. She needs to realize it too.' He said it with a deep sigh. His face again resumed that thoughtful look which said a lot of things that words could not express.

Ramya lowered her eyes to hide her own emotion. She knew that Ganesh would fall apart if she showed her weakness.

She bit her lower lip and looked out of the window. The falling dusk had already shrouded the opposites structures. Ramya thought of Mrunali. Her girl was growing fast. They needed to hurry, or no one would want to marry her. 'We need to put pressure on her. She is aging and she needs to understand that.'

***

'Aai, give me more sabji. Today it is awesome.' Mrunali extended the plate to her mother.

Ramya filled the plate with more sabji. She has cooked today with extra coconut and red chilli. Mrunali likes that extra.

Ganesh took the opportunity, 'So, how is everything going on at work? College, and at the cafe?'

'Everything is fine, baba. There is a lot of work these days but getting a lot to learn.' She was enjoying her dinner, with no hint of where her father is heading.

'It's excellent, I am sure your hard work will pay off.'

Mrunali gave him a smile in answer. Ramya signalled Ganesh to come to the point and talk on the real matter; he nodded back in yes.

'Beta, what have you thought about your future?' he asked.

'Baba, everything is going well. I am happy with my job. This is what I always looked for.'

'Mruni, I am asking about yourself, what about marriage?' he came to the point.

'Baba, I have just become a full-time teacher. Just wait for some time.' The casual conversation from her father now made sense.

'For how much more time should we wait. Firstly, you were a provisional teacher, I agreed. But now the job is fine, what you wished for. Then where is the problem?' he sounded rigid this time.

She didn't respond.

'You know,' said Ganesh when Mrunali's face turned stubborn. 'You have two more sisters. They need to get married as well. If you don't agree to marry, how can I arrange their marriage?' Ganesh knew he needed to add something more to convince Mrunali. So, he said, 'At least let me fulfil my responsibilities before I die.'

Ganesh had seen Mrunali. He knew that under the tough exterior, lived a soft-hearted girl who thought of her family before anything else. He had faith that Mrunali would agree to marry.

Mrunali was quiet for a long time. Her face did not reveal any emotion. But in her eyes Ganesh read helplessness. She did not want the responsibility right now. She was not ready for the additional expectations that a marriage brings. But Ganesh had no other choice. The chawl people had already started talking about Mrunali and his other daughters. If Mrunali did not agree to marry right now, people would spread rumours about his family and eventually, his other daughters would remain unmarried as well.

Then when he thought Mrunali would not reply at all, he heard her speaking. 'I understand, Baba. I will do as you say.' She got up from the place with her empty plate to go to kitchen. 'You decide what you think is right for me.'

Ganesh's eyes met with Ramya, and there was relief. Now they can begin with the next steps.

***

The next morning, Ganesh got onto the job.

He spoke to his colleagues and acquaintances to look for grooms for Mrunali. He also made calls to his relatives in village and other cities.

In the next three weeks, there were couple of options shortlisted. Boy's families visited Tamhankar's house to meet the girl, Mrunali. But for some or the other reason, the proposal did not go farther. Ganesh knew, this is just the beginning. He was ready for the long haul to find the right match for his daughter. His efforts continued.

Three months gone, three more boys; however, the result was same. Guys side had various reasons; some did not like a working girl, girl is overqualified, or she will not fit in the culture; and so on.

Ganesh and Ramya felt disappointed each time. However, they did not lose hope.

Mrunali was depressed too. Five rejections in such a short span. She was more saddened to see her Aai and Baba each time. Though they did not say much, but she could read the emptiness in those faces. She was tired with all this and wanted it to end. But she did not want to break her parents' excitement and happiness. She always got ready with a smiling face and suitable answers for the dozens of questions from the boy's side.

Ganesh had spread word of mouth near his shop. One day, Mr Sharma, owner of a shop nearby, visited him and informed about a nice prospect. The boy's name is Ramesh Sikare, he works in MTNL, a secured job.

Sharma was elated to offer, 'The boy is the only child in the family, with a well-settled background.'

Ganesh really liked the groom, he thought it would be a perfect match to her daughter. He requested 'Sharma Ji, you are a godsend to me. Please introduce me to them so that we can take it forward.'

Sharma spoke to the boy's family and requested for a meeting. Ganesh and Sharma visited their house, met the boy and family. They all seemed patient and cultured. He invited them to visit their home.

Ganesh liked the boy and Sikare family. He was hoping for the best this time.

***

It was Thursday, when Ramesh, his father and mother came to Tamhankar's house. Mr Sharma too joined in. Sikares said, they like to do new things only on Thursdays. Ganesh had come early from the shop. Ramya and Mrs Mhatre had made suitable arrangements for their welcome.

Mrunali had arrived just in time from the college. She took a little longer to get ready this time. She had borrowed some makeup from one of her colleagues. To Ramya's delight, Mrunali looked different after hours of toiling in front of the mirror. Ramya's heart ached at the thought of the series of rejections which Mrunali had suffered during the past few months. She had seen the unspoken pain in Mrunali's eyes. But there was very little she could do.

After the initial customary greetings, and appetizers; Mrunali walked in balancing a tray loaded with steaming cups, and her saree which she had bought for this occasion. Her hair rested on her shoulders in loose waves. Yellow light of the bulb played with the hair strands. Ganesh drew a breath at the sight of his daughter. It was not the Mrunali he knew. Before him stood a woman now who had seen enough rejections to endure anymore.

Ramesh's mother was very pleased with Mrunali, 'You are very beautiful. Come sit by my side.'

Mrunali sat next to Mrs Sikare. Ramesh was sitting nearby. 'My Ramesh is really hard-working. He studied and created a name for himself. You will be lucky to have him.'

Mrunali thought in exception, 'Why is it so, and not otherwise? He would also be lucky if she gets married to him.' But she kept silent. This is not the time to allow any signs of agitation to surface on her face.

Ramesh was shy, but kept glancing at Mrunali, carefully avoiding the glares from others. His mother probably realised. She suggested Ramesh and Mrunali to go out and spend some time in the veranda. 'Get to know each other,' she declared.

'So, you have done master's in economics?' Ramesh asked as they both accommodated themselves in the veranda.

'Yes.' Mrunali replied in one word. She was still scanning the vicinity and onlookers. She was relieved that there were not many roaming around.

'So, what you do? I mean the whole day? your hobbies?' He asked again, he was too nervous but still trying to strike a conversation.

'I do not get much time from my work.' She again kept it to the point.

'You work? Oh yeah, Mr Sharma ji had mentioned. What do you do?'

'I am a teacher at Paikar college, teach math. After the college, I take care of a cafe as a manager.' She was not sure if Ramesh would like this.

Ramesh knew that Mrunali works but did not know that she is busy the whole day. Working at a cafe was not something he appreciated.

'Understood. So, you would quit your job after marriage?' He was direct with his question.

'To quit. Hmm. It never actually occurred to me.' She honestly put it across. 'I just want to be an independent woman. Plus, I have the passion to contribute back to the society through my work. So, hoping to sustain it.' She nodded to herself.

He nodded his head with a smile. There was a pause for some time. Ramesh took the final effort, 'Do you have any questions for me?'

Life On The Edge

Mrunali just smiled, 'Nothing, I'm fine.'

They set silently further on; finished their tea. Ramesh called his mother 'Aai', and they both went inside the house.

Ramya's eyes had followed Ramesh, and then to her mother. There was hope in those eyes. Mother in Ramya was seeing her 'in-law' in Ramesh. There was an excitement in her heart. But she managed to control it, she has earlier seen disappointments.

Ramesh's parents started to leave. Ganesh enquired in a low tone, 'When should we discuss the next steps?'

Ramesh's father looked at his mother. His mother responded, 'Let us talk in few days.'

Ganesh was happy. He wanted to be positive this time. His eyes met Ramya, and he saw the same hope. The father in him, was excited with the prospect of finding a right groom for his daughter. The eldest one. The first one. The most loved one.

Both looked at Mrunali. She was in herself; she had a hectic day. Shruti and Jaya were enjoying the leftovers.

7b. Rejection Again

Two days were gone. With each passing day, it brought more reservation, uplifting sorrows to the next level and distress creeping in deep within. The wait seemed long, years.

Ganesh came back home in the evening. He was disturbed. His eyes were constantly glazing outside the window, with sun already downed, there was nothing much to be seized.

Ramya asked him, 'What happened?' handing the cup of tea to him.

Ganesh, who confines everything in his wife, had to open up, to lower the burden on his heart, 'Mr Sharma came to the shop. He said, Sikares are looking for different options.' He whimpered, 'So, he stopped by to say that he will find other options and let us know.'

'Why? What happened?' 'They cannot just say No.' Ramya could not absorb it.

'They did not like a working girl. Ramesh is earning enough. They need a housewife, just to take care of their home.' As he finished moaning, he looked at Ramya, who was already glaring at him. It followed a brief silence. Their eyes just conveyed helplessness. They knew that all of this will come back to this one thing. It seemed little in their head, they expected the society to be progressive, they expected this to the need of the future. But they were proven wrong again, and again.

Mrunali sat in the corner of the room. She heard the conversation, it saddened her. She had thought, her parents would be relieved of this ongoing pain, at least this time.

'Baba, isn't this enough? I do not want to meet another boy. Let us stop all this.' She looked dispirited. Her conviction was shaken, she started doubting the path that she has chosen for herself. Should she be working any more, the question has hit her many a times in last few months.

'Mrunali, you don't have to get worked up. I am still here.' Ganesh comforted her. He is the father; it is his responsibility. He didn't want his elder to take any stress.

'But Baba...' Ganesh's eyes met hers, and he waved his head left to right indicating, 'No further'. It was reassuring to Mrunali, in the sense that her Baba still has enough energy; and has not lost all the hope.

Hope was on the surface. Internally Ganesh was shaken, slightly disheartened. He was hopeful this time. However, the 'hope' alludes you when you want it the most. It strikes you unexpectedly when you expect it the least.

***

Ganesh was swarmed by deep thoughts. He was not able to decide on the next steps. Should he keep exploring the other boys? Should he talk to Sikare family again? Who else can help find the next groom? So many questions, but no answers. He was getting restless.

Dazed look on his face, Ramya could not ignore. 'Aaho, what are you thinking? Don't be sad, everything will be ok.' She interrupted his thoughts. Her voice was comforting.

'I don't know when will this happen? This is our dream. But when will it come true? I really want Mrunali to be happy, happy for life.' Ganesh said and wiped his tears. He could not control those few drops; they dared to come out.

After a brief pause. 'We are not able to find for one. How will we do it for the other two?' he added. Ramya felt his pain, she herself was in despair. For now, she could only listen to him quietly and did not want to add to her husband's anxiety.

Ganesh fetched Ramya's hands, turned to her to confide. His eyes conveyed some determination, 'I cannot lose hope this time. I will talk to Ramesh. I will try to clear things up.' He seemed resolute.

'But how will you?' she asked.

'I will visit his office tomorrow.' 'Mrunali's job is not that important than her marriage. I want to see her settled and happy in her life.'

Ramya was not sure, if this was the right approach. Their daughter has toiled hard to reach, where she has. It cannot just go to drain. However, she did not have any alternative to offer. She kept silent.

***

'Please wait here. Let me call Ramesh sir.' The peon at the reception showed the place to sit. Ramesh intrigued that people here call him 'sir'. He must be holding a senior position, he thought.

Ramesh came outside, and he was surprised to see Ganesh here.

'Oh Uncle, you here? Namaskar.' Ramesh folded his hands to greet him.

'Bless you.' Ganesh touched his hands. 'Beta, just wanted to have a chat with you.' Ramesh took him inside his cabin.

'Uncle. Truly speaking, I am surprised to see you here. How are you?'

'So sorry uncle.' He realised that he seemed in hurry, 'Please be seated first.'

'Thank you, Beta.' Ganesh took the front seat. Ramesh called the peon and asked him to bring two cups of tea.

Ganesh was nervous, he wiped sweat on his forehead. 'Beta, I am here to talk about Mrunali.'

'Uncle, please tell me.' His eyes had widened.

'Yesterday, Sharma ji told me, that your family did not like Mrunali.' 'You know, I really had started thinking about both of you.'

Ramesh interrupted 'Uncle, this is nothing about her. She is very fine girl, beautiful, educated, passionate about work.' 'But we have to live together and live with our families.'

He continued, 'She is an ambitious girl. I really respect it. But I am not sure if my family, Aai and Baba can cope up with a working girl. It will be unfair on my part to put conditions on them for marriage.'

'I hear you, and I understand it as well.' Ganesh coughed up. 'I know, working women are not acceptable in our society. But Mrunali is very different. She knows how to balance her professional and personal life. Family will always be a priority for her.' Ganesh had conviction in his words. Ramesh was listening to him quietly.

'She always dreamt to be an independent girl. She completed her studies on her own. It never became a burden on us. She used to do all the household work, while doing her college and part-time job. She managed her college expenses herself. Also, helped me financially.'

'Moreover, a working wife will be helpful to you too. It is getting costlier each day, to live in the city. It will be difficult to handle all alone when your family expands. She will be a companion to you. She will stand with you in every problem.' Ganesh persisted with his thoughts, while Ramesh obediently listened to him.

Ramesh finally found an opportunity to sneak in, 'But uncle. This is a major decision in life.'

'See Betaa.' Ganesh interrupted, took a pause. He was determined. 'In case you and your family want her to leave the job. Then she will leave it. I will convince her for the same.'

'I know she won't mind leaving it,' he said, with folded hands. He was greatly pained; he knew the efforts from his daughter to reach to where she is today. It will not be easy.

'Uncle, please. Do not do all this. You are elder and father figure to me.' Ramesh held Ganesh's hands, with a sense of empathy.

'Uncle, I need to step into a meeting,' he indicated to people waiting for him outside his cabin.

Ganesh realised that he has taken too long, 'Sorry beta, did not want to put you in an awkward position.'

'I will go now. Please think about it.' Ganesh got up, and ready to leave.

Ramesh could just nod his head and show the affection through his eyes.

Ganesh waited for few more seconds, and then left.

Ramya was eagerly waiting for Ganesh to return home. But he did not have any positive news. He has brought only more disappointments, more tears. They had avoided this from Mrunali. But sadness was prevalent at Tamhankar's house.

***

It was Sunday morning. Ganesh was late in waking up. He was in front of Lord Ganesha, finishing up his rituals.

'Tamhankar bhau, you there?' Someone shouted at the door. Ganesh knew this voice.

He opened the curtains from the door. He was surprised to see Sharma. 'Namaskar Sharma ji.'

Then he sees, Mr Sikare standing behind. His eyes got widened.

Ganesh greeted them 'Namaskar' with folded hands, 'Glad to see you all here.' He was surprised, but his heart was pumping. There was excitement of hope. He pretended to be ignorant.

All the guests had a seat. Sharma waves at Ramya, 'Bhabhiji, please make tea for all of us.'

'Are Sharma ji, you do not have to ask for it.' Ramya had already started arranging for some quick snacks.

She had Shruti & Jaya bring water to all the guests.

'Tamhankar bhau, Sikare bhau wanted to meet you personally and talk to you. So, I did not want to delay it. Sorry, could not hint you earlier.'

'Are Sharma Ji, this is your family. This is your home. You are always welcome.'

Mr Sikare stood up. Holding Ganesh's hands, he said 'Ganesh ji, we are ready for the marriage.' 'Ramesh spoke to us, he said that you met him. We understand, what a girl's father and family goes through. Mrunali is now our daughter as well. If she wants to work, we will not be a problem to her. We are aged, we will be here only for few more years. So, let kids decide what they want to do, and how to do?'

Ganesh was thrilled to hear this. A father in him has persisted and waited for long to get such a news, he was finally met with a pleasant surprise. He hugged Mr Sikare, 'Thank you Sikareji. Thank you so much.'

'See Ganesh, we were little conservative in our approach. We thought about the society and other things. But we understood that this is the future of this new generation.' Ramesh's father laughed.

Tamhankar's gloomy house was filled with rays of happiness. Ramya was in the kitchen with Mrunali, she took her in arms. 'Lord Ganesha give all the happiness to my daughter. Let her live like a queen.' Shruti and Jaya were watching all the drama unfolding, it looked like something happening in movies.

'Tamhankar and Sikare bhau, now we should not delay any more.' Sharma was excited as well.

'Absolutely.' Sikare said, and Ganesh just nodded.

Sikare pulled his mobile phone and had Ramesh on the phone. 'Ganesh, Ramesh would like to speak to Mrunali, if you do not mind?'

Ganesh asked Shruti to give the phone to Mrunali. Mrunali was hesitant in taking the phone, but Ramya prodded her to speak. 'Hi' Mrunali said.

'Are you happy with this marriage? Before we move ahead, I just want to be sure. It is matter of our lives.' Ramesh asked.

'Yes, I am. Aai and Baba are very happy. Thank you.'

'Thank you for what?' he teased.

'Hmm. Thank you for saying, 'Yes'. Also, accepting me, my job and respecting my views.' She was curt in her reply, but it came from heart.

'Are baba, why so formal. I like you; and hence,' he giggled and said, 'meet you soon.'

Mrunali was over the moon, her face beamed with ecstatic happiness.

Mr Sikare while leaving, with folded hands said, 'Take care of marriage, Ganesh ji. Do not give any reason for complaints.'

Ganesh just nodded.

7c. Sakhar Puda

Both sides priests met. Tamhankars and Sikares agreed on a date for Sakhar Puda, Maharashtrian engagement ceremony. They decided to keep it a low affair. Marriage date was also fixed for a month later.

Ramya started preparing for Sakhar Puda. The excitement on the faces of girls was quite visible. Three sisters got together to make a list for their requirements. Ganesh looked happy, as he watched them laughing and discussing all the things. His eyelashes hugged each other, and the tears of pleasure and satisfaction fell on his cheeks.

Now he needed to ensure that the marriage happens without any complaints from groom side. Fortunately, in Maharashtrian tradition, the concept of dowry is not very prevalent. But he still has to arrange enough to give to his daughter at the time of marriage.

Ramya served the tea to Ganesh, and she joined him. A ritual, that they have continued since their marriage.

'Check this list if anything is missing,' Ganesh shared the textbook with Ramya. He has been preparing this list for many days, it was important for him to not miss anything during marriage.

She took a sip of her tea; it tasted a bit sweeter. She took a deeper look at the list. 'Would we not give anything to Ramesh? Also, what about his parents? And cousins?' She further remarked, 'At least one gold chain and one ring for Ramesh; and cloths for his parents and close relatives.'

'Hmm,' Ganesh sighed.

'Also, I think, your list for Mrunali is not adequate. You should add at least 5 more tolas of gold for her.'

Ganesh took a long breath. Things were getting out of his hands, he realised.

'Ramya, that is easily five to six lakhs of rupees.' 'I am now thinking, how to arrange so much?' Ganesh shared his inner quandary.

Ramya offered, 'I have my gold jewelleries. That will help to some extent. But don't worry, we will do something.'

'I have to break our savings, but we will do what is needed.' Ganesh said, the wrinkles on his forehead had deepened. 'Ramesh is well settled. His parents have not asked for anything, but they will be expecting for sure. We have to keep their prestige as well.'

'We have two more to go, after Mrunali. If God is on our side, we will do all smoothly.' Ganesh said with hope amid a dim face.

***

Ganesh was constantly making and updating the list of things required for marriage; and then the sources from where he can get the funds. The list was growing, but the sources were the same. Many a times he felt, he was stretching himself beyond what he could manage.

His days were stressed busy thinking and planning, and nights were sleepless. In the middle of the night, he started talking to himself.

In one night, he just woke up. He went outside, took fresh air, and came back in. He could see, his three daughters sleeping together. He sat next to Mrunali, looked at her calm face.

'You were just my little Mruni.' He murmured when he reminisced the day Mrunali was born.

'When you were born, it was the happiest day of our lives. Twelve years of long wait. Ramya was ecstatic looking at me holding you in these hands.' He was talking to himself.

'Look now, you are grown. You are doing well in life. You have made us proud.' 'Beta, Lord bless you with all the happiness.' Emotions took over him, thoughts got stuck, he could not do more than staring.

After a while he moved back to his bed with as much silence as possible.

He is lying on his bed, but sleep is elusive of him. He again went back to his thoughts, 'I will manage for a good marriage. I know I have to arrange funds for the same. I will do everything and will not leave any dearth in the marriage.' His desire ran him high.

And then realty struck him, 'but how will I manage all these things? I have already applied for a loan at the bank. But what if the loan is not sanctioned? I should contact few more folks also and ask them for help.'

His blabbering continued that night, and many nights.

***

Ramya was thick into her things, but she could notice what Ganesh is going through.

'Have you arranged the funds?' Ramya pouring more dal to Ganesh. Mrunali, Shruti and Jaya were paying attention to what Baba is going to say.

'No, Not yet. I am trying best to arrange. But still short.' He stopped seeing the attention of his daughters on this topic.

'I think; it will be the problem of every middle-class family. The desire to get daughters married, and to have a good son-in-law. That requires good arrangement, but they always lack funds.' Ganesh got philosophical.

'We need to manage with all these expenses. But I am happy. Our daughter is getting what she deserves.' Ganesh smiled at Mrunali. She tried to smile; she could comprehend the pain that her father is going through.

Shruti was thinking; why do we need to spend so much, why don't we keep things simple. But she did not mutter anything.

***

The day of Sakhar Puda finally arrived. Close relatives and neighbours had gathered at Tamhankar's house. Mr and Mrs Mhatre, and their kids Namrata and Raghav were helping the family in cooking, decorations and making other arrangements.

Sikare family and their relatives also arrived, they got a warm welcome. Members on both the sides were happy, their excitement was palpable.

While snacks and drinks were served to all the guests, Mrs Mhatre arranged to begin the rituals. Priests started performing the puja.

Mrunali was asked to sit on a chair. Ramesh's mother put haldi (turmeric) on her face, hands. She blessed her, and then gave her a gold chain, and cloths. She also handed her a box of sweets, 'Live longer, and live happy forever.'

Mrunali went down on her knees to takes blessings of Mr and Mrs Sikare. They both blessed her.

Priests then call upon Ramesh to sit. Now it is time for Tamhankars. They also put turmeric on Ramesh. Shruti and Jaya enjoyed putting haldi on their brother-in-law Ramesh's forehead and cheeks. Ramya asked them to stop; all started laughing.

Priests did some prayers with a coconut. Ganesh put on a shawl across Ramesh. Also gifted him cloths, and a silver coin.

Ramesh's mother made her face, 'this should have been a gold coin.' Ramya heard it. 'It is better to ignore,' she thought.

Both Ramya and Ganesh bent on their knees in front of Ramesh and requested him to take care of their daughter. Ramesh got up and lifts them upwards. 'Baba, please don't do this.' He now touched their feet to take their blessings.

Finally, Mrunali and Ramesh exchanged the rings. They take the vow to get married to each other. All the faces conveyed happiness, excitement, and enthusiasm.

Meanwhile, Ramesh's father enquires Ganesh about the preparations for marriage.

'It is going well. We have booked a hall. Must tell you it was difficult to arrange this, as it is a peak season.'

'Good. Thank you, Ganesh ji.'

'Also have arranged for a cook, for two-hundred plates. It will cost Rs three hundred per plate. They will give two-time snacks, and lunch.'

'Also, priests are booked for the whole day. They will be available throughout the event.'

'Our wedding card is ready by tomorrow. So, we plan to come to meet you on Sunday to give you the first card.'

'Ok Ganesh ji, good arrangements. I'm sure, you will take good care.' He took a pause, and then delivered what he has been holding for some time. 'Last year, Ramesh's cousin got married in Nashik; his in-laws gifted him a Maruti 800. Please put it in your list.'

'Hmm' Ganesh got the shock, but he did not burst out. 'Sikare ji' he just sighed.

'Ganesh, I know, you will be able to manage. You will not get good in-laws like us. And Ramesh is the best son-in-law.'

Ganesh's stare was a bit too long before he nodded his head.

He thought, Ramesh's parents are soft-spoken and good human beings. But the society has taught them, how to raise the demands. They had not asked Ganesh to do anything specific until now. 'Whatever you give; you will give to your daughter,' they always said.

It was the lunch time. Women started serving food to all guests; Puri, Sabji, Dal, Rice and Shira.

Ganesh's mind was now occupied with what he needs to do now. Maruti 800, Why? And how will he arrange it now. He was overly stressed.

7d. Quest For Maruti 800

'Now, I'm helpless. How do I get Maruti 800? That is easily two and half lakhs.' Ganesh closed his eyes, running his mind to every possible corner looking for a solution.

'Mr Sikare should not have asked for it. They know our financial situation. You had been telling them.' Ramya's voice had annoyance.

'But they also cannot help it. Prestige at times gives you the strength to show your true character; stand and fight for things. But other times, it makes you choose the wrong things; when it takes a different meaning in the society that we live in.'

'He has a son, qualified engineer. He needs to show it in the society.' Ganesh justified the ask with a dim face.

'But what should we do now. How do we arrange this?' Ramya's rational question brought him back to reality.

'I am clueless. Only a few days in the marriage.' Ganesh said, with deep in thoughts.

Ramya put his hands on his shoulder. She could not do anything more.

Mrunali was restless and in deep anguish. She has been watching her stressed parents, and their difficulty to manage the finances for her marriage. They were taking loans left and right, how would they repay them. 'All of this is happening because of her?' She felt worse.

She jumped in, 'Baba, I don't want to marry.' She had tears rolling through her eyes.

'Hey, what happened to you now?' Ramya was agitated.

'Aai, I can't see you both like this. Day-by-day the needs are increasing, it is taking away all your life-long savings. I can see how stressful it is to you.'

'Now I heard about Maruti 800. It is too much. It is going to stress all of you and us. We cannot manage this. Please baba, let us stop all of this.'

Ganesh's eyebrows were tightened. He did not want Mrunali to take any stress during this time, she should be stress-free, and happy; after all it is her marriage.

'Beta, you do not worry about this.' He put up a smile, 'Mruni, every father and mother do this for their daughter. We have been wanting to see you married for so long. We are living our dream.' He put his both the hands on her shoulders.

Mrunali has always taken a lot of strength from her father. It was reassuring to her that her father is still solid in his mind and will.

***

Mrunali knew that her father is still thinking about ways to make things happen. She also knew how impossible it is. It made her tense. You can either remain clogged with trying to achieve what is not possible; or realize that it is not possible and then look for ways to come out of it.

Her thoughts were interrupted. College peon was standing at her classroom, and said, 'Madamji, there is a call for you.'

'Ok. I'm coming.' She instructed the class to remain silent while she is back.

'I have never ever been called while at college. Baba may have some urgent need?' She thought.

It was Ramesh on the call, she was surprised. She took his mobile phone number and told him that she will call him back as soon as free from the class. This was God's plan to her, she thought.

During the break, she called up Ramesh, 'Hi Ramesh. Mrunali here.'

'Hey Mrunali, Thank you for the call. Sorry. Just got your college number, so called you. Have been thinking to connect with you for some time now.'

'Can we meet for a brief?'

'Oh. Sure. How about Today evening?' Ramesh was surprised at the spontaneity of Mrunali.

***

They were meeting for the first time after their first meet at Mrunali's home. It was at a Lassi corner near Ramesh's office.

'Mrunali, you are beautiful.' Ramesh could not stop himself from saying this.

She smiled. But he did notice that she is deep into her thoughts. There must be something important that she wants to speak, he thought.

After they settled at the restaurant, Ramesh asked, 'Is everything all right, you look a bit tense.'

'Yes. There is something important. But not sure, how to say.'

Ramesh got a bit scared. Is Mrunali not interested in this marriage? Does she have some other boy in her life? Lot of related thoughts perturbed him. But he quickly composed himself.

'Just trust me and say,' he said and held her hand and gave an assurance.

'Ramesh.' She took her hand back. Now, his heart was pumping more severely with all wrong thoughts on what she is going to say. But he prepared himself mentally.

'Ramesh, actually my father is a middle-class man. He is used up all his savings for this marriage. My mother has given away all her jewellery. I cannot see so much stress on Baba and Aai. He has two more daughters after me. How will they manage?'

'Sorry, I am not able to comprehend. Can you please clearly explain to me?' he interjected at the first opportunity.

'From your side, my parents are getting some demands, which are out of our budget. My Baba is already struggling to do what he can for this marriage.'

Ramesh was quietly listening to her, not aware of where this is heading to.

'This demand of car is beyond what we can manage. It has taken the sleep away from my Baba. He is so stressed. My Aai is in a different world. It is traumatic. I am afraid that something wrong may happen.' She said with a heavy voice. She was not sure if it would make Ramesh angry; she in a way looked to be complaining.

Ramesh did not say anything for a while. Meanwhile, he placed the order for lassi.

'Mrunali, I am not aware of all this. I knew my parents were not interested in the system of dowry. But seriously no idea of all these demands and all.' He was embarrassed and seemed in guilt after hearing about this.

'I will talk about this at home and make sure that you or your family will not face any more problems.' he said.

He noticed, Mrunali was still thinking, deep, staring at the tablecloth. 'And listen,' he begged her attention, 'I feel happy and lucky to have a girl like you who dared to open up about this. And who thinks so much about her family.' He said and smiled.

'Please. Sorry, I did not mean to be complaining. I just wanted to be myself. And transparent to you.' She wanted to be sure, that she did not come across as complaining. 'Please don't make your parents think, that I complained. It would look odd. They will develop a perception about me even before marriage.'

'Do not worry about it.' He laughed.

'I want you to be happy and to enjoy this period. So that your glow shines, and at the wedding I shall not take my eyes off you.' He said and winked.

This brought a smile on her face. They both enjoyed the Kesar-Pista lassi; and then left for their homes.

Mrunali was relieved a bit. Ramesh's words gave her an assurance and belief that things will be sorted now.

***

Ganesh was in front of Lord Ganesha. He thanked God for taking care of all the problems. He thanked for the kindness showered upon him and his family. He thanked for showing the way, removing all the obstacles. He requested for blessings for his daughter Mrunali and his to-be son-in-law Ramesh.

Mrunali was pleased seeing her happy parents. She was glowing today. She glanced in the mirror, 'Is it the same glow that Ramesh meant?'

She thought 'Ramesh turned to be the real hero of her life. He managed his parents. He is the reason for all the laughter, and happy environment.' 'Else all of this looked remote.'

Indeed, the house was filled with giggles, and laughter of all the family members, relatives who had arrived, and neighbours.

She has one more worry, she decided to speak to her siblings today.

'Hey Shruti, stop here. I'm seeing you running around and doing nothing.'

'Tai, at least for today. Leave us. This is time of fun, and enjoyment.'

'Yeah. But wait here. I want to speak to you.' She also called Jaya to stay back.

'See, Shruti and Jaya.' She pointed to both. They looked at her Tai.

'I am going, but you two are here. Baba and Aai are ageing. Do not become a burden on them. You two are growing up. Do your stuff yourselves, and please take care of them.'

'Baba's medicines in the night. Aai need little help during her day-to-day household stuff.'

'Shruti, you have to help Aai more in her outside activities. She has to go to Chakki to get the Wheat done.'

'They don't have a son. We don't have a brother.' Mrunali got emotional, but she controlled.

'But we; you Jaya, you Shruti and I together made sure that they never felt any gap.'

'Though I am going, I will keep visiting. But it would not be usual. So, please…please be there for them, take care of them.' She started crying, holding Jaya in her hands and Shruti on the other side.

'Tai, I can feel what you are saying. We are really going to miss you. Baba loves you so much. He will miss you the most. But we are here. You don't worry. This is your day, Tai. You cannot cry.'

Jaya's sympathetic voice filled her core. She realised that Jaya has matured; and she has really been the backbone of family, taking care of parents; doing whatever activities that she could, when she was out teaching and managing cafe. Today as well, she has been thick into helping Aai. She got up early, took early bath; and then has been into lot many household activities. Jaya was indeed in charge of domestic activities, helping her Aai.

Mrunali had a sense of relief. 'Jaya, I know. You have been the best daughter to them. Shruti, you too.' She hugged them both.

***

Mrunali is in the Mandap, wedding hall, looking beautiful in her wedding attire. Priests are chanting all mantras. Ramesh is looking the handsome groom.

They both tied the knot of love in the form of marriage. All the rituals and the whole marriage occasion went smoothly. There was love and happiness everywhere.

Ganesh fell on his knees to thank Mr Sikare; he requested Mr Sikare to take care of their daughter.

'She is now our daughter, Ganesh.' Ramesh's father hugged Ganesh.

Ganesh and Ramya had tears of joy, the pain of their daughter moving away, leaving them; she has been their pride. Also, a sigh of relief, that finally it all happened smoothly. They have to live their lives for Shruti and Jaya now.

8. Meanwhile Shruti and Jaya

8a. Shruti Meets Mangesh

Mirror had always played an essential role in Shruti's life. It had done what admiring glances of the beholders could not do. It made Shruti realize that she had been born with stunning good looks. Her reflection had given her the assurance that she would stand out wherever she went. The same mirror now showed her that she had grown up.

Shruti tilted her head to assess her face. Even though she had grown up, her facial feature still clung to the youthful smoothness of a sixteen-year girl. The pinkish hue which had made her think of the last ray of the dusking sun still hung on her cheeks. Yet, deep down inside Shruti was aware of a transformation.

Each time she saw a young married woman, her stride halted. While she stared, in her mind she visualized herself in the woman's shoes. Unknowingly she lived the imaginary life of the woman. Inside the safety of her home, she adorned herself with Ramya's sindoor just to see what she would look like as a bride. Jaya innocently used to ask her, 'Why do you use Aai's sindoor?' And Shruti would simply put her finger on her lips to 'sush' Jaya.

Even though Shruti was aware of her needs, she could not come out and talk to her parents about her wishes. Her past experiences had her ashamed of her desires. Thus, the longing to get married remained suppressed within Shruti's heart. She went ahead with the day-to-day life, secretly playing the role of a wife in her heart. Her desire which she had mistaken as her dream bloomed because of Purvi.

'Have you gone to the grocery shop today?' asked Purvi. The two friends were sitting on a wooden bench of the front yard of the chawl, watching a group of children playing cricket. Indians love the sport, and gullies in Mumbai will be filled with kids and grown-ups playing cricket from afternoon to evening.

Shruti turned to look at Purvi, puzzled. 'No. Why?' she asked, eyeing her friend with alertness. Purvi was not someone who would pop a question just to make a conversation.

Purvi shook her head. 'Just asking.' She went quiet for a while, focusing on the group of children instead of elaborating. 'I have come to know that the guy who runs the grocery shop at the corner of the market likes you a lot.'

This startled Shruti. She dragged a sharp breath to keep herself from gasping. In a flash Deepak and everything Deepak had done to her rushed back. Her face burned in shame. With surprise she realised that the trauma still lived within her soul.

***

The entire day, Shruti spent thinking about the man who liked her. It had been quite a long time since she had been in a relationship of any kind, three years to be exact. Ever since the incident with Deepak, Shruti had avoided being with men. Her heart had recoiled at the idea of being with someone. It had been a kind of fear she had never experienced before. In each man, she saw potential betrayal. Thus, she had maintained a general distance with men. She had even refused to make friendship with them.

However, the longing for affection remained inside her soul. It had her wondering about this man who liked her. Even though, she made every attempt to banish the thought, it persisted like the speck of clouds which clung to the sky even after a downpour.

So next day, Shruti made her way to the grocery store which this mystery man called Mangesh ran for his living. The bazaar bustled with life with early morning shoppers. People loitered everywhere trying to beat each other in getting the best deal. Shruti shouldered her way towards the furthest corner where Mangesh's store located.

Snuggled between two narrow fruit stalls sat a large grocery store. It buzzed with chatter of people. They were all trying to elbow their way to the counter to get grocery. Shruti knew this store. It sold the freshest grocery. She had been to this store many times. However, never before she had turned to notice the man who managed it. But today, her agenda pushed her towards the shop's counter. She needed a good look at the man who ran the store.

Half-way through, Shruti halted on her track. Her eyes narrowed as she beheld the young man managing the store with a frown. Bony and dark, Mangesh had a face that reflected no touch of beauty. His small eyes moved from customer to customer as he took orders. His hands packed grocery with swiftness. In his haste to attend all the customers, Mangesh did not notice Shruti. She did not try to announce her presence either. With slow steps she retreated from the proximity of the store. Then she turned and walked away from the market without a glance over her shoulders.

The remaining day, she successfully pushed Mangesh away from her mind. Yet, the woman inside her heart nudged her for some mischief. Curiosity rose and swept Shruti off balance.

***

She went back to the bazaar next morning as well. However, this time she delayed her approach to avoid the morning rush. Mangesh noticed her at once this morning. He rose to his feet, eyes wide at the sight of her. Shruti felt a sharp sensation inside her heart at the reaction. Past flooded back with force of a wave. She went back in time when boys used to go speechless at the sight of her. The memory brought with itself the desire to be in a relationship again.

Mangesh opened his mouth to say something. But words failed him. Shruti wondered whether Mangesh had this expression every time she had been to this store. Purvi must have picked the hint from his expression only. Funny, she mused, how she had been ignorant to this man and his feeling.

Pasting a wide smile which she knew light up the surrounding, Shruti walked over to the grocery counter. Even though she did not require anything, she still placed order for some common vegetables which she knew her mother would need sooner or later.

Mangesh smiled back. His hand trembled as he put the groceries in the measuring device. Shruti stood looking at everywhere but Mangesh. She played with a strand of her hair as she waited for Mangesh to fill the grocery bag for her. Once the deed was done, she paid for the items and took the bag from Mangesh's hand. As the bag changed hands, their fingertips brushed against each other. Shruti felt a jolt of awareness. It brought her the memories of being with Deepak. During the past few years, Shruti had forgotten how it felt like to be touched by a man. Her body reacted without her consent. Before Mangesh could see the expression of startled remembrance, Shruti turned and hurried away from the market. She did not want to be in a relationship with this man. He did not match her looks. She had been aware of the fact.

Emptiness captivated her the moment she entered her home. The need to be in a relationship with an opposite sex made her go back in time. She thought about all the men who had come to her life till now. The feeling of being fulfilled rushed to her. It had been such a long time, she thought. To take her mind away from the past and to keep depressing thoughts away, she decided to stay engaged.

'I will handle the cooking,' said Ramya. She had been handling the kitchen for such a long time that now it seemed strange to allow someone else to enter the space.

'Ma, I am getting bored,' Shruti said. 'I need to do something. Should I take up a job like Mrunali?' she asked, knowing the answer.

Ramya's hand froze at the suggestion. The amused expression she had worn a few moments ago, faded. For a moment, only the rattle of cooking utensils stirred the silence of the kitchen. Then in a low voice, Ramya said,

'You don't have to. Your father earns enough to support us all. Mrunali also sends money every month.'

Shruti retaliated slightly. 'But Ma, she is married. She should not be sending us money. I am old enough to handle a job.' She knew well that her parents would not allow her to work outside. Maybe she could get to teach some children of the chawl. It would occupy her time.

'You can spend some time with Jaya, she is your sister. Help her in studies.'

'Aai, she doesn't need my help.'

'You can go out with Purvi,' said Ramya. 'It would take away your time.'

The prospect of going out with Purvi did not appeal to Shruti. She did not want Purvi to question her about Mangesh. Even though she did not want to have a relationship with this man, she still liked to go and tease him a bit. It felt good to be watched by a man, even though he was ugly. Maybe she would go back to the market tomorrow but would not buy anything. Or maybe she would take Purvi with her. Together they would tease Mangesh. Her feminine soul came alive as she visualized herself walking back to the grocery store without even looking at Mangesh. 'It would be so much fun,' she smiled at the thought.

***

'Mangesh is a very good human being,' said Purvi. 'My father knows his family.' Shruti and Purvi were walking down the street aimlessly. They did not have anything particular in mind. Their slow walk created resistance for the people hurrying around. But the two girls did not pay any attention. They went along with their own pace.

Shruti considered the statement. Her eyes took a faraway look as she thought about it. In her mind she saw Mangesh. Then she saw Deepak and the other men who happened to cross paths with her. 'But he is ugly.' Her young heart did not even feel a touch of guilt for judging someone because of their appearance. She paused for a moment then spoke up again. 'I don't think he would be a good match for me.'

Purvi had been raised by her grandmother. The old lady had a strict moral value which she had inflicted in Purvi. 'It is not right to judge anyone by the looks only, Shruti.' Purvi said in a firm voice. 'Yes, he may look bad. But he is a very good human being. He comes by our home sometimes to talk to my father. I have seen him.'

Shruti did not reply. She could not bring herself to get beyond the outer surface of the man who liked her. In her mind she had already created an image of the kind of man she would marry. He should be good looking and smart. He should be able to turn heads while walking down the street. Mangesh was someone who would not even gain a first glance. No, she decided with firmness, she would not get involved with Mangesh.

Purvi was watching her expression. She spoke after a moment of silence. 'No one is asking you to marry Mangesh. You don't have to get involved with him. All I am saying is – don't judge anyone by their skin.' She paused to flash a smile. 'We were about to go to the grocery shop, remember?'

Shruti nodded. The hesitation evaporated in a moment. She forgot the seriousness of the conversation as the prospect of having some fun rose. It had been years since she had gotten the chance to tease a man. Eagerly Shruti and Purvi walked into the market. They wanted to stand a little distance away from Mangesh's grocery shop to make him uncomfortable.

Mangesh froze at the sight of Shruti like a programmed robot. His mouth gaped open. Purvi chuckled despite herself not wanting to do so. She looked at Shruti with amused eyes. 'He feels your presence even from this distance.' The laughter in her voice made Shruti giggle.

Mangesh's eyes remained fixed on her. He was unable to look away. The spectacle would have been embarrassing but Shruti felt feminine exhilaration at the bewildered expression of Mangesh. She decided to take the matter forward to another level. Without stopping to consider the consequence, she walked up to the grocery store and stood with her hands on her hips, glaring at Mangesh.

'Why are you staring at me?' asked Shruti in a stern voice. Even though her voice reflected anger, her eyes were full of amused girlish mischief.

'I have been noticing this for a long time.' She added, her hands remained on her shapely hips and her chin high with pride.

For a moment Mangesh appeared to be replying to the jab. But then he shut his mouth. His eyes fell on the ground. Because Shruti had kept her tone low, only Purvi got to hear the comment. She came forward to haul Shruti by her arm. But Shruti remained steadfast. Her eyes glared at Mangesh. She refused to move from the place.

'Shruti,' said Purvi. Her voice was guarded. 'Let's get away from here.'

'No,' Shruti shrugged off Purvi's hands. 'I need to know why he keeps staring at me.'

Mangesh looked around. His face had lost all colour. Now, he appeared to be shaking in shame. Twice he opened his mouth to reply. Twice he shut it being unable to find a word.

'I am sorry if I have offended you any way.' He sounded so ashamed of his behaviour that Shruti dropped her gaze for her irrational act. She should not have acted on reflex.

'Please forgive me.' Mangesh's voice carried out genuine sorrow. His humble manner made Shruti take a step backward.

She walked away from the market with Purvi on her toe. On the way, neither girl spoke a single word. Then after reaching their chawl, Shruti turned towards Purvi. Her heart had shattered at the sight of the Mangesh's helpless expression. He appeared to be so guilt stricken that Shruti wished she could turn back time and undo what she had done.

'I think I have crossed my limit there,' said Shruti. She looked down at the ground. Her face flamed with shame. 'He looked so guilt stricken. I…I.' Words failed her as she tried to express her feeling.

Purvi nodded. Her face too turned ashen. Colour had drained from her cheeks. She looked behind her back. 'I also think we have crossed the limit. Thank God people around the store did not hear you speaking.'

Shruti nodded. In her mind she saw the colourless face of Mangesh. The young man would have run away from the market if he could. 'I will go tomorrow and apologize to him,' she said. Her eyes refused to meet Purvi's, even though she knew her friend would only look at her with affection.

8b. Not To Be, Or To Be

The whole day Shruti spent in a restless state. Her mind kept reminding her the wide-eyed expression of Mangesh. When she could not bear the burden of guilt anymore, she went down to the front yard of her chawl, just to look at people moving around to take care of their daily chores. She desperately needed to push away the memory of the morning event.

Some women of the chawl exchanged some pleasantries with Shruti. They came to ask her about future plans now that she had finished her school education.

'I don't know,' Shruti said absently. Her focus continued to fade. Yet, she made her best effort to hold on to the conversation. 'I am not sure I want to sit again for the exam.' As she said it, her heart twisted in pain. The women knew that she had flunked the class ten's board exam. Yet, they had to come and rub it on her face.

'If you don't want to pursue study what will you do?' one of them asked. They just would not go away. The curiosity which spread over their faces looked almost gawking. Shruti tore her gaze away from their faces.

'I think I will get a job like Mrunali,' she said. 'Let's see.' With this she brought an end to the conversation. Life in a chawl came with many benefits. People stood together in any problem. They helped each other in time of needs. But the downside was the curiosity. People thought it was their right to gather knowledge about everyone. They did not hesitate to ask questions about the personal lives of the others.

Suppressing her irritation, Shruti turned to head towards Purvi's house. She needed to talk to someone. But Purvi was not at home. Even though unwilling, Shruti had to head back towards her home.

***

'You look strange,' Ramya said. She looked at Shruti closely. 'Has something happened?'

Shruti's heart ached as she realised that her own mother did not trust her. Ramya must have suspected some misgiving and for the reason, she was asking such question.

'No mother, I am fine,' she said in a low voice. But Ramya kept staring at Shruti. Her gaze remained glued on the girl's face for a long time. 'I am sure you will tell me if anything is wrong.' Ramya's voice was low. But the chill it carried out froze Shruti from inside. She nodded without looking at her mother.

For the next three days Ramya did not leave Shruti alone even for a moment. She remained home most of the times and when she did leave, she made sure to take Shruti along. The protective stare of Ramya kept Shruti from going to the market and apologizing to Mangesh. Finally, on the fifth day, Shruti crept away from her apartment and knocked on Purvi's door. Now only Purvi could save her from the mess.

'Shruti,' said Purvi. 'What happened? You look pale.'

'Mother would not let me leave home,' whispered Shruti. 'Would you please take my message to Mangesh and tell him that I am sorry for my behaviour?'

Purvi thought about it for a moment. Her eyes scanned the background to see who loitered around the apartment. Then she looked over her shoulder. 'I cannot go now. Dadi wants me to clean the house while she is cooking.' Noticing Shruti's pale face and disappointed expression, she said quickly, 'I will go tomorrow. If I can, I will take you along with me as well.'

Shruti was relieved to know that her friend would try to help her. She had been wanting to express her apology to Mangesh herself. But with Ramya's interference, she had not been able to do it until now.

'Great,' she said with a bright smile. 'It would be great if you can cajole me away for a few moments.'

All the way back home, Shruti counselled herself, saying that the apology did not mean anything. She told herself that the yearn to make amends with Mangesh was nothing more than a show of respect. Young that she was, Shruti did not understand the complication of human psychology of talking oneself to fall in love. With slow and steady motion, she propelled herself towards the edge after which love would be born.

***

Purvi succeeded in coaxing Shruti away from her home in the morning.

'Yes, she can go with you,' said Ramya in her usual low tone. 'But she must come home in an hour.' Ramya though unwilling did not object because, even she understood that keeping Shruti under house arrest would not yield a lasting result. Some day she would have to loosen the leash and that day Shruti might again go astray. So, it was better to allow the young girl to meet friends outside.

Purvi brightened at the permission. 'Oh, aunt, don't worry. She would be back in twenty minutes.' She looked at Shruti with meaningful eyes. They quickly walked out of the house before Ramya changed her mind.

The bazaar displayed the same busy life it did every morning. People hauled things around to set their stores. People competed with each other to get the best buy. No one paid any attention to the two young girls ambling by.

'How should I talk to him?' Shruti whispered to Purvi. 'I am feeling awkward.'

Purvi looked around with doubtful eyes. 'I am wondering the same thing.' She tried to get a view of Mangesh's store. 'It is somewhat empty.' Her voice depicted the relief she felt.

Shruti stopped in the midway. She appeared a little disoriented. Never before she had done this. But it had to be done today. With racing heart, she approached the store. Like every morning, today also Mangesh attended everyone with the same attentiveness. He did not notice Shruti until she stepped close to the grocery store. His face paled immediately. He looked around to look at the heavy number of people loitering around.

'I am sorry,' Shruti said before she lost her gathered courage. Mangesh stared at her. He did not find his voice for a moment.

Shruti mumbled, 'I did not mean to behave like that with you. I reacted.' The more she spoke, the more nervous she became. Her face heated up as she lowered her eyes to the ground. 'I was just joking with you.'

'No.' Mangesh could utter something finally. Shruti was looking at him.

'You were right in behaving like that,' he said finally, startling both Shruti and Purvi. 'I should not have stared at you like that. It just happened. I know it is not appropriate.' He drew a deep breath to steady himself. 'I am really ashamed of my ill behaviour.'

His soft voice and mild tone made Shruti look up. She felt at ease with Mangesh. Her initial fear of being treated rudely evaporated. Relieved, she smiled. 'So, you are not angry?' She asked.

Mangesh smiled back, shaking his head. 'No.' They looked at each other for a moment. To Shruti's amazement, Mangesh did not look that ugly to her that day. Rather Shruti noticed that Mangesh had a sweet smile that brightened up his eyes.

'Thank you,' Shruti said. She felt light now that she had taken off the burden from her heart. 'I need to go now.' She was painfully aware of the fact that her face had flushed. Mangesh noticed it. His eyes shone like two precious jewels at the sight of her discomfort. They exchanged a smile before Shruti walking away from the store.

'That went rather well,' said Purvi after they walked out of the market. The sound of morning buzz faded slowly. The two girls began to walk in slow pace. That day heavy clouds had veiled the sun. Cool breeze promised a downpour anytime. Yet, the two friends were not in hurry to get back home. They loitered on the street to talk to each other.

'Yes,' Shruti said with a smile. 'He was not angry with me.'

Purvi nodded. 'I know. I told you that Mangesh is a great guy.'

Shruti nodded. She said nothing for a long time. Her steps fell methodically as she thought about the event that just took place in the market. Her experience with the opposite gender had created a particular image of men in her mind. She took them as arrogant and controlling. For the first time in her life, she saw someone who did not have that arrogant streak in his mind.

'I think we should hurry home,' said Shruti thoughtfully. 'It is getting darker with time.' She craned her neck to look at the sky. The grey mass of clouds had turned a shade darker. The wind had picked up it pace as well, blowing dry leaves around the street. Shruti loved rain. But she did not want to stand in a downpour right now.

Purvi scanned the sky too. 'Yes,' she said. 'Let's hurry.'

By the time they returned home, pattern of rain had started to drum against the roof of the houses. Shruti felt grateful that she could come home before the real downpour started. She took her usual seat in the veranda by the window to look outside. The raindrops had created a misty curtain around the chawl. Everything appeared to be hazy. She could not help thinking about Mangesh. His smile had showered her with something she had not felt in a long time. He could become a good friend, she thought. Then before the thought became a nagging voice, she pushed it away. Mangesh was not the type of man she wanted in her life. She would not even think about anything that would relate her to Mangesh.

The resolution lasted for a few minutes when Ramya came to talk to Shruti about the evening meal. Once Ramya disappeared, Shruti got totally engulfed in the thoughts of the young man who managed the grocery store. A strong gust of wind crept inside the room to brush Shruti with its loving touch. Goosebumps rose all over her bare flesh at the caressing. In her mind formed some images which she had come to regard as forbidden.

She dragged a deep breath, wondering whether dwelling in the depth of the images, an appropriate thing to do. Because of all the complications life had brought to her, she did not want to get involved in any kind of attachment. Even thinking about a man seemed like a wrong thing to do. But unable to turn her mind away from the visions which stubbornly refused to fade away, she finally gave in. The reverie took her to places and made her do things which she had not done since Deepak's departure from her life. All of a sudden, her face flamed. To hide the expression, Shruti moved away from the veranda and went inside in the corner. Feigning headache, she remained there for hours, hiding from all the prying eyes.

***

Two days later, the memory of Mangesh had been fading thankfully. Shruti was inside their small kitchen, helping her mother with the cooking. She hummed a little under her breath as the good spread across her heart, making her light and jovial again. The front of their house rattled as someone pushed it open.

'That must be your father,' said Ramya. She looked over her shoulder expectantly. 'He went down to buy some essentials.' She then looked at Shruti. 'Please go and fetch the spices.'

Shruti set aside the potatoes she had been peeling. Voices rang from the living room. She rushed to see who her father was talking to. However, when she appeared in the tiny square shaped room, she found her father standing alone with a smile on his face. At Ganesh's feet rested a huge bag, loaded with groceries and other required elements.

'That must be heavy,' commented Shruti, looking down at the bag with concern. 'Why did not you call me or mother? We could have helped you carry this thing up.'

Ganesh shook his head. 'I did not have to.' He reached up to wipe sweat from his forehead. 'The young man who manages the grocery shop in the market, helped me carry this. In fact, he carried this huge bag all by himself.'

Shruti drew a deep breath at the mention of the young man who managed the grocery store. 'What a well-behaved young man he is.' Ganesh went to drop his weight on a chair of the living room. 'I requested him to come inside, but he refused, saying that his store would need extra helping hand at this time.'

Shruti nodded, not trusting herself to speak, lest she gave away her feeling. 'Must be a great person.' She mumbled instead.

'Yes,' said Ganesh. 'A very well behaved and decent man.'

'Who?' the question came from behind. Ramya stood with a questioning gaze. 'Who are you talking about?'

'His name is Mangesh,' said Ganesh. 'He runs the grocery store in the market.' Ramya nodded as she bent to pick up the bag of grocery. The name has touched Shruti's soul. She hurried to help her mother. As they made their ways back to the kitchen, Ganesh said, 'I will have to invite him for snacks or meal one day. He has returned from our doorstep. Our custom does not permit it.'

***

The next day, Ramya proposed Shruti to come along with her to the market. Shruti emotionally backed away from the task, shrinking inside her soul mentally. But she could not refuse Ramya's request.

'The grocery bags get too heavy to carry alone,' said Ramya as they made their ways to the market. 'This is the reason I prefer to bring someone with me.'

Shruti nodded in silence. She wished to stay at the opposite side of the market. So, she would not have to meet Mangesh. But in the seclusion of her heart, she wished to go to the grocery store and meet him for a moment.

Ramya bought some groceries from the outside stalls of the market. To Shruti's relief, her mother did not seem likely to go inside. But then her eyes fell on a moving figure. A tall, lanky, young man was hauling a couple of heavy packages down from a cart. Her breath caught inside her throat at the sight of the man, Mangesh. She hurriedly looked away before their eyes met. But like a magnet attracted to iron, she turned to steal a glimpse, promising herself that it would be quick. But when she looked, she found herself staring into the eyes of Mangesh. He had noticed her and now had his gaze fixed on her face.

Without her permission, blood rushed to her face. She tore her eyes away but Mangesh noticed her blush. He smiled at her from the distance, nodding his head to let her know he had seen her flamed face.

'What happened to you?' asked Ramya with concern. 'Are you ill?' She reached out to touch Shruti's forehead.

Shruti shook her head. 'No mother, I am absolutely fine.' She touched her cheek which she knew had flamed up and looked flushed. 'Must be the heat. Let's go home and get something cold to drink.'

Ramya nodded absently. The sun blazed like a ball of fire in the middle of the sky that day. According to the weather forecast, the heat would remain for a couple of more weeks. 'Yes, I guess, we should get home now.' She looked down at the bag she had been carrying, 'I have gathered everything I need.'

The mother and daughter made their ways through the crowd towards their chawl. Shruti chanced a glance over shoulder at the market entrance. Her heart fluttered as she saw Mangesh still standing at the gate staring after her.

***

That evening while taking a walk with Purvi, Shruti again came face to face with Mangesh. The unexpected shock of seeing Mangesh there made Shruti gasp. She looked at Purvi and found her friend to be displaying unawareness.

'I came to visit your father,' said Mangesh in a shy manner. His eyes brushed Shruti's for a moment. Then he looked away. 'How are you?'

Purvi nodded, still recovering from the shock. 'I am doing well. Thank you.'

'Would you like to have some tea?' asked Mangesh.

Shruti shook her head. Purvi followed too. However, Mangesh insisted on having tea. Finally, the two friends accepted the offer and followed Mangesh to a nearby tea stall. While taking their beverages, sharing laughter, Shruti felt her initial shield about Mangesh's looks fading. She did not look at Mangesh as an ugly looking man anymore. Rather she looked at him as a man who respected women. To Shruti's surprise Mangesh turned out to be a great person to talk to. Their conversation flowed without restrain. The three of them stood in the disappearing ray of the sun. The heat still made the air heavy, yet Shruti hardly noticed the discomfort.

She almost felt sorry when the tea session came to an end. This meant they would have to go back home now. She did not even know whether such chance meetings would ever take place or not.

'It was nice having tea,' said Purvi. 'Maybe we could do it often.' She pushed strand of hair out of her face as she said this. Sweat had gathered on her forehead, making the hair look limp. Shruti worried about her own looks. With caution she touched her hair. The need to check her reflection rose the moment her finger pads came in contact with her thick mane. It seemed sticky. She did not want to appear ugly before Mangesh.

'I think we should go back now,' she in a hurry, not wanting to linger outside any longer.

Her sudden need to get away, caught the others by surprise. Mangesh appeared to be protesting. He opened his mouth to say something. But then he closed it without saying a word. 'I guess, that's it then', he said. 'How about meeting for tea tomorrow evening as well?' he said this with each word standing apart. But Shruti saw the effort it took him to propose the idea.

'Yes,' said Purvi. 'Let's meet tomorrow for tea as well. We will be here at the same time.'

'Why did you do that?' asked Shruti as the two girls walked back to their chawl. 'Why did you tell him that we would be waiting here?'

Purvi laughed at the question. 'It would be nice to socialize, you know.' She did not stop to elaborate further or linger to give Shruti the chance to protest. 'See you tomorrow evening,' she said over her shoulders before disappearing in the crowd.

8c. Shruti Too

'What do you like about me?' asked Mangesh. This was a common question between Shruti and Mangesh. Each time they met for tea or snacks, he made sure to ask her this question. Each time Shruti had to struggle to come up with all the adjectives she liked about him.

Their friendship had deepened over time. They started to meet twice a week for ten to fifteen minutes. Initially Purvi used to accompany Shruti. However, lately she refused to come along. Most of the time, she feigned headache or illness or some college work. However, despite Purvi's absence the tea or evening snacks session continued.

Finally, one day Mangesh expressed his love for Shruti. Even though Shruti already knew about his feeling, she felt herself flushing at the confession. That day, Shruti had not said anything about her feeling. Mangesh remembered, how she stared at him without blinking her eyes. She looked beautiful. He was worried, that him proposing should not take any adverse turn of events. But their continuous meeting made it clear that she accepted his love.

'I like the fact that you are humble,' said Shruti. Today they were having ice cream instead of tea. The heat had risen high in the air. It was a bit difficult to breath. Therefore, the young couple gave the hot beverage a miss. 'I like that you are easy to talk to.'

Mangesh nodded. If he looked for compliment about his looks, he never got it. Shruti did not want to say something just to please Mangesh because that would be a lie. 'You have many admirers,' said Mangesh. It was a statement, not a question.

'I…' Shruti began to speak. Then her throat choked up. She could not come out and tell Mangesh about her past affairs. The incident with Deepak was still a sore spot in her heart.

'I don't know about any admirer,' she said after several attempts to speak. 'I have always focused on my studies.' It was another sore spot which Shruti wanted to amend. Her academic status had shamed her parents. They wanted her to study further. But her inability to pass the class ten's board exam had silenced them. Now, Shruti did not know what she would do. Her only option was to get married.

'I think we should tell your parents about our relationship,' said Mangesh. 'They need to know about it.'

Shruti was not willing to talk to them just now. She knew what would happen if they come to know about the relationship. Deepak was a wound yet to be healed. Her parents still had not forgotten about him. If she spoke about another man right now, they were sure to get angry.

'Let some more time pass,' said Shruti. 'I don't think this is the right time.'

But Mangesh wanted everyone to know about the relationship. Shruti understood his insecurity. His appearance played a big role in this.

'Why don't you want people to know about us?' he asked. Accusation layered his tone. He looked at Shruti with such pleading eyes that she had to agree to talk to her parents about them.

'I want people to know about us,' she said, unable to explain her reluctance. 'I will talk to them tomorrow morning.'

Mangesh shook his head. 'Not you alone,' he said. 'I will come down to your house. So that we can talk to them together.'

Shruti had to agree because she did not want to offend Mangesh. She did not want anything to create a rift between them. Yet, each time she thought about the matter of revealing the secret about her relationship to her parents, fear twisted her heart. 'See you tomorrow then.' Her voice dropped to the level of whisper. Even if Mangesh noticed her discomfort, he did not say anything.

With anticipation of a disaster, Shruti went back home that evening.

***

Shruti was late in reaching home by her usual times. Ramya threw her doubtful glances a few times. But her pale face and unfocused eyes kept her mother silent. Shruti performed all her domestic duties with perfection that night.

The nervousness has taken over Shruti. At the dinner time, suddenly her appetite vanished. She tried to force herself to eat. But the food would not go down her throat. Nausea spiralled up from the depth of her stomach. She swallowed hard to chase the feeling away. But it remained with stubbornness. Finally, she looked up to see Ramya watching her every movement.

'I am not hungry,' Shruti said. 'I think I am coming down with fever.'

Ganesh looked at her with concerned eyes. 'At least try to eat a little. If you come down with fever, you would need strength.' The affectionate advice made Shruti push some rice into her mouth. But anxiety did not allow her to eat. Once again, she felt nausea rising.

'I think I should lie down,' she said.

Ganesh looked at his wife for confirmation. Ramya looked worried. Shruti could clearly understand what formed in her mother's mind. 'If you are not feeling well,' finally Ramya said. 'You can lie down.'

Relieved Shruti fled the room. Tomorrow was Ganesh's day off from his duty. 'How would Baba react after learning about Mangesh?' the question loomed like thick clouds over Shruti's mind as she lay still in the darkness of her room.

***

Mangesh sat in their small living room. He had brought sweets for the family because it was his first official visit. Ganesh welcomed the young man with a hearty smile.

'Please come in,' said Ganesh. He was delighted to see the young man who had helped him carry the heavy bag a few months ago. Since then, Ganesh and Mangesh made it a point to make small talks whenever they met. Ganesh was overly amused as well, as there was no reason for this man to be at his house today.

Life On The Edge

Mangesh crossed the threshold of the house, scanning the room for Shruti. But she stayed away from the area as her courage had faded by then.

Ramya came to the living to meet their guest with a surprised smile. Her surprise intensified when Mangesh handed her over the boxes of sweets. 'Thank you.' She looked at her husband with questioning eyes.

Mangesh cleared his throat. He did not believe in delaying a task. He has prepared for this the whole night. 'First of all, I want to apologize that this is happening this way. But some day we had to do this.' Ganesh and Ramya were puzzled, looking at each other; and then focused on Mangesh.

'I have come here to tell you.' Mangesh paused.

It looked dramatic. But he was falling short of words. 'Shruti and I love each other.' He paused to allow the shock or surprise to register. Jaya's eyes had widened at the declaration, she looked at Shruti, who had lowered her eyes in shyness.

Ganesh's face turned blank at the direct revelation. To his credit he controlled his reaction and did not let his mouth hang open. But Ramya did not have that kind of control over her expressions. She stared at the young man sitting in her living room. In her eyes, Mangesh was a man who did not match her daughter in any way. Even before speaking out, Ramya knew that the relationship was headed towards struggle. Yet, she could not blurt out her feeling.

'How...when?' Ganesh asked after a while. He could not remember seeing Shruti and Mangesh together.

'We have been seeing each other for a while,' said Mangesh. 'I would like to marry her.'

Ganesh nodded in confusion, with closed eyes. His face did not reveal his feeling. Twice he cleared his throat before speaking. 'I am not sure that this is a good idea.' Finally, when Ganesh spoke, his voice sounded hollow. 'Shruti and you have come from two completely different background.' He paused to look at Ramya, who stood with a disapproving expression. 'But I would like to talk to Shruti about this, alone.'

Mangesh understood immediately. 'I understand. I will wait for your decision.' With that he walked away from the tiny house where Shruti lived with her parents.

Once Mangesh departed, Ramya called Shruti. Ganesh with his expression restrained Ramya from being rude. He wanted to sort everything out without any dispute. Shruti walked in with hesitant steps. She had heard everything from the kitchen. Her heart was beating furiously against her chest as she came to face her parents.

'How have you come to know this boy?' Ganesh raised his palms.

Shruti was silent for a moment. Then she raised her head and narrated the incident of the market few months ago. Ramya and Ganesh heard with patience. They both looked bewildered at the narration. For a moment everyone drifted into a solid silence which could build anything.

Once again, Ganesh cleared his voice. 'So, since then you are secretly meeting this man,' he said to clarify the events.

Shruti did not trust herself to speak. She nodded her agreement, bracing herself for a bashing. But Ganesh said nothing for a while. He sat in silence, allowing his head to hang over his chest. Looking at her father Shruti felt a pang of guilt for putting the family in an embarrassing situation again.

'Are you sure, you want to marry this man?' asked Ganesh. He looked at his daughter. As she grew up, her good looks bloomed. Now she looked like a freshly blossomed flower. Mangesh's infatuation for Shruti, Ganesh could understand. But he failed to guess why his daughter reciprocated.

Shruti took her time before saying anything. Was she sure? She had made so many mistakes in her short life that she was not really sure of anything anymore. 'I love him,' she said at last when nothing seemed like a fitting reply.

It did not satisfy Ganesh. However, his unwillingness and disapproval showed on his face. 'Shruti, you are still young. You may not realize this right now. But in the long run the difference between you two will create many problems in your life.' He lets out a deep breath. 'I am not willing to allow you to marry this man. Though he is a great human being.'

Ramya speaks out before Shruti could say anything. 'You have made a big mistake, Shruti.' Her harsh voice made Shruti flinch. 'I am against this relationship. There is no match between you two.'

Ganesh attempted to calm his wife down. 'I think you understand that we have your best interest in our hearts.' He got up to his feet. 'You are not going to meet this man from now.'

Ramya looked angry at the event. She glared at Shruti. To avoid being in the middle of the wrathful glances, she moved away from the hall. Jaya stayed in the corner stunned at the entire episode.

Inside her room, Shruti lay on the bed, buried her face into a pillow and cried. During these past few months, she had come to love Mangesh. She had come to appreciate his way of caring for her. For the first time in life, she had felt valued with Mangesh around. She heard her mother calling her.

'Shruti, come for dinner,' Ramya had said in a harsh voice.

Without arguing, Shruti pulled herself to a sitting position. She wiped her eyes. 'Yes, mother,' she said in a low voice. 'Coming.'

Ganesh tried to make the dinner time cheerful. He spoke about his plans for future. He also complimented Ramya for her cooking skills. But nothing could make the little family come out of the sudden gloom that had taken place due to Shruti's pale face and reddish eyes.

***

'Where are you going Shruti?' asked Ramya the next morning as Shruti opened the main door.

'I am going to Purvi's house,' said Shruti.

'I will come with you,' said Ramya.

'Don't imprison her inside the house,' said Ganesh that night after the girls went to sleep.

'What am I to do?' Ramya asked. 'If I allow her to go alone, she will meet that man again. And not sure, how many others.' She taunted.

Ganesh was silent for a long time. His inner core was tormented at how they were shamed in the past cases with Shruti, and she has yet again invited another episode of disaster. His heart cried, 'Why does she not understand the implications; huge emotional distress for the family and losing prestige in the society'. He knew that Ramya was right. Yet, he wanted to make his house cheerful again.

'You cannot keep her inside the house forever,' he said.

'We will find the right match for her,' said Ramya. 'We will marry her off.'

Ganesh looked away from his wife's agitated face. He stared at the sky that had not shown its starry face tonight. 'That would be forcing,' he said after a while. 'It would not make her happy.'

***

For three days, Ramya had kept Shruti under her surveillance. Most of the times, she remained in the house. When she did leave, she took Shruti along. Ganesh could see the withdrawal in Shruti's eyes. The young girl was retreating from the world. He could feel her helplessness but Ramya was determined to keep Shruti away from Mangesh.

Finally, on the fourth day, Shruti found her escape route. Ganesh had gone to his work that morning. Ramya was preparing lunch when the tap water stopped running. In desperation, Ramya went down to inspect the matter. Seizing this opportunity, Shruti went down to Purvi's house.

'Tell Mangesh that mother is not letting me out of the house,' she told her friend. 'Tell him to find a way to get away from here.'

Purvi looked over her shoulder. Then she turned towards Shruti. 'Mangesh is at the grocery store right now,' she said. 'You can go to him.'

Without thinking, Shruti turned and began to run. She was out of breath when she reached the grocery store. Mangesh jumped up to his feet at the sight of Shruti.

'Shruti,' he said with concern. 'What happened? I was waiting for you.'

'Mother would not let me out,' Shruti said. 'My parents will not allow this marriage to take place.'

Determination set on Mangesh's face. His jaw tightened at the news. 'We will get married right now,' he said coming to a sudden decision. 'Let's go.'

***

'I told you not to imprison hers' said Ganesh. He could not keep irritation out of his voice. The sun had gone down towards the western side of the sky a long time ago. Yet, there was no sign of Shruti. Ramya had gone in search of Mangesh at the market. But she found the store closed.

'I am not her enemy,' said Ramya in desperation. 'I was trying to protect her only.'

With defeated eyes Ganesh looked at Ramya. 'She is not mature enough to understand this. In her eyes, you are her enemy, Ramya. If you had allowed her to go out and meet this man, her infatuation might have died after a while.'

Before Ramya could say anything, a knock on the door, got their attention. Shruti and Mangesh walked inside. Shruti had sindoor on her forehead. She still had a thick garland hanging from her neck.

'Baba, Aai; we have gotten married,' declared Shruti.

Ramya gasped at the declaration. She took a couple of steps backward as if pushed by someone physically. She could only say, 'Lord Ganesha!'

Ganesh only stared at his daughter's face. His horrified eyes told the tale of intense pain. From his face Shruti could feel that her father felt betrayed by the way this event had unfolded itself.

'How could you?' gasped Ganesh after a while. His eyes glazed as tears formed there. Shruti had seldom seen her father crying before. He had been a strong man who had worked hard to keep the family together. Now because of her, that man was shedding tears.

Ramya looked at Shruti with accusing eyes. Jaya appeared to be a little angered by the event. Ganesh fell on the worn-out couch in the living room. He buried his face into the palms of his hands.

Looking at the distressed parents, Mangesh came forward. He fell on his knees in front of Ganesh. With his hands, Mangesh held Ganesh's feet. 'Please forgive us,' he said. 'Please. We acted out of desperation. We love each other.' His desperate pleading made Ganesh look up. 'I will keep her happy.' The promise came out with honesty.

Ganesh's face broke into a smile. It reflected no sign of joy. The melancholy touch of the smile made Mangesh look down in shame.

'When you become a father, you would understand my feeling,' said Ganesh. He looked at Jaya with sorrow. 'I will have to think of all my daughters. The community is cruel, and they talk.' He let out a deep breath as he said so.

Mangesh looked at Jaya. Shruti bit her lower lips as the realization hit her for the first time that her action would impact the entire family reputation and especially her younger sister.

8d. Meanwhile Jaya

One can crib about the difficulty and cruelty of a situation only until the realization happens. The realization of the fact that it could have been cruel-some, it could have been more catastrophic. Once it occurs, then you start looking for ways to live, start adjusting your living to accommodate the cruelty. It is a movement from knowing, it is not normal, to accepting that it is the new normal. This prepares one to take anything head on.

Jaya has fought with her inner conscience many days and many nights. Finally, she has accepted the realty. She feared seeing herself in the mirror, and the missing eye, swollen scary portion in place of eye. She used to question herself, 'Why am I born? Can someone be so ugly looking?' She did not have an answer.

She would go further, deeper into understanding what has happened to her, 'Why didn't my father and mother kill me, when I was born?'

'But. No.' Her conscience always intervened, 'They never ever looked at me like that. My Aai is the kindest person on earth. Baba behaves the same way to all his three daughters. They never ever discriminated.'

'Are they happy to have me? Like this?' She was tormented internally many-many days of her growing up.

Now, she has moved away from the fake world. She has come to terms; she is what she is. God has given her, what they thought is right. If her parents are okay with her, why should she crib with her life.

She has become aware of what she had, beyond the missing eye. She used goggles, now. Not that she wanted to hide her eye, but wanted to avoid unnecessary glances in the society, from people.

She would glance into mirror with confidence. She felt beautiful. 'You are a kind soul, Jaya,' she remembered what her mother always said to her.

***

It was late afternoon. Typically, the gullies were deserted at this time. Jaya came into the veranda to spend some time.

'Oh, what is going on?' She saw a group of four-five boys jumping on a boy, beating him up.

She quickly hid herself. 'What is this going on?' 'Oh my gosh. He is badly being beaten.' But she did not pull herself out, and shout. She did not want to be part of this mess.

'Is this Sam? Yes, he is the one.' She knew Sam. He was famous for his bad reputation, a fifth-class failure. His father is a known advocate. People called Sam as a curse to his parents. Good for nothing.

'Oh, please stop.' Jaya murmured. She peeked a bit into it.

Unconventional face. But she knew, he had a starry attitude. He tried a variety of jobs. Each time he realised it soon that those jobs were not meant for him.

'Ah. He is bruised. When will they leave him? Are they trying to kill him?' She could feel his pain.

Sam was drunkard and often created nuisance in the community. He was never liked in the neighbourhood. Caught stealing pockets and been into jail. Being abusive, always involved in abrasive fights. All of these were nuances of a failed man. He did not have any respect in the society.

'By now, someone should have come out to save.' Jaya thought, she was getting nervous.

'Hey, what is going on there?' She finally screamed her heart out.

The shout alerted the boys. They knew, it is only a matter of time before people wake up and a big gathering takes place. They hurriedly punched on Sam, threw expletives, and ran away.

Jaya came out running, she was concerned. Sam was not in his senses. She quickly picked up his hand, helped him stand, brought him in her veranda.

She cleansed all the bruises on him, put turmeric on them. 'Ah…ah,' he cried in pain.

'Don't worry. It will help you.' He felt the smoothness of her hands, and her voice. It was still hurting him; however, her touch has evoked a chord within him.

'If you would not have come, I would still have been lying there.' Sam muttered to Jaya; he was barely conscious. She shushed him. She gave him water to drink.

Ramya noticed her movements in and out of house so many times. She came out, 'Jaya, what are you doing?' She saw Sam now. 'Aga re bai, what happened to you?'

'Jaya, this needs more than turmeric. They should go and see a doctor. Go and call his Aai.'

Jaya quickly rushed to call Advocate's wife, Sam's mother.

Sam's mother came running, crying, and shouting. 'Arre what happened to my kid? Why is everyone after my kid?'

She picked up Sam around his shoulder. He was finding it difficult to stand up, but he had to go.

He walked ahead, and then he realised something. He turned back, looked at Jaya. Eyes met. 'Thank you.' Jaya blinked her eyes, accepting it humbly.

Only she could notice, it was much more than just, Thank you.

***

Another afternoon. Jaya was standing in her veranda. She was surprised to see, Sam coming. He was wearing his usual flashy style cloths.

'He, funky guy, could be visible from anywhere,' Jaya thought.

'Hi'

It surprised Jaya, that Sam was direct in his approach. 'But this is what he is famous for,' she thought. 'Hi', 'Sam, right?'

Sam nodded, and then he closed his eyes, breathed heavy; 'Thank you.' Almost a heroic act.

'For what? Oh, that day. It is okay.'

'You came to help. Probably no-one else would have come.'

'You think so?'

'Yeah, for sure. One, no-one dares to come-in amid people fighting. Secondly, when they see me, they seem to have all the reasons to back-off.'

'Hmm. You are bad?' Jaya took a chance with that question.

'Really, don't know. But people think, I don't deserve to live here.' After a pause, 'Rather don't deserve to live, at all.'

'That's very rude to yourself.'

'Ah…I do not care, what other's think.'

'By the way, who were they? Why were they beating you?' Jaya diverted to another topic.

'Leave it.' Sam made 'schh' noise through his tongue.

'Okay.'

Sam gave a deep stare at Jaya, 'You really want to know?'

'Yeah, if you want to share,' said Jaya, moving her eyes away from him.

'Not much. Those fuckers.' He suddenly stopped. 'Sorry.'

'One of those guys were after a girl in our society. So, I had bashed him up. This time, he came with his group to take revenge on me.'

'My gosh. Why do you get into all of this?'

'So, you think, I should not have acted?' Sam had put on a histrionic display.

'Yeah, why you?'

'If I don't indulge and stop; then tomorrow they will go after other girls in our society. Tomorrow it could be you.'

Anger was palpable in Sam's eyes. It followed a brief silence.

'How come, here today?' Sam was surprised with a sudden question from Jaya.

'Yeah. Actually.' After a pause, 'Just to say, Thank you.'

'Aha. Good.' 'So, you are bad enough to get beaten, and don't expect anyone to come forward to save you. But.' She emphasized more, 'But, you are good enough to come forward, and say 'thank you'.'

'Yup. I'm like this.'

Jaya heard her mother calling. 'Yes Aai, I'm here. Coming.'

'So, Bye for now.' Jaya quickly turned back to go inside. Then, she was startled. Sam has touched her pinkie finger. She turned back in a sudden.

'I love you.' Sam was spot-on, without wasting any time.

She could not immediately grasp it, 'Whattt?'

'I do.' And Sam waved his eyes in affirmation and repeating his over-ambition.

Jaya could only nod her head, left-right, possibly indicating 'No'. And she ran inside.

***

Jaya has never experienced this feeling. What happened today, has never ever occurred to her mind, not even remotely. She has never thought of, dreamt of this ever.

She has won the battle over minds in front of mirror; but she knew deep inside what an absence of an eye means to the world.

'Was it Sam again, one of those fancier tricks of his?' 'Isn't he famous for this?' Jaya could easily blame Sam for this misadventure. Deep within, she was waging for love, for someone who could love her for what she is. At the same time, she was a girl with modest mind.

'But why would he express it like this? There was a bit of truth in his expressions.' She recollected how he left her.

'Na, Na…' 'He must be faking it.' 'Isn't he famous for this.' She repeated that line in her mind.

'Or, what if he has not seen me, without my goggles.' She was in front of the mirror, looking into her other eye. She played the game that she plays each day in front of mirror. Hiding, and then showing. For many a times.

'Why did Sam do this today? Why does he have to tease me like this? Is this what he has to give back, for me to help him that day?'

She has kept her life simple. Possibly, until today.

9. Nature, Disaster, And Injury

9a. Heavy Rains Causes Havoc

Ramya stood by the window of her living room. She watched Jaya from a distance. 'My young girl has grown up now. Lord Ganesha has taken away one eye from her but gifted her with so much patience.' Her heart ached.

'We will have to get her married soon.' It pained Ramya to think soon Jaya too would leave the house forever. The tiny space that they called home, once seemed small with the three girls roaming around all the time. They frequently got into each other's way. But now with Mrunali and Shruti gone, the house appeared to be huge and empty.

Without any warning a drop of tear slipped from Ramya's eyes. Getting daughters married was a privilege to any parent. Yet, Ramya's heart rebelled at the thought of letting Jaya go too.

Whistle of the pressure cooker got her attention. She hurried to the kitchen to attend the lunch. She was cleaning up the kitchen when someone knocked on the door.

Ramya came out of the kitchen. 'Mrunali', she saw her elder daughter at the threshold. Mrunali's small son stood by his mother with a confused look. For a moment Ramya felt delight to see her daughter. But then she looked closely at Mrunali's feature. A dark shade had wrapped itself around Mrunali's otherwise bright face. Even her eyes had sunken into two holes.

'Mrunali,' whispered Ramya. 'What happened? Are you okay?'

Mrunali crossed the threshold with reluctance. She knew that her sudden appearance would not be welcomed with heartiness. Yet, she had no other way.

'No, Aai,' said Mrunali. 'I am not okay.'

She still lingered at the doorstep, wondering how her life took such a downward turn. 'Can I come inside?' she asked like a stranger when Ramya did not invite her in.

Ramya's eyes widened at the request. She realised her mistake immediately. 'Yes, of course. This is still your home.' Even though Ramya said this with as much honesty as she could master, it sounded a little hollow. Even Mrunali understood that. Her next statement confirmed the fact that Mrunali was ashamed to come home.

'I am sorry Aai,' she said. 'I had no other way. I could not tolerate it anymore.' The desperation in her voice must have given out a tremor of pain.

Ramya moved immediately. She came forward and embraced Mrunali in her arms. Mrunali had been holding back her tears for a long time. In the warmth of her mother's embrace, she allowed herself to release the pent-up sorrow. With a heave, she began to cry. Like flurry of monsoon rain, the drops of tears emerged out. Mrunali's body shook as she sobbed. Ramya felt helpless holding her daughter. They had found Ramesh for Mrunali after much effort. They wanted to give her a better life, a secure life. Every parent wanted that for their children. But the sense of security was a misleading notion. Nothing was secured, no place was secured and today Ramya understood that.

'What happened?' she asked with dread after Mrunali's sob subsided. They sat down on the worn-out couches. Jaya had taken Mrunali's son inside the house. 'Is it too bad?'

Ramya knew that the situation at Mrunali's home was not happy. The relationship between Mrunali and Ramesh had been deteriorating. Mrunali had hinted about the rising tension several times. But as every mother of the world, Ramya too denied the inevitable. She had refused to believe that the matter would turn so bad that Mrunali would someday return home. Living in denial had its advantage. It allowed people to live in makeshift peace. But Ramya forgot that such peace never lasted. Someday reality comes out with its cruel teeth and claws. Someday life comes crushing down.

Mrunali sat in silence for a long time. Ramya could feel the silent debate going on inside her. Then after a long time, Mrunali looked up to meet her mother's eyes. 'Should we not wait for Baba?' she asked.

Ramya wanted to find a solution of the problem before Ganesh returned. She hoped to make Mrunali understand that everything would be fine in the future.

'Yes, sure. Together we can find a solution of the problem,' said Ramya in a hopeful tone.

Mrunali shook her head. 'No Aai,' she said with such sadness that Ramya blinked. 'There is no solution of this problem.' She paused for a moment. 'Everything is over for me and Ramesh.' She dragged a lungful of air through her mouth, before collapsing against the couch.

That struck hard at Ramya. 'Lord Ganesha, rescue us.' She mumbled. Maybe Mrunali was thinking too much. Maybe there would be some solution. Ramya's concern was Jaya. If Mrunali did not go back to her in-law's house, the entire chawl and society would tear them apart.

***

Ganesh returned home after sun set. Darkness had enveloped the earth by then. He smiled, as he saw Mrunali sitting with her mother and younger sister. He noticed something unusual in those eyes today. He ignored for a moment and asked, 'Where is Bala?' referring to Mrunali's son.

'Baba, he was roaming all around the house for the entire day. Tired, and went to sleep quickly.' Jaya responded.

He could sense the gravity of the situation; however, he did not express anything. He washed his hands and face in the veranda; and came to sit with his family. 'How are you, beta?' He asked calmly.

'Baba', Mrunali halted for a few seconds. 'I need to talk to you.' 'I have things to discuss.'

'Have you had lunch?' asked Ganesh with such calmness that Ramya looked at him with surprise.

'Yes,' said Mrunali with a smile. 'We ate.'

Ganesh nodded. Seeing no space to avoid the revelation, he sat down beside Mrunali. His eldest daughter had been his pride. She has stood her ground in difficult times. With dread, Ganesh invited her to speak.

'What happened?' he asked, even though he did not want to know about it. He wanted everything to be normal again. But right now, that seemed unlikely.

Mrunali began her narration in low voice, careful because she knew the chawl people. Eavesdropping had always been their favourite pastime. She did not want anyone to know about her personal situation, right away.

***

It all had begun with Ramesh's drinking habit. He was not fond of booze earlier. However, with time the habit somehow had crept itself into their lives. Ramesh had begun to drink for pleasure. Initially, Mrunali had not raised any objection. She had remained calm and strong as she always did, hoping that Ramesh would change eventually, hoping that the habit would pass like everything in life did. But drinking habits did not pass. Mrunali had little idea about this. Finally, she set her foot down and told Ramesh to get rid of the drinking habit.

'You cannot come home drunk every night,' said Mrunali. She did not try to hide her anger and frustration. 'Everyone is getting affected because of this habit.'

Ramesh had been a calm and peaceful man. However, that day he reacted in a different way. He barked at Mrunali. 'I don't take money from you. It is my money and I have a right to spend it as I wish.'

That made Mrunali turn around in rage. 'Just because it is your money, does not mean you will come home drunk every day.'

Life On The Edge

Ramesh took a couple of steps towards her. His reddish eyes turned wide in anger. For a moment Mrunali thought he would hit her physically. But Ramesh curled his hands in tight balls and stood still for a moment. Then in a low menacing whisper he said, 'If you cannot tolerate my habit, you can go back to your father's home.' With that he spun around and left the room, leaving Mrunali standing by the double bed where their little was playing.

Mrunali was left speechless, in utter shock. She looked at her kid, Bala was startled with what just happened.

***

It had been raining continuously since the previous night. The streets of Mumbai had been washed off with water. In some areas the water went waist high. The news channels were filled with the news of the floods across all of Mumbai. It said, Mumbai came to a standstill due to flooding. Railways stopped, buses and auto-rikshaws immersed in water, roads filled with traffic. There were people who lost their homes, many stranded on the roads, and there were scenes of people walking amid deep water to their necks.

Mrunali looked out of the window of her home at the street. Ramesh had not returned home for two days. She had tried to call his office. But the number was out of service as expected.

'I am scared,' said Ramesh's mother. She came to stand behind Mrunali. The elderly woman's face was marred with lines of worry and fear for her son. 'Have you tried calling?'

Mrunali nodded. She looked down at her hand. In it she still clutched the telephone diary. 'I called. But the phone is not ringing.'

She looked at the wall clock. It was past ten in the night. She had called Ramesh's office for more than eighteen times. But the telephone on the other side remained stubbornly silent.

'I will go to his office tomorrow,' said Mrunali with determination. Her mother-in-law looked at her with startled eyes. She opened her mouth to protest but then looking at the tight jawline of Mrunali, she swallowed the words.

***

Mrunali had hoped that the rain would stop that night. But the downpour continued. All night long the sky cried without restrain. It seemed that the sorrow of the heaven would never cease. The earth flooded with the teardrops falling from the eyes of the divine.

The morning appeared without even a blink of sun ray. Mrunali prepared herself to step out in rain. Her in-laws tried to stop her. But that day Mrunali was not ready to listen to anyone. Ramesh had not returned home for three consecutive days. She worried about his safety. Each time she closed her eyes, she saw Ramesh meeting with an accident in the heavy downpour. She asked that question, 'What if' so many times.

Outside raindrops hit her with fury blinding her for a moment. Mrunali blinked twice to clear her vision. Gritting her teeth, she began to walk. In this rain, walking was the only option. Thankfully the road across her house did not get affected by the flood. The relief lasted only for a few moments. As she circled the lane, her eyes widened at the sight that unfolded itself. In front of her eyes was a vast realm of water. A few cars stood abandoned at the sides of the road. The water had reached the mid-level of the cars. Even though it was morning, Mrunali could not find a single human being anywhere near the road.

Her breath caught in her chest. After crossing this water-logged street, she would have to walk through the main road. For a moment, she considered going back home. But the next moment her determination made her change her mind. With hesitation, she stepped into the water. First it lapped at her ankle. Then as she walked ahead, the water level went up. Finally, in the middle of the street, Mrunali found herself walking through waist high water. She cursed the municipal corporation and governmental offices on not doing enough.

A couple of times, she trembled, losing her balance. 'Oh Deva, please help.' She prayed with everything she had for a smooth path. In this flooding water, she could not see anything. In case, she stepped into a hole or walked to an uneven part of the road, no one would be able to save her from falling.

Walking through water slowed her down. She took each step after elaborated calculation. First, she felt the surface of the road with her toe, then after satisfying herself that everything was smooth and safe, she placed her weight on the extended foot. It took her almost four and half hours to reach Ramesh's office. She was exhausted.

Ramesh's office building stood amidst knee high water. It looked like a tower in the middle of a sea. Mrunali shivered as a gust of cold wind slammed against her. She hurried towards the building. Now that she saw her destination, her patience had worn out.

Inside the office she found only a few people working. One of them recognized her and came over to assist.

'Is something wrong?' asked the middle-aged man. His knowing eyes made Mrunali go straight to the question.

'Where is Ramesh?' she asked.

Ramesh's colleague stood in silence for a moment. Then he went up to his table, took out a piece of paper, wrote something in it and returned to Mrunali with the paper. 'Ramesh has left the office three days ago. I believe you would find him in this address. This is not far away from here.'

Mrunali's eyes narrowed as she looked down at the paper. 'Whose house is this?' she asked.

Ramesh colleague sighed. 'I think you should find it out yourself.'

***

Mrunali found the address in thirty minutes. She had also learned about the owner of the house. It belonged to a bar girl. She prayed not to find Ramesh there. She prayed to be spared of this humiliation. But sometimes the God turned cruelly deaf.

Ramesh himself answered the door upon the knock. For a moment they both stood speechless, staring at each other. Then Ramesh reacted with rage.

'What the hell are you doing here?' he shouted.

Mrunali could not contain her rage either. She reached out and held Ramesh by the collar of his shirt 'What are you doing here?' she asked with equal anger.

Ramesh forced her hands away and thrust her away from the door with such a force that Mrunali almost went flying on the ground. Before she could move, Ramesh came forward and held her by her hair.

'Get lost,' he said through gritted teeth. 'Or I will kill you with my bare hands.' With that he stood up and disappeared inside the house, slamming the door behind him.

9b. Divorce, A Social Stigma

A pregnant silence fell around the house. Everyone wanted to speak. But no one knew what to say. Ganesh knew, as a father he should support his daughter. Ramya knew, as a mother she should console her daughter. Jaya knew, as a sister she should stand by Mrunali. But none could say or do anything to make the situation better. No one knew how to make it all go away, how to erase the past in its entirety.

Mrunali's eyes were all red, with rage, and helplessness. Her inner core was filled with sadness. Finally, after a lengthy silence, Mrunali spoke. 'I want a divorce.' Her grim voice echoed around the house. The words slammed against the corners of the living room and got back to haunt each member of the family.

'I think we should talk to Ramesh once about this,' Ramya jumped, she could not believe what her daughter has just said. She looked at her husband with a baffled expression. Ganesh was still absorbing the magnanimity of situation.

'No,' said Mrunali. The sharp denial made everyone flinch. 'You would not talk to him about anything. There is nothing to talk about. He had completely failed me and his son. I am not going back to his house ever again.'

In her agitation, she spoke with such force that Ramya thought everyone in the chawl had heard the words. She looked at her husband again for solution. But Ganesh had nothing to offer at the moment. He sat without speaking a word.

'Have you told Ramesh that you want a divorce?' asked Ramya. She hoped that Ramesh would come to fetch his wife and son.

'Yes, I did,' said Mrunali. 'He does not care about us.'

The last hope shattered before Ramya. She too resigned to her fate and sat back like Ganesh. Together they had battled a lot of things. But this divorce would ruin them. Ganesh knew it. Ramya could understand his state of mind. He was after all a father.

'Ramesh, you did not do right.' Ganesh thought to himself. 'What would society say? What would people in the chawl say? A divorced daughter is not treated well. It would also impact Jaya's life.' Ganesh's worry surfaced on his head.

He looked at Jaya with compassion. The girl had seen a lot since the childhood. Shruti's multiple affairs and her sudden marriage had left a scar behind. Even though the chawl people had come to term with the event, they still talked about it. The wound might have healed. But the mark still remained. Now if Mrunali's marriage ended, Jaya would have to bear the consequences without any fault of hers. The entire family would be stigmatized.

Yet, Ganesh could not ignore the fact that Mrunali was a responsible and sensible young woman. She would never take such a drastic step without thinking it through. He could not allow Mrunali to feel ashamed of the situation. He could not leave her alone. He was the father after all. It was his duty to stand by his daughter. With a humble drag of air inside his lungs, he calmed himself down.

Finally, Ganesh spoke. 'It's ok, Mrunali. I know you have tried your best to handle the situation. You can stay here. This is still your home.' He smiled reassuringly at his daughter. Ganesh's eyes met his wife's questioning ones. She wanted to talk to her husband about the situation. She could not accept the way this situation was unfolding.

'Let's not talk about this now,' he said. Mrunali scrubbed her face with her hands. She looked at her father with a smile. On her face, the smile looked forced. But Ganesh was relieved to see her easing up for the moment.

That night, no-one was sure, if the others had gone to sleep. Weird thoughts, and what would happen next had engulfed everyone. However,

Ganesh had decided what he would do next. He was just shaping up how to do it.

***

The next day Ganesh stepped out of the house early in the morning. He has set out to meet Ramesh. He had hoped that the situation would be sorted out. There had been problems between him and Ramya as well. Yet, they had not talked about divorce. They did not even think about it. Even as Ganesh thought about it, he admitted that Mrunali's situation was different from theirs.

Ganesh went straight to Ramesh's office. He wanted the situation to be sorted as early as possible. For this reason, he went to meet Ramesh without intimating him first. But he was not in the office. Upon Ganesh's enquiry the office boy said with hesitation that Ramesh had lost his job.

Ganesh almost fell on the ground at the information. 'How?' he asked in a heavy voice. His heart thudded against his chest wildly.

'The boss had caught him taking bribe,' said the office boy.

Even in the cloudy sky with cool wind blowing, Ganesh sweated as he walked down the road. It had been difficult to find a match for Mrunali. They had to make an effort to find a right groom in Ramesh. He had to spend a lot during the marriage ceremony.

Finally, after walking for fifteen minutes, Ganesh reached the bar which Ramesh's office colleagues had told him about. It did not take long to find Ramesh. He sat near the door with a half empty bottle of whiskey. The sight of Ganesh did not bring out any expression. Ramesh poured a little whiskey in the glass and kept sipping without looking at Ganesh.

'Mrunali has come back home,' said Ganesh. He had no idea how to start the conversation.

'Let her stay there,' said Ramesh in such harsh manner that Ganesh looked at him with a startled expression. 'To hell with her.' Ramesh said that with as much venom as he could gather in four words. He clutched the half-finished glass of whiskey in his hand and looked at a shadowy corner of the bar.

Ganesh cleared his throat, not knowing how to deal with this situation. He had not thought about meeting Ramesh in a bar. Therefore, he sat back for a while, trying to think of something wise to say. Then he resorted to pleading. 'She wants to end the marriage.' His voice trembled as he said this. 'People would gossip about this. You need to understand the gravity of the situation.'

But the pleading did little to deter Ramesh. He sat without speaking a word for a while. Then he said. 'I did not ask her to go away. She did. Why should I go fetching her?' The question came out in a slurred voice. 'I am not going to plead to her. I don't even have any need for her.'

For a moment, Ganesh felt like shouting at Ramesh for the behaviour. But then he thought otherwise. The situation was indeed sensitive. 'You two are grown-ups. You have a child. You should sort everything out or else it would affect your son.'

Even that did not make a difference to Ramesh. He looked at Ganesh with an indifference expression on his face and said through gritted teeth. 'I am not responsible for her or her child. She should have thought about her boy before leaving my house.' With that Ramesh drained the glass and before Ganesh could say anything else, he stood and left the bar.

Ganesh sat in the shadowy hall of the bar, staring after Ramesh. The dream of sorting everything out today evaporated before Ganesh's eyes. He understood that the chance of talking Mrunali into going back was slim.

He tried to swallow the shock which he had received by the behaviour. The young man had changed, Ganesh realised that. In these past few years, Ramesh had gone through a big transformation. Ganesh wished he could brand the changes as positive one. Ramesh had become rude. His manner of speaking which had been polite years ago, now had become harsh. The memory of meeting Ramesh for the first time came back to Ganesh. He remembered how politely Ramesh had behaved with him.

With a sigh and a sense of loss, Ganesh pulled himself up from the chair. He would have to get back home bearing the news of the failed meeting now. He could imagine Ramya's expression. Their only hope lied in Mrunali's in-laws now.

***

Two days later, Ramesh's parents Mr and Mrs Sikare appeared at Ganesh's doorsteps. By that time, the chawl people had started asking about Mrunali's return. They enquired about the well-being of Ramesh. Ramya and Ganesh could see the curiosity in their eyes. People could sniff bad news without trouble. They kept the news of Mrunali's decision a secret from the chawl people. But how long could they hide it?

Ganesh and Ramya felt grateful and relieved at the sight of Ramesh's parents. They rushed to greet the elderly couple. The four of them sat in the living room for a while. Each wondering how to break the ice and what to say to alter the situation. Finally, Ganesh began with a meek, 'I went to meet Ramesh.'

Mr Sikare nodded. His sad face told the tale of many sleepless nights. 'Can we talk to Mrunali once?' he asked after a while.

'Yes, sure,' said Ganesh. He hoped that the situation would be solved that morning and Mrunali would go back to her in-laws' house. But when Mrunali came to join the conversation, the prospect of getting a fast solution faded. Mrunali had a blank and stoic expression on her face. Ganesh knew this expression very well. This was Mrunali's armour. She would not break even under the hardest push with this expression on her face.

'I am not going back,' said Mrunali when her in-laws asked her to return home. 'I am not being able to tolerate it any longer. The situation is getting worse. You all know it.'

'But my dear,' said Ramesh's mother, Mrs Sikare. 'What would the people say? They would not accept the divorce. We don't live in such a free society.'

Mrunali's eyes turned hard at that. 'So Aai, you are asking me to live in misery because people would not accept me?'

Ganesh spoke in a mild tone. 'We are living in a society.' He tried to reason out. 'We must abide by its rules.'

Mrunali shook her head. 'I don't think so. Society is for the people. It must change according to the welfare of those who are living in it.'

'But my dear,' began Ramesh's mother. But she could not say anything else. In loss of word, she did what she had always done. She turned to look at her husband.

Ramesh's father smiled to soften the situation. 'You come back. Together we can solve the matter. People have already started to ask about you.'

Mrunali remained silent. She understood that the reason everyone pledged the reconciliation was because of the people. They were scared of rumours, they feared gossips. Most importantly, they feared being left alone by the society.

Mrunali bit her lower lip as guilt began to rise. What made her shrink from inside was the fear of being questioned about her marital status at work. People would no doubt want to know. What would she say? That her husband was an alcoholic? How would she make them understand that it was impossible to live with a man who smelt foul and roughened her up each night? Those were the secrets she would not be able to tell anyone. These happened behind the closed doors only.

9c. Train Blasts, Hit The City Hard!

Mrunali sat by the window of the living room where she had grown up. She had been to her in-law's house once during this one year. The relationship which she had built with Ramesh had completely fallen apart. Not even a tinge of the thread had remained now. They had completely lost the bonding that they had created together. She looked at the living room's floor at the toddler who played with a plastic car. They had created the child together. Those had been the days when she still thought of happily-ever-after. She still believed in true love for she thought what she shared with Ramesh was true love.

Now, she knew better. Ramesh had lost touch with his life. After losing his job, he had become even more rude. Less and less, he returned home. Even his parents had failed to make him understand the situation. He refused to accept anything or tried to see anything from a rational point. Life had crumbled right before Mrunali's eyes. She let out a deep breath.

Her parents had not said anything. But she could see the tattered hope in their eyes. She remembered the entire situation during her marriage. At the end, it looked like a solid match. Yet, she had failed to hold on to her marriage. None of her parents had accused her, for the failure. But time and again, she detected the sparks from the society and people around that held her responsible for the entire event.

In her trance Mrunali did not see Jaya rushing inside. The young girl tried to catch her breath. Mrunali looked at her youngest sister with questioning eyes. 'What happened?' she asked. 'Why are you running?'

Jaya raised her hands to speak. Then she stopped and then she opened her mouth again. In her eyes, Mrunali saw frightened excitement.

'Bomb blasts, Tai.' Jaya finally managed to say. 'I heard that there is a blast in Mumbai train.' She went towards the television set to switch it on.

Ganesh had come a bit early from his work that day. He came out from the above floor, hearing Jaya's breathless voice. Ramya left the preparation for meal at the kitchen and came out to watch the news along with her family.

The news anchor was screaming his voice out 'What happened in Mumbai is a terror attack.' The other one said, 'Mumbai lifeline is under attack.' There were seven blasts, seven different places, seven trains, all at the same time; bringing Mumbai to a standstill. Many-many deaths, many injured. The rescuers were not sure of the actual casualties as yet. The number increased with time.

Ramya dropped on the floor, beside Mrunali. 'Ago Lord Ganesha.' She sighed 'These things are increasing every day.' Her heart breathed heavily. 'I am frightened even to go to the market.'

Ganesh watched the news in muted surprise. 'seven blasts,' he said to himself in disbelief.

'Nothing would happen,' said Jaya as she looked at the number of dead people. 'These people would not get justice. It is like this always.'

Ganesh sighed. 'What are our investigative agencies doing? With a more responsible Government this could have been avoided. I am thinking about the people who had died in the blast.'

Jaya looked at him. 'Baba, think about those who had been injured. Blast injury is the worst of them all. They have to live the life, with something missing.' Ganesh could sense the pain that she just communicated. It was her own suffering.

Mrunali even though watched the news and heard the conversation, kept drifting back to her life and the problems surrounding it.

A black and white shot of the blast scene appeared on the TV screen. Everyone dragged a deep breath. They felt bad for the people, who had been travelling by the train.

The telephone rang at that moment. Mrunali picked it up absently. She mumbled in a low voice 'hello'. And then paused to listen. Moment later the receiver slipped from her hand and she sat with an unfocused look in her eyes.

Ganesh and Ramya forgot the news. Ramya touched Mrunali's shoulder. 'Who was that?' she asked, fearing the worst.

Mrunali licked her lower lip before speaking. 'Aai. Ramesh's mother. Ramesh has been in one of the trains.'

She looked at her father with wide eyes. For a moment, she resembled the little girl who did not want to go down to play with the other kids. Her face lost all its colour in that moment. Ramya sat frozen to her chair. The room turned stuffy all of a sudden.

'He...he has suffered intense injury.' Mrunali said this with trembling voice. With effort she dragged a deep breath inside her lungs. Then her shoulders started to shake. The news, its intensity, and the probable consequence finally dawned in. The prospect of losing Ramesh forever came with a strong blow. Mrunali's chest began to heave as dry sobs emerged out. She could not even manage to make sound. The months-old rage and anger had faded now. Mrunali could not even recall the bitterness she had been experiencing even a moment ago. When the tears emerged out, only the happy memories rushed back to twist her heart.

'Ma, Ramesh,' she cried in helplessness. 'He...' She could not even bring herself to speak the words out.

Ramya untangled herself from the shock. She would have to act now. Her daughter needed her. Ramya wrapped Mrunali in a tight embrace. Ganesh looked at the mother and daughter. He had gone speechless at the news. Blast injury, he could not even fathom how serious that could be. Just a while ago, they were watching all of this tragic stuff on the news; not knowing how it would hit his own family.

After a while, Ganesh managed to gather his strength. He made a call to Ramesh's house. The maid picked it up. Ganesh enquired about the hospital where Ramesh had been admitted. 'We would have to go right now,' he said.

***

The hospital area had been flooded with people, the relatives of the blast victims. Amidst the sea of people, Ganesh found Ramesh's parents. They were in a wreck. Mrunali immediately went to them and hugged Ramesh's mother. Together the two women began to cry.

'How is he?' Ganesh asked Ramesh's father.

Mr Sikare found it difficult to speak. His eyes glazed as he looked at Ganesh. His mouth trembled. Twice, the old man opened his mouth to speak, but no sound came out. Then he took a couple of deep breaths to steady himself. 'Not good,' he said. 'He has suffered severe injury. Has not gained consciousness for once.'

Ganesh looked at the place where Mrunali, Ramya and Ramesh's mother stood huddled together. He did not know what to say about this. The desire to console people around him suddenly died as everything began to blur. He had hoped for a reconciliation. But now it seemed…Ramesh's father's words got his attention.

'This is not acceptable,' he said. 'How could these people plant bomb in so many trains without the authority's knowledge.'

Because he was expected to say something, Ganesh replied. 'They allow these things to happen.'

Ramesh's father wiped tears from his cheeks. But more drops followed. 'My son…' He looked at Ganesh. 'I know he has gone astray, has started to drink. But he is a good human being.'

Memories of the day Ganesh met Ramesh in the bar came flooding back. It made Ganesh wonder how someone could change so much in such a short while. Even though he wanted Mrunali to reconcile with Ramesh, he found it difficult to accept the transformation which Ramesh had been through. Fortunately, Ganesh did not have to reply.

A young woman in white saree came hurrying towards them. She eyed Ganesh for a moment before turning towards Ramesh's father. 'Your son's condition is worsening,' she said. 'Please steady yourself.' With that she turned and disappeared.

Mrunali came hurrying towards Ganesh and Ramesh's father. 'What did she say?' she asked. 'Can I see Ramesh?' she asked.

Ramesh's father was in a terrible state of mind. He looked at Mrunali in muted silence. This time he did not even try to speak. Ganesh touched Mrunali's shoulder. 'You need to be strong dear,' he said as there was no point hiding.

Mrunali's eyes were staring blank. She staggered. Her already bloodless face turned pale. She swallowed, trying to gather control. But she could not hold herself for much longer. Tears came out in flood again. Ramya and Ramesh's mother hurried towards her. They all waited for further news about Ramesh.

It did not take long for the news, anticipated yet, impossible to accept, to come. The same nurse came hurrying once again. Her eyes moved from face to face. It was clear that she had not delivered news of so many deaths in one day. Ganesh looked at her questioningly. She did not come close this time or said anything. With a short shake of her head, she shook her head, delivered the news, and disappeared from the waiting room.

World blurred before Ganesh's eyes. He stood staring at the nurse. The sound of moaning and crying around him did not reach his ears. 'Mrunali' he thought, 'is a widow now.' 'She had been free from all the miseries her married life had brought along. The incident solved the problem of divorce. Now no one would raise their eyebrows at the sight of Mrunali. No one would ask any question.' Suddenly a thought struck to him, 'Am I so cruel to think like that? For my own daughter?' He turned to look at his daughter. She was on the floor crying.

The guilty question then formed in Ganesh's mind, what was better a widow daughter or a divorced one? In that moment, looking at Mrunali and her grief, he could not decide that.

10. Chandekar Builders

10a. Builder's Entry

Modernization comes at a cost. Civilizations have lost its true character in the name of modernization; some may have lost its existence altogether. Some must die, to be reborn into the new form and shape, wearing the shade of modernization. Society, and cities have transformed and changed their look and feel, way of working and many more things in that process. It is a draining process involving financials, erosion of history, emotions, relationships, and many-many lives.

Mumbai chawls were also going through a change in and around that time. Modernity meant, chawls needed to lose its place, to towering structures called buildings, towers. It is destiny. At one time, the chawls mushroomed at rapid pace to accommodate the ever-growing population. Now theirs razing was the answer to the demand-supply imbalance when the continued growing population needed more houses. Also, to the elites, chawls are spoiler, a bad scar to the global image of financial capital of the country. The chawls had to go. That was never meant to be an easy exercise, some took it as means to exploit to their benefit, some took it as political gambit, and some wanted to give the image makeover to the city. But for people living in chawls, it took a toll.

***

Summer was about to dissolve soon, Ganesh thought with pleasure. He stood by the window of his tiny house. Occasional cool breeze brushed past him and entered the stuffy hall. Even though Bombay never experiences harsh winter, this year it seemed the air had cooled down sooner than the other years.

A hard knock on the door interrupted Ganesh's thought. He looked at the door. Even though it was morning, and everyone was home in the chawl, he had still latched his door. The time was changing, Ganesh let out a deep breath. He opened the door to find a few of the chawl residents standing with bewildered expressions on their faces.

'What happened?' He asked this with curiosity.

'It is Chandekar,' said one of the residents. His face showed naked fear. Chandekar was not an easy man to deal with. In his mind Ganesh knew exactly what had happened. He knew this from the rumours he had picked up. He had been anticipating this day for a long time. He had attempted to delay this event from taking place. But the meeting was inevitable.

'He had brought his big gang along.' The added information did nothing to ease the discomfort that had started to build itself inside Ganesh's heart.

'What does he want?' Ganesh asked. He stepped out of the house. There was no other way. He would have to go down now and face whatever was waiting for them.

The men who came to fetch him were quiet for a moment. Then one of them said, 'He wants to talk.'

Ganesh nodded. Without another word, he left his house, and started going ahead. The group of men followed him closely. They had elected Ganesh to be the spokesperson. No one wanted any dispute. They just wanted to be left alone with their lives.

***

Chandekar was waiting for them in front of the chawl. Behind him stood a couple of men. They all chewed their usual paan masala. The rapid movement of their jaw said they would start spitting the masala any moment now. Proving Ganesh right, Chandekar spitted the masala on the ground, sending out a splatter of red saliva around. Ganesh stepped away from the proximity to protect his trousers. He linked his palms together to gesture a pleasant greeting. Chandekar ignored it completely. 'He is probably here for hard business today,' Ganesh thought.

Ganesh waited for Chandekar to speak. But then the builder did not make any attempt to say anything, he understood that Chandekar was waiting for him to open the conversation.

'So, Chandekar Saheb, what brought you here?'

'People told me; you are Ganesh. Tamhankar?' Chandekar asked with a staring eye, and expression-less face. Ganesh could just nod.

'Hmmm. Don't you all know? Didn't Dev provide all the details?' chewing each word, he continued.

The directness un-nerved Ganesh a bit. Before he could interject, 'Why is the delay? What is the fuss all about?' Chandekar raised his palm.

'We need to discuss a few things,' said Ganesh in a polite tone.

Chandekar nodded. 'We are here to discuss things as well.' He looked around the chawl with observant eyes. 'You see we cannot wait for much longer. We need to get this done soon.'

Ganesh drew a deep breath. He constructed his sentences carefully. He did not want any dispute with anyone. 'Can we sit and talk for a while?' He requested everyone to take a chair.

'You see, this is all we have. Here our families are residing for so long.' He paused to look around. The chawl had been their homes for long.

The last comment made everyone nod in agreement. Chandekar nodded his acknowledgment as well. 'I understand everything. I am a businessman, not a monster.' He curled his lips in an attempt to smile. It looked grotesque on him. Clearly, he was a man unaccustomed to smiling. 'I am offering you all a separate flat.' 'Imagine, brand new,' he gave a godly smile. 'I am giving you luxury. Who does it for people in today's times? Think about it.' Chandekar was emphasizing on his act equating to God, pointing his finger to upwards in the sky. Before anyone could utter a single word, he concluded, 'also, I am going to offer you all money for leaving this chawl.'

Ganesh shook his head. 'That's very kind of you. But it is not that simple.'

'We just cannot leave like that. We have our lives invested in these homes. People are emotionally attached. Here we have married ourselves, had our kids born. They have done their schooling, they made friends, all of us have so many memories.'

'So? So, Tamhankar. What is it? Come to the point. You don't want to leave?' he uttered each word with eyes moving swiftly up and down. He spat again.

'We do not have any place to go?'

'I said, I am offering you some initial money; that will help you find temporary stay.'

'Would that suffice?'

'Ganesh Tamhankar, you and people are testing my patience. I'm trying to uplift you.' 'Where you live today, you call it homes. We call it trash' he made face and was very direct. 'Foreigners call it dirty place. They laugh at us for dumping people in such dirty spaces.'

'Here I'm thinking about you; trying to move you upwards, trying to get you to a luxury life. From 'Jagardev Compound' to 'Chandekar Heights'. But you all still want to continue living in dirty places.'

'But Chandekar Saheb. Whatever other call it, we live here.'

'Tamhankar, control.' Anger in Chandekar was palpable. 'You all know it. I can easily get things done. Don't have to talk to you. You all know it very well.' He was hinting at his connections. 'So do not take advantage of me coming here and trying to listen to you.'

'Come to the point. What is the main problem?' Chandekar's sudden powerful thundering voice made everyone silent.

Then Mhatre podded Ganesh, 'Double homes.' Ganesh composed and said, 'See, there are few, who have put in a lot of money to upgrade their homes.'

'Some have made duplexes; some have made their homes equivalent to the amenities in flats.'

'So, what do you want?' the man behind Chandekar intervened.

'They are looking for two flats.' He put it across as politely as he could. These builders were powerful. Yet, the people in chawl could not just agree to everything they wished for.

'Forget it. Demanding too much. Because of those selective folks, why should the broader Janta suffer?' Chandekar's man was direct.

'They are looking for some benefits over the others; who have not spent a penny on their rooms?' Gupta said from behind Ganesh.

'Everyone will get same house,' Chandekar roared again. His voice turned tight this time. He was losing his temper; Ganesh could see it. 'I cannot give anything more than this.' He heaved a sigh before saying, 'I am also giving you money to settle down.'

'Tomorrow, there can be an earthquake.' Chandekar paused, and then deliberately lifting his head and his finger 'Hmm...Maybe I can get it for all of you.' 'Then...Then?'

'Then all of you will be equal. Homeless. 'Right?' he himself answered.

'So, be happy in equality.' Chandekar's cruel smile only made things calm.

Ganesh could only watch Chandekar with a calm expression. Even though his face was neutral, his heart thudded against his ribs. He could not show his fear. There were many rumours about Chandekar and his people. Some Ganesh believed, some he discarded as spiced up gossip. But right now, standing here in front of them, Ganesh felt that all the rumours surrounding the builders were true. They really were the 'bad guys', people called them.

'Saheb, we have heard that building does not get ready in time.' Shetty dared to bring a question, breaking the long silence.

'We will get it ready in 3 years.' Chandekar was quick to retort with pride.

'But Saheb, your other property is stuck for 5 years, and it is not even half-complete.' Someone said from behind.

Chandekar's jaw tightened at the question. 'Hey. Who is this?' He was surely more than angry. 'Who is teaching you all this nonsense?' 'I am here. I am telling you I will deliver the homes to all of you in 3 years. No if and but.'

'You see, my offer will remain the same,' there was a sudden change of tone in Chandekar, imitating empathy. 'I understand your problems. I understand that this chawl is your home. Here all of you have spent all your lives. Therefore, I am offering you brand new homes. So, that you all remain happy and safe.'

'But what I ask for, is cooperation. Let us move fast.'

Ganesh took the courage to put it out 'Saheb, we understand. We will need some time to get back,' he said at last. 'We cannot come to a decision just like that.'

Chandekar's grim face appeared to be ashen under the sunlight. 'I don't have much time. My party has invested big money on this. You need to make up your mind soon.'

He left the group standing with a baffled expression. No one had expected to come to a decision that morning. But no one had expected to be threatened by the builder either.

***

After Chandekar and his men left in their white Sumos, the people in chawl waited for some time. It is customary for people in the chawls to stay back even after dispersing; for some who cannot speak in public to share their thoughts; for some it is a way of continuing with their views; for some just to be silent listening as if they have all the time in the world; for some it is just out of respect as if they leave the show it will be considered against them.

'So', Ganesh was exhausted. 'Are there any ideas?' He openly looked at group of people.

'Should we go to court? He is openly challenging us.'

'That is an option. But that should be the last one. Chandekar is a difficult man, he has no propriety. He will take it personally.' Mhatre provided his wisdom.

'How about taking help of Shinde bhao?' Shiva jumped in, flaunting his possible reach in the political affiliation.

'Oh, don't think, that is an option here. This builder has all the backing of Shinde bhao. You saw he was talking about influences? Shinde bhao is one of them.' Gupta jumped in.

'Yeah, you are right. Shinde bhao was holding that rally in the other area. People said, Chandekar had completely funded it.' Shetty added in.

The discussion which started out peacefully then turned into a verbal marathon. Everyone wanted to be heard. Everyone wanted to place their opinion. But no one listened to the other. Finally, Ganesh put an end to the mess.

'Go home, all of you. Sleep over it. We will have better ideas. Our mind is not working, with what we are pushed to just a while ago. May be Chandekar will come back with a solution. Or we come up with better ones. So, for now, let us disperse.' Ganesh looked at Mhatre, he got the silent support in his eyes. Both got up and moved back to their homes. While on their way to home, they did not speak. Probably they were thinking about what lies in future.

10b. Jaiswal's Murder

'Why are they silent?' Mhatre looked at Ganesh.

'Hmm. Not sure.' Ganesh was thinking.

A lull had fallen around the chawl all of a sudden. No word had come from the Chandekar builders. No one from the group had paid any visit to the chawl either.

'Not sure, if it is a sigh of relief. Or worst to come as yet.' Ganesh continued. They had been looking over their shoulders for a while. Each day they used to wake up with the dread that the builders would come to visit them. The last visit had shaken them all up.

'Remember, the clout of political threat from Chandekar? I still remember his grinning teeth. See, we could still go to police, and not wait for them to come back?' Mhatre's old voice was cautious.

'See, Mhatre. You know, and I know. What will police do? They are not for us. They are just other tools of Chandekar. They will come and harass us every other day.' Ganesh knew that the police would not help the poor chawl people. No one would stand by them and go against the powerful builders.

'At the same time, this sudden silence from the builders has me worried.' Ganesh had seen a lot in his life. Thus, he could not summon any relief from the depth of his heart. Even though those people had not come for a few days, it did not mean they had disappeared. But he had not shared this with anyone. They did not have to know the harsh truth from Ganesh.

'Truth' Ganesh thought as he made his way towards his house, 'had a way of revealing itself to everyone. Most of the revelation left ugly mark. But that too could wait now.'

'Ganeshji.' The call made Ganesh stop on his track. He turned to see Yadav, who lived in the same chawl and ran a small tea stall. Yadav looked amazingly pale that evening. Immediately, Ganesh knew what had happened, Chandekar builders were back.

'What happened?' he asked going forward to Yadav. 'Is something wrong?' When Yadav faltered, Ganesh dropped his voice, 'Have they come back? Have they said anything bad?'

Yadav dragged a shaky breath inside his heart before answering. 'You remember Jaiswal?'

Ganesh was taken aback for a while as he found it a little difficult to attach a face to the name. Then the face of Jaiswal formed in his mind. The middle-aged man lived with his family not far from the chawl.

'Yes,' answered Ganesh. 'He owns that open space near the main road. Our grand Ganesh festival is celebrated on the space, each year. Shree party members do the arrangements, right? Jaiswal is kind enough to offer that space at no cost.' He could remember Jaiswal's smiling face in his mind.

Yadav cleared his throat. Ganesh could see that the young man had been shaken. 'Jaiswal's body has been found this morning near the bus stop. He was possibly coming back home late night.' Yadav swallowed before continuing. 'He died of brutal sword wounds.'

'Sword wounds?' whispered Ganesh. He could not believe his own ears; he was visibly shaken. 'What do you think has happened?'

'Chandekar builders,' said Yadav. 'Apparently. Chandekars wanted to purchase that very space, where Ganesh festival is celebrated each year.'

Ganesh reached out and clutched a wall, feeling unwell for no reason. 'Has police said anything?'

Yadav shook his head. 'Police had nothing to say, as usual.'

Ganesh stood in the darkening dusk long after Yadav was gone. The builders would do anything to get their way. They had murdered Jaiswal with swords. What would they do to the chawl people? Worse, what would they do to the spokesperson?

Life On The Edge

***

'Aaho, will you come in the house?' Ramya noticed the hesitation in Ganesh.

'You heard about Jaiswal?'

'Yeah. People in the chawl are talking about it.' Ramya answered. 'I personally never met Mrs Jaiswal. People said, she is a kind woman. It is a big loss to her. You know, she has two minor kids. How would she feed them?'

Ganesh looked at Ramya, 'What else did you hear?'

'Hmm. The murder and its brutality had evoked a lot of gossip around. There are various angles being thrown to the murder story.'

'Some said, it is related to Chandekar builders. But some said it is a personal situation.' Ramya continued.

'Probably Chandekar Builders are engaged.' Ganesh's eyes were telling the tale of horror.

Ramya noticed it, 'How do you know? It may not be related to the Chandekars,' she said. She deliberately added a firmness in her voice that she did not feel in reality.

Ganesh gave a tired smile at Ramya's attempt to make the matter light. He shook his head as he considered the event. 'Who does such a killing if it is a family affair?' His voice sounded hollow and exhausted. Then he went quiet for a long time.

'I want this murder to be a personal vendetta or some other things like that. I don't want it to be the Chandekars.' He raised his eyes to look at Ramya. 'I am not sure I want to be up against such cruel people.'

Ramya spoke in a quiet voice. 'That's why I am saying don't think about it.' She looked at her husband's pale face. 'You will be ill soon if you allow yourself to worry so much.'

Ganesh did not reply. He looked out the window at the darkening sky. Even though the sun had disappeared a tinge of orange still hung on the horizon. Light breeze lapped the thin curtain he had hung on the window the previous year. Multiple washes had worn the cheap cotton down. Yet, it displayed a cheerful aura.

Life had been so simple, thought Ganesh. The only problem had been making the ends meet. Somehow, they all managed to survive the poverty and lack of adequate money. But the builder had exposed them all to a new struggle, a deadly one. Even though there was no evidence, yet Ganesh knew that the Jaiswal murder had close connection to the Chandekar builders. It was their doing and the chawl people should be careful about the future.

***

It was 11:40 PM, last bus from the station has arrived. Jaiswal got down, he had two bags on either side. 'Jaiswal, Namaskar. How are you?' Mhatre padded him at the back.

'Are Mhatre ji, good to see you. Namaskar. I have not seen you earlier in the bus.' Jaiswal was cheerful. 'Are you late today?'

'Yes. Had gone to visit my daughter-in-law. Her father-in-law was admitted to a hospital. Got a sudden heart attack.'

'He was hearty and healthy. Was getting ready to go to his office, and he felt some pain. It was good that everyone was at home and they could take him to the hospital.'

'What to say. Heart attack comes for no reason' Jaiswal just added to it.

'Hey Jaiswal, you come here.' Startled with the hefty voice, Jaiswal and Mhatre turned back. They were four men.

'Who are you?' Jaiswal asked.

'Come, we have to talk.'

'But who are you?' 'What's the matter?'

'Matter. We will explain you.' They looked at Mhatre, 'You go'.

'Mhatre ji, you stay. I don't need to speak to them.' Jaiswal said. Those four men were visibly angry, holding hand of Jaiswal, staring at Mhatre.

'Dada said, come back.' One of those men said holding a phone near his ear. It looked as if they were getting instructions over the phone.

'Jaiswal, we are going for now. But follow the order quickly.' And the men left.

***

Mhatre was visibly shaky. 'Ganesh, I was scared that night. I told Jaiswal to take care of this soon.'

'He looked brave, had something in his eyes. But I never thought that I'm seeing him the last day.' He sobbed, 'This episode was trailer of what to come next for that poor man.'

Ganesh's heart began to thud against his ribs. As he aged, his ability to tolerate shocks faded. He forced his voice to remain calm. 'so, what do you think?'

Mhatre drew a long breath inside his heart before speaking. 'Those men were probably from Chandekars. He is the one, who has him killed.'

A pregnant pause materialized then. They both stood silent. Neither knew what to say. Then Mhatre spoke again. 'The police department probably knows everything about the killing. But no one will do anything to catch the killer.'

'Probably we should drop at Jaiswal's house once tomorrow evening,' suggested Ganesh. 'It will be unfair to speculate anything.'

Mhatre cleared his throat. 'I agree. But do you understand who we are up against?' he asked. 'It is the same builder who wants our land.'

Ganesh had considered this. In fact, he had thought about nothing else during the past few days. 'Yes, I understand the risk we are exposed to,' he said after a long pause. 'I know that the builders will not stop at anything.'

'We should be careful,' said Mhatre.

Even though he had spoken for everyone, Ganesh heard the actual warning in Mhatre's unsaid words. Afterall it was Ganesh who had been dealing with the builders. By then the Chandekars had understood that no one else had the courage to speak on behalf of the chawl people.

'Let's pay Jaiswal's home a quick visit tomorrow evening,' Ganesh said ignoring the growing unease inside his stomach.

In the falling darkness, Ganesh could see Mhatre's anxious expression. Despite his own calm exterior, Ganesh too was frightened.

***

Next evening Ganesh found Mhatre waiting for him at the decided place. Mhatre looked better. But when the old man smiled at Ganesh, his expression revealed the anxiety.

'No one knows about this visit?' Ganesh asked. He did not want anyone to know about it right now.

Mhatre nodded. 'I know. I did not tell anyone either.'

Even though Ganesh did not want to bother Jaiswal's family right at the moment, he had to make this visit. They walked in silence, both restless, both lost in their own thought.

The situation at Jaiswal's place gave the vibe of both sorrow and fear. Jaiswal's eldest son met them at the entrance. Ganesh explained that they were known to Jaiswal and came down to pay their condolence.

'Father had…' Jaiswal's eldest son who introduced himself as Pravin was barely out of his teen. He looked shaken and Ganesh felt deep sympathy for the kid. 'Father had so many plans,' said Pravin. 'But they killed him.'

Ganesh's heart began to thud at this accusation. 'Who did it?' he asked even though he knew who had done this.

Pravin looked over his shoulder to confirm that his mother was not within hearing distance. Then he said, 'The Chandekar's. They have collaborated with the members of Shree party.'

Ganesh exchanged a worried glance with Mhatre. It was news to them. They had no idea about the involvement of the Shree party members.

'They want the land. They came to father and demanded that he signed all the papers.' Pravin's voice dropped down to the level of whisper. Ganesh could hear a slight tremor as well.

'Father refused multiple times. Last week, they thrashed father for not signing the papers.'

Ganesh nodded. 'Jaiswalji again said no?' he asked, knowing the answer.

'Yes,' Pravin said. This time a sob escaped his throat and the mask of bravado he had been wearing slipped. 'They also had come a night earlier and warned him that they will have to take a 'big' step.' 'But…but he remained adamant. Father was ready to face them. But they.' He cried, 'they killed him.'

Mrs Jaiswal could not control herself; she cried her heart out 'He was saving the land for his kids. The only savings of his life. His wish was that kids use it to do something bigger.'

'Now he is gone. What will we do with the land? They will now come after my kids. I don't want the land.'

Pravin got up, to console his mother. Pravin and his brother were too young as kids. A lot for this family to face, Ganesh thought.

Ganesh comforted Pravin as best as he could. Then he, along with Mhatre headed back to their chawl.

Neither spoke on the way back. The danger that they had envisaged, was proven to be imminent. Ganesh kept playing the conversation with Pravin in his head. Each time, he experienced the same shock. Chandekars killed Jaiswal for his land. What would they do to the chawl people to get their way?

The question hung over him like a winter curtain of fog about to engulf everything.

10c. Ganesh To Not Pursue

Night never seemed that long. 'Now he is gone. What will we do with the land?' this question kept coming back to haunt Ganesh. He questioned himself, 'What was the fault of Jaiswal?' 'Why should he have died, rather murdered?' He answered, but then he negated. He further negated, that negation. When you let your mind do the games with you, it creates mesh of thoughts, a maze that you cannot come out of. Until something happens all of a sudden. He just got up from the bed. Morning has hit the city, basking in the warmth of Sun.

'Ago, what are you thinking?' Ramya placed the cup of tea next to him. This broke the chain of thoughts, a relief for Ganesh. His eyes met hers, the same solace, he never has to search the world for. It filled him with the comfort, as if clearing a lot of confusion. But he had to let it out first.

'Please have a seat,' he said. After a short pause Ganesh added. 'I need to speak to you about something important.'

Ramya's face immediately drew into a frown. She knew this would be something important. She had expected it to be casual, but today, he had the look of a drowning man who needed to hold on to something to stay afloat.

She just placed herself on the floor, next to the worn-out chair that Ganesh was sitting. She waited for him to speak. He had been looking out, at the dusking sky. A tinge of orange still remained on the horizon. The chawl created a starling contrast against the shiny bright sky. Years had left many bruises on the walls and the rooves of the houses. Dusty curtains and greasy clothes filled the windows and the railings of the veranda. Children played in the front yard of the chawl. Their happy voices floated inside to fill the lengthy pause.

'Chandekars' Ganesh could mutter only this much. Ramya was aware about the on-going conflict with the Chandekar builders. It raised her eyebrows. Women in the chawls, all had been following the progress. It created fear, raised emotions, doubts about the future in them.

'Chandekars and Shree party workers murdered Jaiswal,' said Ganesh. His heavy, and hesitant voice sent a chill down Ramya's spine. She shivered at the information. Even though they had discussed this earlier, and had their own suspicion, learning it for truth was difficult. 'They could not pursue him to sell his property. So, they killed him.'

Ramya looked down at her hands. She did not know what to say. All she knew that Ganesh could be their next target. Chandekar could go to any extent. Still, one could always hope, so she asked. 'What the police is doing?'

Ganesh gave a mirthless laugh at that. 'They will not do anything. Shree party workers are too powerful.'

Ramya fell quiet as the grim reality bared its menacing teeth to the aging couple. 'What are you planning to do?' Finally, Ramya asked Ganesh. Her face already lost its colour. She was thinking about the life that had been snatched away because of a piece of land.

Ganesh has had already spent countless hours into self-debates. He had pondered on this question numerous times. 'What will he do now?' He appeared speechless for a moment. His eyes look in the shining Sun with careful consideration. When he spoke, his voice appeared to be distant and worried. 'I don't know. Chandekar want the chawl. He is now taking the active support of the Shree party. They will not accept refusal. They will not stop until they claim it.'

'Then,' Ramya hesitated for a moment. 'I think you should back out of this. You should not stand in the way,' she said, with a finesse firmness in her voice. 'Why should you be responsible for the entire chawl? No one is risking their life. They all want you to solve the problems for them.'

Ganesh already knew this. The entire chawl depended on him from the beginning. The dependence had turned into an expectation. They wanted Ganesh to get them back their chawl.

'But they depend on me.' Even to his own ears this sounded weak and uncertain.

Ramya roared like a wounded mother at that. Her face flushed as she spoke in a low, yet harsh voice. 'They don't depend on you.' She hissed. 'They want you to die for their houses. They just want to stay away from any trouble and push you to the face of danger.'

Ganesh knew it for truth. He knew that the chawl people wanted someone to face the Chandekar builder and his syndicate for them. But he did not expect Ramya to be so blunt in her statement. 'They rely on my words. If the chawl gets saved, we will be benefitted as well.' Ganesh tried to reason out. 'We also get to keep our home.'

It did not work on Ramya. She held his hands in hers. 'We will get a home even if Chandekars takes over the chawl. But if you end up like Jaiswal, what will I do?' She sighed then. Ganesh did not have an answer to this question, which has been lingering in his mind too. Her shoulders slumped. 'We only have Jaya to marry,' she said finally. 'We don't need a large place. A small one-bedroom house will be sufficient for two of us.' She stretched her arms. 'We have lived in this tiny house for so long. Why can't we live in one-bedroom house?'

The question hung between them. Ganesh looked down at the floor. His eyes scanned the fading flooring colour. But his mind kept drifting. He had already taken up the responsibility of the chawl. How could he back out now? It made him uncomfortable. 'What will I tell them?' Ganesh asked finally.

Ramya looked at her husband hard. 'I know, you will find a way. But you get out of it.' That gaze unnerved Ganesh.

***

It is not usual morning for the people in chawl. The notice has read, 'Mandatory to join this meeting.' Such a notice has never been sent earlier, so it triggered curiosity, suspicion, and uneasiness.

Everyone whispered all around behind the urgency and the need to meet Sunday morning. People in chawls worked hard over the week and woke up late on Sunday morning. Obviously, they did not know the urgency as yet. Seniors were expected to be aware of the situation. However, Shetty, Mhatre too raised their hands in ignorance. That raised the level of suspicion again. It could be hefty fines by municipality, or it could be heavy water bills. Or the need to clean the nearby overflowing gutter. Or it could be about the corporator elections. But nothing seemed to make sense.

'Let us wait for Tamhankar. He is usually the first.' Mhatre said. And then people just got into discussing the usual gossips, studies about kids, politics, mafia nearby and so on.

'Namaskar, everyone.' Ganesh was finally here. 'Where were you, Ganesha' Mhatre in his typical tone asked.

'Jaya just stopped me for something.'

'All well, Kaka?' Mhatre and Ganesh turned their eyes. It met the young man, asking the question. He was Tanay Agre, son of Maharshi Agre. After Maharshi Agre died with cancer a few years ago, Tanay was frequent to join the society meetings, seemed very active in handling society related activities assigned to him.

Ganesh raised his both the palms to him, with eyes closed and shaking of his head. It may have indicated that all is well, but he knew deep within that the turbulence is in sight.

'See my friends.' Ganesh thought it would not be good to delay the proceedings any further.

'Arre, wait, Tamhankar Saheb. Let me order the tea for all. How many are here?' Yadav interrupted. He always hosted all the society folks joining the meeting. He counted everyone, and then went into his house. People waited patiently; it has been a ritual for some time now.

He came back with a tray and offered tea to everyone.

'Thank you, Yadav. You always take care of us.' Mhatre appreciated the kind gesture.

'Without your tea, how can we start our meeting as such. Yadav, you really are kind.' Ganesh too weighed in. That brought cheer on everyone's faces.

'Okay. Let us talk about why we have gathered here today.' Ganesh started. 'First of all, thank you Mhatre, Shetty, Gupta and Patel. I really need your wisdom. Also, good that Tanay, Mishra, Yadav and all of you could manage to join us this Sunday morning.'

The opening sentence brought the atmosphere to a standstill, people were now waiting to hear more. Some prayed in their minds, that it is nothing alarming.

'Chandekar builders' Ganesh took a pause. But two words were enough to raise the anxiety amongst chawl people. 'Did he come again? Is he going to come later today?' Patel asked, with fear in his voice.

'He has not come back. He may be busy in other things for now. But he has not forgotten us; he will come back.' Ganesh continued.

'We have to make a decision. We cannot make it an infinitely long process.'

'What happened, Tamhankar ji? You seem agitated.' Gupta was cautious in his question.

'You all know, Chandekars. The longer we take; it will irritate him further.'

'The last time, he issued us a verbal threat. This time he could do a physical assault.'

'Your worry is genuine. Chandekar is dangerous.' Mhatre aided to Ganesh's concerns.

'But what he is offering is not fair. Other builders have given more for the other chawls, for albeit smaller sized rooms than ours.' Tanay justified.

'Agreed. We could get more. But those are other builders. Here we are dealing with Chandekars.'

'One, he will not allow other builder to come in our case. Secondly, none would dare to come in since Chandekar is engaged.'

'Also, it is not that he is offering something very unfair. Getting one-bedroom flat for our one room kitchen is sufficient for us to make our living.' Ganesh tried to be rational.

'But that is like we know, someone is cheating us, and we are accepting that cheating. That is really not done.' Shiva retorted.

'See, we will never be happy with what we get from our one room kitchen. If we would have been getting a bit bigger house, then the desire would be to have bigger.' Ganesh got philosophical.

'But we all know. Chandekar's are not offering us a decent deal. The rooms are really small-sized.' Tanay finally showed signs of anger in his voice.

'See, I understand, what Ganesh is thinking. Chandekar's are powerful. They have connections with Shree party too.' Mhatre aided.

'See, I care for you, all of you. It is not worth the fight. Our lives are more important. They say, live today to see another day. And another day may bring better opportunities.' Ganesh reasoned it out.

'You are scared, Kaka. You know it, it is hard earned property for us. It is our sweat. Our only earning of our lives.' Tanay had anger and emotions flowing together.

Then, it continued for some time. While the seniors were cautious with their approach, being careful, caring for their lives was important; the young brigade displayed passion, anger, frustration, fighting for their right.

Some brought in their political connections, some raised bhagat singh and willing to give their blood for their right. Some even went to the extent of exercising their right and going to court to fight the matter.

'I understand all of your wishes.' Ganesh was calm. 'But I am unable to continue. I am ageing, I must take the back seat. I am happy if one of you take the battle in your hands.' He got up and slowly moved away.

Others just watched him going. It was plainly sudden and caught everyone by surprise.

Mhatre quickly got up from his place and followed him. He could catch Ganesh only after a few quick steps. He caught hold of Ganesh's hands from behind, 'Ganesh.'

'Arre, Mhatre.'

'You have always led the way. You were the bravest of the lot. But I understand, my friend.' Mhatre said, while nodding his head with closed eyes. His words felt sympathetic. But Ganesh knew deep within himself, he has let himself down.

11. Life Has To End, Once!

11a. Life Is Uncertain

'Sorry Saaheb, what are you saying?' Ganesh did not understand what this disease meant. He could not understand a single word of what Dr Tiwari just said.

He has had severe ache on the left of his abdomen and chest for several days. A week ago, he coughed blood, noticeable. That prompted him to visit the local doctor at nearby clinic. Dr Parab advised him to visit a lung specialist. Hence, he visited Dr Tiwari, who is a Lung Specialist; works at this charitable trust.

Dr Tiwari did a few scans for Ganesh and had asked him to visit after a week for results. Ganesh found this nuisance, but Ramya forced him to visit each time. He had hoped for this meeting to be a casual meeting. He had taken a break from his shop for today.

'Ganesh ji, simply put, this is lung cancer.' Dr Tiwari knew he has to do his job, he put it straight to Ganesh.

Before Ganesh could understand, what he heard, doctor picked up his hand. 'Ganesh ji, this is at an advanced stage; it cannot be cured.'

Doctor was still observing Ganesh, probably waiting for him to speak, ask a few questions. It has been a few seconds; Ganesh has not yet said anything. 'Ganesh ji, whatever life is left, you should enjoy. Do not live in stress.'

'How....' He gulped. It was all black in front of him. 'How much...' Ganesh could not complete his sentence.

Dr Tiwari was kind, he patted him; held him at his shoulders. 'Ganesh ji, possibly a few weeks if you got lucky.'

Ganesh was numb. A State of shock, he could not utter a single word to doctor. The thought of not having to live for long was pre-dominant. He never had a pleasing experience with doctors, hence he always avoided visiting these professionals. He didn't visit Dr Tiwari to get this news at least.

***

'Is it true?' he murmured, on the way to home.

'What does it mean? What should I do?'

'Am I unhappy? Should I cry?' Ganesh was destroyed from within; his soul and mind were fighting a battle for the losing cause.

'I have a family behind me. My two daughters are married. I must thank God. But I have Mrunali, I should get her married again, she has a long future. How will it happen now?'

'Ramya too is not keeping well. I thought, I will take care of her. But now?'

The thought of cruel-some has occupied his mind.

'Never thought, my departure will be so soon.'

'Is it so soon?'

'Hmm. What is so soon?'

'Ramya must be waiting for me. She will ask me, what happened? What did Dr say?'

'What will I say? She will get depressed. What if she does not handle well?'

'Should I talk to Mrunali? She is mature, will handle well.' He calls up Mrunali.

The call rings on the other side. One ring. Ganesh cuts the call.

'What am I doing? Why am I informing her so soon? She has responsibilities to manage.' He hated that he has the mobile phone. Otherwise, hurried mind and heart would not result in a hurried action; he would have waited. While he was thinking, he got a call back from Mrunali.

Life On The Edge

'Hello. My Pori. Mruni, how are you?'

'I'm fine. Just called you. Felt like calling you.' He was shivering. He waited, wiped his sweat, and closed his eyes. He was in a different world.

'Sorry Beta, what did you say?'

'No. No. All well. Are you planning to come down to house? Ramya has been saying, it is long.'

'Take a break. You can do that from here as well. Come for a week or so.'

'When? Not this week. One week later?'

'Ok. That is perfect. See you.' 'God bless you.'

Ganesh kept the phone back in his pocket. He sat there down, on his knees. It was highway, vehicles were passing by at a fast speed. There was music, there was chaos. But he was at peace, himself engulfed in white smog all over. His mind has calmed down, heart has slowed pumping the blood.

A loud self-realization just kicked in. He came back to senses. Someone has just sprinkled water on him. He saw lot of people running to him, someone lifted him up. Lot of questions, but he could not answer any. He could just signal, all is okay.

***

As he expected, Ramya asked him at the doorstep. 'Aaho, I was waiting for you. How was the doctor visit? What did he say?'

'Arre, all well. Just a casual visit.' Ganesh realised that his response was too quick. 'Is the tea ready?' he added, to divert the attention.

'Yes, you wash your hands. I will bring'.

Ramya and Ganesh enjoyed their tea together. Ganesh has loved this part of his day every-day. They have done this together for past many-many years. This has probably been the only moment of their day, that was for them.

Ganesh has not yet opened about the Dr, or the lung cancer. He was still not sure on how to share this news with Ramya. It is only a matter of few months, or weeks may be. He will be no more. He will not exist in the world. 'Should he share this, at all?' he debated with self.

***

'What have I done in my life? Has it been enough?'

Ganesh was staring at the full moon outside the window. There is life in this dark sky as well, he thought.

'When I was growing up, I had lot of aspirations. My parents died early, but I got on my own feet. Reached here in Mumbai.' His gaze at sky has deepened.

'This is the house that I bought. I had hoped for a better house, a bigger house. But.' It was blank again.

'Ramya has been with me forever. She supported me in all situations, thick and thin. I have not been able to give her the happy life. I wanted the happiness of all the world under her…but what have I?'

His thoughts were not steady, albeit intermittent.

'My native place, a small village. Isolated from the stubbornness of these cities. I had to walk tens of kilometres to go to school for studies. Wanted to build a small school. But now how?'

It is about death. A certain death. All kinds of thoughts have grappled him. Sanity was in the randomness. New thoughts were emerging out of nowhere, and the current thoughts were vanishing for no reason. And, Ganesh was immersing, deeper into it, to an extent he can drown himself to death of unwoven thoughts.

'I wanted to do more. Really more, for me, my family, my society, my village. More than what has happened through me.'

'Destiny has not helped me enough.' Ganesh was into reality.

***

Ganesh woke up fresh. His head was aching. His hands automatically went to his left chest, 'Ah, it is hurting'. He realised, why.

He finished his prayers in front of Lord Ganesha.

'Ramya, I think.' 'I am thinking, I should go and spend some time in our native place.'

'All of a sudden? Anything happened?' She turned to him, amused at what she just heard.

'Have been thinking about it for some time. But.' Before Ganesh could complete, Ramya shared her thoughts.

'Let us go in three months from now. Kids will have holidays.'

'No,' Ganesh emphasized, 'I'm going tomorrow. We will go in three months again, that's not a problem.'

'Why now? What is the hurry?' Ramya asked, it was not just enquiring. She wanted to know if this is something that she should be worried.

'Ramya, just like that.' Ganesh's eyes met with Ramya's raised eyebrow. They spoke, without words spoken. Ramya understood.

11b. Back To Native Home

Ganesh was finally at his native place, Singaar. He was standing in front of his ancestor's house. Made with clay, it still stood tall surviving all storms and typhoons frequently occurring during summers. Most of the houses in Singaar were made with clay, broken from the edges, walls fallen. Probably only a few had their homes cemented, a symbol of being rich and holding power in the village.

He opened the doors, they were still very solid, and heavy. The condition of the house showed that it was closed for a long time. It was filled with spider webs and so much of soil. Ganesh coughed.

It took him 3 hours to clean-up the house. He was tired, but he was happy that he still had the energy to clean it up. He fetched fresh water from the ground, his house was one of few which had their own hand pump.

Suddenly he saw someone standing at the door.

'Arre Ganesh? You came and did not inform us?' Ganesh's eyes sparkled.

This was his child-hood friend, Sharad. 'Hey…Sharad. How are you?' Ganesh took Sharad in his arms, they hugged tightly and long to cover up for the lost time.

'How is life? How is your little one, Kiku?'

'Are Ganesha, now where are they little. She got married. Now, me and Sushila are by ourselves. Our times are now over. Anyways it has become so difficult to live.'

Sharad continued, 'Good that you moved out of this village. There is nothing left here. We hardly produce anything in the lands. And then during summers, we have to struggle for waters. The struggle gets so much severe, that we feel like dying. Anyways, just waiting for our times.'

'Sharad, don't say like this. We should respect what we have, what God gives. Life is precious.' Ganesh was reflecting upon himself. Sharad nodded.

'How is my Mehvani?' Ganesh referred to Sushila, Sharad's wife.

'Sushila is doing fine. Just that she has pain in her legs and knees. She cannot walk much without the support.'

'So why don't you take her to a doctor? Now a days it is easy surgery.'

'Ganesha, you are coming from Mumbai. You will surely advice all this. There is very little changed here. You remember the State hospital, right? It is 200 km away. It takes hours to go; and after reaching you are not sure you will get the doctor. And if there is a doctor, he will give the same medicine to all the patients.' Sharad's face showed helplessness. 'Anyways, leave all this, come to house, she will be surprised to see you'.

***

'Aago, look here, who is here?'

'Aaho Bhau, when did you come?' Ganesh bends down to take blessings from Sushila. Then they had greetings, and small talk catching up with personal lives.

They were seated at the self-woven bed, a distinction of villages.

Sharad shouted at the boy who came in, 'Hey porya, tell your baba; Ganesha is here.' Ganesh looked at the boy, he resembled someone.

'Mehvani, your tea is still the best.'

'Arre Bhau. In City, Ramya would make much better.'

'But Mehvani, what you get in villages, is special.'

'What is going on?' The noise outside distracted Ganesh.

'Let me check.' Sharad got up; he found a group of people storming into his house.

'Way,' Sharad shouted, 'Kaliya, Dhanaji, Shurma.' They came inside, and lifted Ganesha on their shoulders. 'Ganesha, Ganesha, Ganesha…' Ganesha hugged each one of them, he had tears in his eyes. A strong man, mentally and at heart; but could not control his emotions having seen his childhood friends.

'It's been seven years, Ganesha.' Kaliya was overwhelmed seeing his friend.

'What to do? Life is as such. Mumbai's life is fast. The day starts, and it ends. Lot of times, what left hand has done during the day; the right hand does not know about it…I miss all of you. I miss the life at Singaar.' Ganesh felt emotional, 'Sharad, you were telling that I did good in moving to city. But let me tell you, many a times I felt I should have never left Singaar.'

'Arre Ganesha…Leave all this aside. We are so happy to see you.' Shurma exclaimed.

'But what happened? What brought you here?' Dhanaji was curious.

'Nothing like that. Can't I come to meet you all?' said Ganesh.

'Why not, my friend.' Kaliya again hugged Ganesh.

That night, Ganesha felt the happiness in him. He forgot his miseries. He forgot his chest pain. He forgot his coughing, which has become incessant.

***

'Time flies by fast huh?' asked Ganesh absently. He paddled through the once familiar road where he had grown up. These roads held countless moments of happiness for him. Even today, at the threshold of death, he still found it serene and peaceful here. As if by some magic the town of his birth had erased everything from deep down within. A bout of dry cough, he had become accustomed to it now, brought him back to the present. He stopped paddling his cycle to allow the bout to pass.

Sharad stopped beside him. He got off the cycle and looked around. Sharad had never left the village. He would not understand the nostalgia Ganesh experienced. Ganesh envied Sharad's lack of knowledge in that part. 'Yes, I guess. You had been away for too long.' Sharad looked up at the clear blue sky.

'Yes, seven years is too long, Sharad.' said Ganesh. He had counted each day that had been spent away from his hometown. Life had taken away a lot from him. But the love for his childhood town remained like the distant stars. 'I came here seven years ago.'

Sharad nodded. He looked at Ganesh. 'You should do something about the cough. It could be dangerous.'

Ganesh could not help smiling at the suggestion. Yes, this could be dangerous. This could be deadly even, he thought. But strangely he did not feel any touch of malice in his ask. 'Yes, I will. Soon.' They started to paddle again.

On the way, Kaliya, Shurma and Dhanaji also joined them. In a flash, Ganesh went back to the past. They used to go to school in their worn-out rust eaten cycles back then. Nothing much had changed here.

As they descended in front of a three-story bruised building, Ganesh spoke again. 'It's a pity that we still don't have a school near our homes.'

'But we are glad to have our school here,' Shurma said. 'Our kids come here by cycle. They bond better this way.'

Ganesh sensed the positivity amongst his friends in village. This has always been the hallmark of all of us. He realised, he thought about 'us', that included him.

'True' he further thought. It had helped them create a strong bond as well. This bonding is what Ganesh has always missed while in Mumbai.

They went inside the building to look inside. Children were rushing out as the last bell rang. The school was over for the day. Looking at the young faces, flushed with happiness, Ganesh could not help but to take a tour back to his own childhood when happiness was simple.

'Dhanaji, let us run, who will reach your home first.' Kaliya shouted. They laughed. Ganesh remembered, how the mere last bell of school used to make them all cheerful.

Ganesh looked at Sharad, 'Weren't we happy even with the simple meals that we used to bring from home. We were happy with the simple way of life that our parents could give to us. We were happy because we did not know what unhappiness was.' Ganesh felt a little lost as he held Sharad's hands. Sharad was not sure, what is his friend thinking, and saying. 'Why has life become so complicated.' Ganesh finally delivered.

'What happened, Ganesh?' Sharad gestured to him. He was amazed at his friend being philosophical.

The principal of the school was an elderly man, slightly overweight, yet fit enough to walk without hunches. The man had been Ganesh's senior. They used to share very good relationship.

'Ganesh, welcome home,' said the principal of the school. He flashed Ganesh a smile. 'You look fresh. You have lost weight, I guess.'

To this Ganesh smiled. Yes, he had lost weight. He knew the reason for this. So, he kept quiet and steered the conversation towards the school.

'It had been six years, since the building seen the last patch of fresh paint,' said the principal with regret. They were taking a tour of the building. It smelt of book, ink, and wood. Ganesh was familiar with this smell. He used to inhale deep before the summer vacation.

'I am capturing the smell of school in my heart,' he used to tell his friends. Yes, Ganesh loved his school that much. Today also he took a deep breath to capture the smell in his heart because he would never be able to stand here and smell this fragrance. He opened his eyes, and he saw everyone was staring at him. With shame he realised that the principal of the school had said something which he had missed.

'I am sorry,' he said with a mild smile. 'I am a bit overwhelmed with nostalgia.'

'I asked does this happen to the schools of Bombay as well?' asked the principal.

'No,' said Ganesh. 'They paint their schools every year.'

They climbed a wide staircase to go to the second floor. Ganesh saw the classroom, where he has spent those proud days in the school during his fourth standard. Just outside the classroom, the board was still up to date with all the prime-ministers and principals that India had.

'Remember Ganesh, you used to dance to the famous Dandi dance. We used to watch it from there and die laughing.' Shurma reminded him.

Ganesh shied, and then had his take. 'Don't forget, our math sir, Ghadage sir used to always throw you out of the class. Math tables were always trouble for you.'

'And then, you all forgot, how Dhanaji asked the History teacher...haha...and how badly he was spanked.' Kaliya reminded. Friends laughed their heart out, remembering this anecdote.

They were now in the 'Science' lab of the school. 'Ganesh, in today's times; our kids fight for pen and pencil. They ask for good quality stuff. And what we had during those days?' Sharad said from behind.

'Yeah. You are right. We did not have pen and pencil those days. We used to make our pen and ink by ourselves. Those were days of fun.' Ganesh reminisced.

'Must tell you, schooling in Bombay is very tough. Kids pick up heavy bags...' Ganesh exhaled.

The school tour ended soon enough, probably sooner than Ganesh would have liked it. On the way back, Ganesh and his friends joked with each other. In the falling darkness, the once familiar street looked a little ghastly. It made Ganesh recall the time when they used to scare each other silly by making up ghost stories while crossing this muddy road in the winter evenings. They told stories while paddling back home. The last one to be on the road always protested the storytelling sessions.

'Remember the ghost stories, we used to tell each other?' asked Ganesh. Even today, years later, he could still hear themselves muttering in heavy tones the tales of nightmare and monsters.

'Yes, now my son does the same thing,' said Sharad.

'Yes, same with my son,' said Kaliya and Dhanaji in unison. The five had been inseparable as children. Ganesh had to go to the city looking for better opportunity, and to be able to take care of his ailing father, but his friends stayed back. They all looked happy, a little worn-out due to the hard times. But joy had permanently plastered itself on their faces.

Ganesh paddled in silence. He savoured the brush of cool breeze on his face. With sun going down, the temperature usually dropped. Ganesh was shocked to realize how little had changed in his village. It was as if time had stood still here and refused to turn. Everything had remained the same.

'Tomorrow, we will go to the lake,' said Sharad.

The lake, Ganesh smiled. He had so many fond memories of the lake and its calm, glass like water. 'Yes, sure.'

They said good night at Ganesh's doorstep. In villages night fell quickly. Silence engulfed the earth without warning. Ganesh stood at the front yard of the house for a moment longer and watched his friends paddling away. They chattered with each other as they went. The serenity of life, the village gifted to its residents seemed almost heavenly.

Ganesh inhaled the night air. He felt exhausted from cycling for so long. Time to rest. He thought. Tomorrow would be a long day by the lake. The memory of the lake enlivened him immediately. His slumbering heart began to race at the prospect of the visit, so long dreamt and so deeply desired.

***

They started out early the next morning. Today, Sharad, Kaliya and Shurma joined; they took their cycles to go to the lake. 'What happened to Dhanaji?' Ganesh puzzled.

'He is a busy man; he is getting his daughter married.' Kaliya shouted as he would usually do. It is, indeed, Ganesh knew what it means to get daughters married.

For a moment they simply paddled, enjoying the cool early morning breeze. Then Ganesh asked, 'Yesterday had been a great experience. Suddenly everything came rushing back.' He looked at his friends. Sharad smiled as he allowed himself to drift back to the time, they had been mere children.

'We loved school,' finally, Sharad said.

Kaliya laughed at this comment. 'We did not love school as much as we hated farming back then.' He sneaked a quick glance at his friends before paddling through a narrow space which only allowed two cycles to pass by each other. 'Mostly we went to school to avoid work and baba at home.'

Ganesh remembered rushing to school just to stay away from the farm and the plantation work. 'That and Sarita,' he said with a sidelong glance at Kaliya.

The comment made Sharad & Shurma laugh and Kaliya paddle faster. Driven by the instinct of adolescent, he had expressed his love to Sarita. He had plucked the best and freshest flowers from his garden to offer her. It had ended badly by Sarita smashing the flowers on his face.

'Yeah,' said Kaliya. 'Sarita. We used to come to the lake to see her as well.'

Ganesh nodded. He remembered the fun they had at the lake. They stole glances at the girls while fishing in the lake. 'We had caught so many big fishes back then.'

Sharad's face darkened a little at the memory. 'Back then the lake had been free for everyone to use. Now it belonged to the Sarpanch.'

The unfairness though glared at him; Ganesh did not allow the moment to fade. He changed the topic quickly. 'Do you remember the fishing competition?'

'Yes,' said Kaliya. 'Shurma went to the other side of the lake and then came back with a bucket full of fresh fishes.'

Ganesh looked at Sharad. 'I still believe you bought the fishes with your lunch money.'

With desperate force Shurma shook his head. 'I did not. I caught the fishes that day.'

'You could not catch those fishes,' said Kaliya. 'We knew your fishing skills.'

'You all are jealous because I won the competition.' said Shurma. They paddled in silence for a while and then they burst into laughter.

Ganesh kept throwing questions about the past. He wanted to know whether his friends remembered their childhood with as much clarity as he did. Sharad, Kaliya and Shurma kept answering the questions.

Finally, they came to stand in front of the village lake. The water was still clear and calm. Ganesh looked at the water for a long time, then he turned to look at his friends.

'We cannot go fishing or swimming like we did in the past,' he said with a little regret. 'But we can sit here and enjoy the view.'

They dropped on the ground under a tall tree. The friends sat creating a circle.

'Remember how we used to come here for picnic?' asked Ganesh.

'Yes, with apple and guava.' Kaliya looked around. In his eyes Ganesh saw regret.

Ganesh chuckled. 'Yes, and that too stolen from others garden.' Together, they all started to laugh.

'There is something about stolen fruits,' said Sharad. 'We actually stole a lot of fruits from others garden.'

Ganesh nodded. 'Yes, if stealing fruits had been a crime, we would have gone to jail for our lives.'

Kaliya hooted at this as he used to do as a child. 'I am hungry.' Finally, he said. 'Let's get back.'

With surprise Ganesh realised that they had been sitting here for more than two hours. He did not feel hungry. His appetite had been down nowadays. Yet, he did not protest. 'Yes, let's get back,' he said. 'I will have to pack my things. Tomorrow I am returning to Bombay.'

His friends looked at him with sad eyes. They did not want Ganesh to go. The time they had spent together had made them all relive their childhood.

'Cannot you extend the stay?' asked Sharad. 'A couple of days.'

Ganesh wanted to extend his stay too. Yet, he could not. He needed to go back to his family. Despite the temptation to remain in his birth town, he could not deny his affection for his family. He would have to spend his last few days with Ramya and his daughters.

'No,' he said. 'I have my ticket booked.' He stared ahead at a wide field. They used to bring their goats and cows here to give them fresh food. 'Our animals enjoyed the grass of the field.' His sigh was a lengthier than it was necessary. All the green grass that he remembered, had now turned brown due to lack of care.

'Yes,' said Shurma following his gaze. 'The families have become so poor now that they all had to sell off their animals. I am holding on to the last cow.' He paused for a while. 'But I think I will have to sell it off soon enough.' He took a deep breath.

They paddled back with the sun dazzling over their heads. Even though it was summer, the heat was bearable. Sweet smell of ripe mango had scented the air. Ganesh inhaled with happiness. He remembered stealing mangos from the neighbours' gardens and eating them without pealing the coating. Three days disappeared in a blink of an eye. Now he had to return to his life.

***

Next morning, Ganesh stood on a deserted platform, waiting for his train. Sharad, Kaliya, Shurma and Dhanaji; all had come to see him off, like they did seven years ago. Nothing really had changed, thought Ganesh with gratefulness. The hurried life and the yearn for money had not contaminated the air of his village. The people who lived here still valued the primitive joy of taking a stroll under moonlight.

'Dhanaji, you should have stayed back. I know, how busy it is for you.' Ganesh looked at Dhanaji.

Dhanaji almost beat Ganesh and hugged him tight. 'Friend, when will we see you next?'

'Come back soon,' said Sharad. 'It was nice that we can get together. Otherwise, we are just busy with our lives.'

Ganesh looked at Sharad. Emotions laden with a touch of sorrow swept him over. Looking at his childhood friend, he felt like looking at someone from the other side of the world, someone he would leave soon. But before the emotion reached his eyes and Sharad read it, he lowered his head. Thankfully, the wave passed. With time everything passed.

'Yes, I will come back soon,' he said with a smile that came easily. He did not have to force his smiles anymore.

They would feel betrayed, Ganesh knew it. They would curse him for not telling them. But he did not want to spoil the moment. He wanted to live it and take the moments with him.

A shrill whistle in the distance announced the arrival of the train. Kaliya slapped Ganesh's back as he always did. 'So, we see you in what?' he asked jokingly. 'In next seven years?' Shurma completed it.

Ganesh laughed at the joke. The train slowed and then stopped at the station. He placed his lone bag on the train and climbed the flights to enter the compartment. From the window of the train, he waved at his friends, smiling. 'I will see you in the next birth.' His cheerful voice made Sharad, Kaliya, Dhanaji and Shurma laugh heartily. They stared at the train as it disappeared into the oblivion.

11c. The End, For Another beginning!

'Arre Mrunali', Mrunali bent to take blessings from Ganesh. She asked his son to take blessings as well.

'Come here.' And he lifted his grandson in his arms. 'You grown-up, my boy. Lord Ganesha bless you with lots of power.' Ganesh gave a bear hug to him.

Ganesh looked at Mrunali with lot of sympathy. Mrunali was growing old too. In her late thirty's and having to manage her in-laws and son was a tough job for her. He wished if he could get her married again. Indeed, her in-laws were ready too. However, it is not easy to get a good groom at this age for girls, and that too widowed. That feeling of not being able to do anything with it, was distressing him. For now, he was happy that he could see his daughter before his end arrives.

In a few days, Shruti also joined. She looked in happy space. Ganesh and Ramya had already forgiven her misadventure. Deep within they were happy. Mangesh is really a nice human being. He had expanded his shops, and financially doing very well. Shruti has settled well with her husband. Ramya's happiness lay in the stability that Mangesh has brought in Shruti.

Jaya came with her husband Sam. Ganesh's worry was still him. He still was a character, still into doing tapori stuff. 'It will take ages before he realizes what life is,' Ganesh thought. 'Don't worry, his father has a lot left for him. He does not have to do much.' Ramya always consoled Ganesh. They were always happy, that whatever be the nature of Sam to outside world; he was very caring towards Jaya and both shared a great chemistry.

Their family reunion was complete. The small house was filled with so many breathing creatures all at once, after a long time.

***

Next day, Ganesh was about to do his morning prayers. He asked his grandson to join in, 'Bala, come join me for prayers.'

Ganesh folded his grandson's hands and asked him to follow him. Both stood in front of Lord Ganesha. Bala mimicked what his baba did, folding hands, closing eyes, and chanting mantras.

'Baba, why do we pray?' An innocent question was hurled at Ganesh.

He laughed. 'Looked like Mrunali did not tell you, what I told her.'

'See, at least one time of the day; we stand in front of the supreme power with all humility.' He continued.

'People who believe in God,' he took a pause, 'also, those who do not believe in God. All of them should take away some time to bow down their head in front of a visible or invisible entity. We might call them almighty. The atheists need not assume it to be a God, they can assume their own sole, or their super icon, or whoever they cherish the most.'

'One aspect is that when you stand with your head down. You accept the fact that you are not superior. There is someone in some form or shape above you. It brings humility in you. It brings a bit of fear in you for doing wrong things. It brings alignment in your mind to always do the 'right' and 'just' things.'

'Second aspect is when you pray, wish or ask for something; you actually reiterate what you want with your life. Your priorities for right now. It may be about what you want to achieve. It may be about health, or about wealth, or it may be some recognition, or something else. It may be about your near and dear ones.'

'When you reiterate this every day, it helps a lot. It helps you sort things out in your mind. You know, why do you want to live that day. You know, what will bring you happiness. You will be at peace.'

'This, as they call, self-realization, knowing about self. But lot of people cannot answer this question for themselves. It is deep within them, but they run around the world looking for answers. They also seek external help.'

Ganesh was not sure, if Bala understood all. 'I will tell you all this when you grow up.' Bala nodded his head. Ganesh realised that he must correct his mistake. 'Or may be your Aai will tell you when you grow up.' He looked at Mrunali.

Mrunali could reminiscence her growing up days, when her baba would explain this concept to her, Shruti and Jaya. Her parents never imposed anything on them, about what needs to be done, and what not. In her mind, she was always baffled, why people fight over religion, as her religion never enforced a particular way of doing things. She enjoyed the liberty, to worship, or not to worship, or how to practice the rituals. She has had all the freedom on who, what, when, where and how to profess, pray and pursue. She looked at Jaya and noticed that Jaya was listening to the conversation between Baba and his grandson. Their eyes met, they smiled, and nodded their head in unison.

She noticed that her baba was coughing, coughing heavily. This did not look normal. 'Baba, you doing okay. You, coughing too much?'

'Baba, I also saw you doing this.' Shruti mentioned.

'Nai re. All is hearty and healthy. May be, I will take ginger, and all will be fine.' Ganesh said, rather lied.

***

Situation became difficult. Days passed, rather hours. And it deteriorated further. None in the family knew what Ganesh was going through. They provided the home remedies, they served him ginger tea, kadhi, honey, etc. There was advice to go and visit Ayurvedic doctor. Ramya even questioned what medicine Dr Tiwari gives. But all of this fell on deaf ears of Ganesh. He knew the truth.

Ganesh coughed so much that his inner sole felt weightless. He felt as if the lungs would pop out open through his mouth. Oozing drops of blood has become common. He was losing weight quickly. It was time when he would just be skeleton.

What he could afford is medicines to just keep the pain down a bit. But nowadays that was also not helping him.

***

The night was taking over. Ganesh was lying in the bed battling his unending pain.

There is a small baby, 6 years old running around. That was Ganesh himself. His Aai (mother) running behind him. Her mother is so elegant, so beautiful with dark and long hair. She came closer to him, clutched him in her arm. 'Aai, where were you?' Ganesh hasn't gotten this feeling of calm and composed feeling for years now.

Ganesh is a small boy, walking the road, and he saw a truck coming at him with speed. He is confused, sweating, and the thought of almost getting hit with the truck left him blank. But his mother pulled his hand hard, fetched him in her arms, and hugged so much with tears rolling all over. Still in shock, what just happened; Ganesh is happy that his mother is there for him every time.

Baba is asking him, 'Ganesh, come on this side.' 'Baba, it is fun to do farming, No'. Baba laughed. 'Boy, it is. We feed ourselves and feed the world. It is work of Saintly.'

His best friend, his brother Mahesh is fun to be with. His eyes are so caring; his eyes are so soothing. 'Thank you Bhau. You made it look so easy. I would never have learnt it.' Ganesh was driving the bicycle by himself, and his Bhau Mahesh was running behind him.

A tragic moment. Mourning in the home. Aai (mother) is crying. She is in bad shape. Bhau Mahesh is in the middle of everyone. Why is he lying like this? He is sleeping. A white cloth has been put on him. Ganesh is not sure, what is going on. His Bhau was not well for last few days. Now, why are they taking him, and where? He was told, Mahesh will not come back; he is gone. What does it mean? Why? Ganesh cried, only cried…for days. Many days.

He came back to real world with eyes wide open. He was in tears. He has been dreaming all along. He was not able to move, it looked like he was stuck, folded with tight ropes. He wanted to shout, but his neck was choking. He was losing his breath. He decided to not try; not try to move. That calmed his mind, he closed his eyes.

Ganesh is happy. It is his day of marriage. Ramya is the most beautiful women he has seen his life. His marriage brought all the happiness to his family. Her family was considerably wealthier than his. He heard that she and her family really liked his

Life On The Edge

simplicity. This thought always gave him goose bumps that there are people in the world who like his simplicity.

Ramya is stunningly beautiful. He cannot take away his eyes off her. She has always mesmerized him. She is fasting today to pray for his long life. 'Why do you have to fast?' Ganesh has innocently asked. 'For your long life, my beloved.' This sentence of his wife was echoing in his ears and mind.

Another flash.

Mrunali looked cutest girl on the earth. He is on the moon. He is dancing with Joy, Ramya is amusingly watching him. This was years of wait. Twelve long years after their marriage. This moment of happiness seemed heavenly to him.

Bappa are at home. Only once in his life, that he has brought Ganapati bappa at home. Bappa is everything for him. Lord Ganesha has always guided him and Ramya, on the path of right over wrong; kept all ominous things away from his family. He only has a sense of gratitude towards The Lord.

Ganesh has grown old, middle aged. He can spot grey hears and beard. He has come home early; they were celebrating the festival of Dussehra. Mrunali, Shruti and Jaya were excited to visit the neighbours and give Sona (leaves) as good wishes. His heart was filled with positivity. People were visiting him, paying respect to him, taking his blessings.

There are group of people, quarrelling with each other. Ganesh is helpless. He cannot stop them. There are questions hurled at him. Mhatre said, 'Ganesh, can you please do your magic. Builder is threatening to vacate the entire society by force. Something to be done.'

He is helpless. He wants to do something. It is pinching him with acute pain, he cries his heart out.

***

'Ah, this is heavy. Who kept this stone on me? I cannot move. It is hurting. Ah, it is hurting.' Ganesh was shouting, 'Move this.' 'Move this.'

Then he heard Ramya's noise, 'Aaho.' 'Aaho.' 'Aaho, wake up.' That soothing voice, again. It calmed him.

'Thank you. Thank you, Ramya.' He felt his weight has been removed.

Ramya shook him. 'Aaho, what happened?' And he woke up from sleep, still coming into senses. 'You were saying, move it.'

'Ahh'. It hurt him near his chest. But he realised, this is what it is…A dream. He smiled, but the ache was taking over him. His eyes wide open, tears rolling down. He could control the pain mentally, but his body was not able to support any more.

'Nothing Ramya. Nothing.' He coughed. Coughed non-stop. He was losing his breadth. 'Water. Water.' He just could speak a few words.

Ramya ran to get water. 'Here it is.' His hands fell before he could hold the glass.

'What happened?' Ramya put his head on her lap. 'Take it.' And she fed water to her husband.

Ganesh's eyes were open, showing gratitude, love, respect, relief.

'What?' said Ramya, with affection in her eyes. She realised only after a few moments that his eyes had no motion. His heart was not pumping. His body was becoming cold. She got to terms.

She shouted, 'Poris. Mrunali, Shruti, Jaya, Baba…Baba.'

Ganesh was gone.

***

Sanvaad came into the house. He saw Ramya aunty sitting in one corner. Mrunali was in another just below the temple in the house, her hair was all over her. Shruti and Jaya were in the kitchen. It was silence all around.

He flew from Delhi to Mumbai to be part of the final rituals of his Ganesh Kaka. He was always in awe of how Ganesh conducted himself. He grew up with lot of preaching and learnings from Ganesh.

He went to Ramya, 'Aunty, Kaka called me just 2 weeks ago.' She held him in his arms, but a bit puzzled; looked at him with disbelief.

'Hoy, Aunty, he was a bit worried. Agitated, not true to his character. He was upset with how builder was taking all of us for granted.'

'He asked me to come and see what I can do for our society.' Ramya was staring at him in amazement.

'But I didn't know, he will not be there to guide.' Sanvaad wiped his tears.

'We will take it ahead. If this is battle of our existence, then we will fight for it.'

'We will not let the builder take away our hard-earned houses.'

About the Author

Sandesh Singh is an author, trainer, and Technology leader. He is born and brought up in the city of Mumbai. His wife too hails from Mumbai. His deep love for the city is obvious. Sandesh debuts in the writing world, with 'Life on the edge' bringing what is dearer to him, the stories of people who make the city of Mumbai.

He loves experiencing different cultures, traditions, and architectures. His work does allow him to travel places across the globe. But Mumbai holds a special and unique place in his heart.

His life is filled with the laughter, chatters of his three lovely kids. His favourite time is being with the family enjoying the moments together - watching movies, tv serials, and playing cricket.

Follow Sandesh

Email: sandeshtheauthor@gmail.com

Twitter: singh_sandesh

Instagram: sandeshsingh001

Facebook: sandeshsingh001

CPSIA information can be obtained
at www.ICGtesting.com
Printed in the USA
LVHW011919140723
752117LV00002B/251